WHOSE REALITY IS THIS ANYWAY?

First Published in Great Britain 2016 by Mirador Publishing

ISBN: 978-1-911473-70-1

Mirador Publishing
10 Greenbrook Terrace
Taunton
Somerset
UK
TA1 1UT

Whose Reality Is This Anyway?

By

David Luddington

Dedication

This book is dedicated to the memory of James Stewart, one of my greatest fans and a true story lover who was taken from us far too early.

Author's Note

Although this book is a work of comedic fiction, it is impossible to write a story which touches this subject matter without acknowledging the sterling service given by those who work in the Care Sector. So, to those who each day, not only provide care for our loved ones but continuously struggle with mountains of bureaucracy and funding cuts, I thank you.

Also by the author

The Return Of The Hippy
The Money That Never Was
Schrodinger's Cottage
Forever England

www.luddington.com

Chapter One

"Is there a John in the room?"

A ripple of subdued laughter spread across the audience.

"I'm hearing Booker? Baker?" The medium ignored the disturbance. "Barker? Yes it's Barker."

"She's very good." The elderly woman in a woollen bobble hat seated next to me nudged my arm. "I saw Madame Clara in Bognor Regis last week. She raised the spirit of Cleopatra."

"Surprising how often it's Cleopatra," I said. "She always seems very busy for somebody who died two thousand years ago."

"Is there a John Barker in the room?" the medium called again.

That would be me but I'll make her wait. I'd started using my own name lately, nobody would recognise it now. It had been a long time since I'd been in the public eye and even then it had been under my stage name. The Great Xando, seer of secrets and creator of illusion.

"John Barker?" A slight note of panic tinged her voice. "I have somebody here for a John Barker."

I stood. "Me," I shouted towards the stage. "I'm John Barker."

"Come, come and join me," the medium called as the spotlights swung in my direction, blinding me.

A gentle applause greeted me as I threaded my way through the packed auditorium. The spotlights illuminated the steps for me and I climbed up and made my way to centre stage. It felt familiar and comfortable and I tried to remember if I'd ever performed here. The house lights were still up as I looked around. The Victorian vaulted ceilings, yellowed now and flaking, the Romanesque pillars supporting the balconies, all generic for this type of theatre. Where was I? Weston-Super-Mare. I'd seen so many theatres recently that I'd lost track. It felt like being back on the road.

The medium took my hand and moved me centre stage. She was a small woman, probably in her sixties and dressed to look like everybody's favourite grandmother.

"Don't worry, dear," she said. "The spirits are all very friendly. They only want to bring comfort."

She went into her trance again and her eyes rolled impressively. "She tells me her name is Jessica. Do you know somebody called Jessica, John?"

"Yes, is that really her?"

"Yes, John. She's come back to tell you everything is alright and you're not to worry. She's at peace."

Any second thoughts I'd had for what I was about to do evaporated in that moment. The carefully manufactured homely image, the subtle scent of lavender and peppermints. Peppermints, that was a nice touch, all neatly orchestrated to lure the heartbroken and distraught.

"Does she forgive me?" I asked. "Tell her I'm so sorry."

A hush fell on the audience as the little woman clearly faltered. "Yes," she said finally after a precisely timed pause. "Yes, she forgives you but you must tell her yourself, John. For your own peace, John. You must say it to her."

Her aid held the microphone in front of me, waiting.

"Jessica?" I took the microphone, it felt comfortable and familiar. "Are you there?"

"Yes, yes! She's here, John. She's standing right next to you."

"Jessica, Jessica I'm sorry." I turned to the medium. "Did she hear me?"

"Yes, John, she's listening. Tell her, John, tell her." She held my arm in a display of support.

"Jessica, I'm sorry. But you were so tasty." I felt the woman's fingers tighten around my arm. A warning? "We really didn't want to do it," I continued. "But with the potatoes and gravy, well, you were just... just too delicious."

The medium's hand dug into my arm as she swung round to glare into my face. "What?" she shouted, her gentle granny persona slipping. "What?" she repeated.

"Jessica," I said. "Our rabbit. We ate her for Sunday lunch. Didn't your researcher tell you Jessica was a rabbit? Oh, whoops. I must have forgotten to tell her that bit."

Her eyes blazed with the fires of hell. One day somebody was going to take a swing at me, it was probably well overdue. But not today. Not from this little woman who now stood frozen and speechless on the huge stage. She seemed to shrink even more as the silence in the room turned to uncomfortable mumblings. But I wasn't going to let her off the hook. These people fed on the bereaved and the lost. Parasites bleeding the last hope from desperate people.

"Your researcher," I continued. "The attractive woman who seemed overly interested in me in the bar before the show. She forgot to ask if the deceased was human. Easy slip, I suppose. You should get more reliable help." I gave the microphone back to the dumbstruck aid and left the stage.

As I walked through the aisles towards the door I heard the

medium pleading for everybody to remain calm, that mistakes happen, that I was drunk, crazy. I left the theatre leaving the growing noise of an unhappy audience behind.

***

The early evening still felt warm as I headed towards the sea front and I found my car where I'd left it near the Grand Pier. I pulled the yellow ticket from the windscreen. It seemed the complicated colour coding on the roadside meant I couldn't park there except on alternate Tuesdays during November. I threw the ticket on the back seat with the rest of them and headed for the motorway.

Satnav squawked at me just as I approached the junction. I pulled over to the side of the road to investigate. It was showing the M4 motorway completely blocked just beyond Bristol, twenty-three miles of stationary traffic. I pulled up the traffic reports on my smartphone, looking for an alternate route home. Apparently, the M4 blockage was caused by an overturned caravan. Ah, late summer, the perfect season. The birds are happy, the lambs are scampering in the fields and the caravans are falling over on the nation's arterial routes. I programmed in the A303 but that was also blocked. Not a caravan this time though. A slow moving convoy of military vehicles heading back to Salisbury. The joys of modern technology. Instead of actually sitting in a traffic jam, I could relax here looking at infographs of traffic jams. I pulled my map from the debris on the back seat. After a few minutes I thought I'd found an alternate route across country. It looked like I could use the A39 to go through Glastonbury then pick up the A303 again further east. I reprogrammed satnav and set off once more.

The road to Glastonbury was busy but at least it kept moving. I guessed all the other people had the same idea. As I approached the town the traffic slowed so I slipped through the side streets, it was time for a break. I parked behind the abbey and wandered up the hill. The King George pub welcomed me with its bright lights and comfortable seating. I ordered a pint of local ale and a plate of fish and chips. The ale was good and the meal hit the spot perfectly. I relaxed for a while until I decided that if I stayed any longer I'd be nodding off.

By the time I'd resumed my journey night was settling in but at least the traffic had thinned slightly and as I left the town, the road was surprisingly clear. I relaxed into the drive and my mind wandered back to the theatre. Had I been too hard on the woman? When I'd first started my personal exposé missions I'd been a bit gentler, feeling that at least some of them believed they were genuine and just not understanding the damage they were causing. But the more I saw, the more cynical I'd become.

The headlights of an oncoming car flashed in my eyes and seemed to be heading straight towards me. I instinctively pulled to the nearside and then a face appeared on the windscreen and I felt a bump. I hit the brakes, kicking gravel as I brought the car to a standstill. Shock kept me locked in position for a moment as the image of the face replayed in my mind.

Hell, I'd hit somebody.

I jumped from the car and scanned the side of the road. It took a moment to find him. A shadowy figure stumbled up out of the muddy rhyne and then collapsed in a heap on the grass verge. His face, cast in the pulsating orange glow of my hazard lights, blinked in and out of sight. Okay, don't panic. Mustn't move him. Where had I heard that? E.R.? Or was it House?

Was that right? Should I trust American dramas for first aid reality? I panicked and moved him into what I hoped was a more comfortable position. He groaned and tried to push my arm away. He was still alive at least. The flashing lights made it difficult to see him clearly. His long grey hair tangled with mud and bits of grass and lay straggled across his face. Several days' worth of beard showed through the mud. I pulled my jacket off and wiped his eyes clean with the sleeve. He grumbled again.

"You alright?" I asked. "I didn't see you. The other car... I'm sorry. Are you hurt?"

"Cockenpoop," he spluttered.

"What?" I helped him into a sitting position. It was probably all wrong and no doubt I was dislodging some crucial vertebrae or something but I couldn't leave him lying in the mud like that.

"Demon owls." He picked some soggy leaves from his hair and stared at them for a moment before folding them neatly into a bundle and putting them in his pocket. "Demon owls," he repeated. "They come here with their eyes full of the lights of Luna." He gripped my arm with a strength that gave lie to his frail appearance. "We need to find the caves of Trewar Venydh. Where's Harold?"

"Harold?" Oh, hell. There's somebody else here. I cast my eyes around trying to see through the flashing car lights.

"Ah," he said as he reached into the bank behind him. "There you are." He pulled a large walking stick from the grass and I assumed that was Harold. "Come along, we have work to do." I wasn't sure if he was talking to me or Harold.

I helped him to his feet just as another car approached.

He yelled at the glaring headlights as they approached. "We're too late. The owls have found us." He waved his stick at the lights as they drew closer. "Demons begone!" he shouted at the car as it passed then stumbled from my guiding hands and fell back into the rhyne.

Somewhere I knew all the things I should have done. Don't move the victim. Call the emergency services. But when one can't get a mobile phone signal and the victim is shouting curses at passing cars? He was probably drunk, although I couldn't smell alcohol. Drugs then. He was certainly high on something. I bundled him into the car and interrogated satnav for the nearest emergency hospital. Taunton, twenty-two miles.

My passenger seemed dazed as we drove through the night. I tried to focus him with light chatter.

"You live round here?" I asked.

"Where's Harold?"

"On the back seat."

"Who are you?"

"I'm John. John Barker. What's your name?"

No reply. I glanced across at him. He was asleep. Probably best to leave him like that.

The journey to Taunton took less than half an hour and as soon as I pulled up outside the A&E, staff rushed out with a gurney.

"What happened?" a nurse asked as she bustled me inside.

"He just appeared in front of me. I couldn't stop in time. I think he's high on something he looks like a hippy. It was just outside Glastonbury so he's probably from the festival or something. Is he going to be okay?"

"I'm sure he'll be fine." She guided me into a side office. "You'll have to wait here; the police will want to talk to you."

"The police? But it wasn't my fault."

"Just a formality," she said. "I'll get somebody to bring you a nice cup of tea in a minute."

"He was just there, from nowhere. He's talking nonsense. Do you think it's ecstasy or something?"

"We'll find out," she said. "Do you know his name?"

"No, but his stick's called Harold."

"Harold? Hmm, that's a new one." She left the room and closed the door.

I wondered if she'd locked me in and tested the door. It opened. That was okay then. I settled into a high backed chair and tried to gather my thoughts.

The door opened and a female police officer entered the room. She was slim built and stood around five-two in her police boots. She looked laden down and somewhat lost under the weight of her police kit.

"That was quick," I said.

"I'm on duty here." Her accent was pure Somerset and reminded me of the Archers. "Friday nights, usual drunks, hip-hoppers and gangstas. No point in having somebody to and fro all night so here I am. So, which are you?"

"Huh?"

"You a drunk or a hip-hopper? You don't look much like a gangsta."

"Neither. I'm an illusionist. Or I was, sort of retired."

"Illusionist, huh? What like David Blaine?"

"No, not a bit like David Blaine. That guy's a fraud."

"Aren't you all? I mean, isn't that sort of the point? Blow into this for me." She handed me a breathalyser. "One long breath until it beeps."

"No, what I mean is –"

She took my hand and guided it and the breathalyser towards my mouth. "Just blow."

As I exhaled into the tube I wondered if the beer I'd had in Glastonbury had had time to wear off.

The machine issued a bleep.

"Okay, that will do." She took the device and held it up to view the readout. "You pass," she said flatly. She seemed disappointed.

"Can I go now?"

"When I've taken your statement." She pulled a notebook from her pocket. "Driving licence?"

She copied details from the licence as she said, "What's his name?"

"I don't know. Like I told –"

"You didn't ask him?"

"Sorry. I don't usually ask people their names before I run them over. I find it tends to spoil the surprise."

Her eyes warned against more attempts at sarcasm. "I meant afterwards, during your journey here?"

I gave her what details I could and then she left me alone in the room again with a request that I report into Taunton Police Station in the morning. I spent the next hour reading the notices on the walls. By the time the nurse returned I knew how to wash my hands, lift heavy things safely and was confident I could inform the staff in Polish that I was pregnant.

"You can go now, Mr Barker. Your friend Mervyn is sleeping quietly."

"No, he's not my... Mervyn? Is that his name?"

"Well..." she hesitated. "He *was* a bit dopey. To be honest, I thought he said Merlin but Sister said it was Mervyn and must have been the diazepam slurring his words. We don't argue with Sister so I wrote Mervyn on his notes. That's probably what he was trying to say anyway. We'll give you a ring in the morning when you can take him home."

"Okay. What? No, he's nothing to do with me. I just brought him in."

"After you ran him over when you'd been drinking?" She looked at me as if challenging an argument. "He's not eaten for some time, his clothes are in tatters and he doesn't seem to have had a bath in... well for all I know he's never had a bath. The least you can do is drop him home."

***

I spent the night in a nearby Travel Lodge. These places had been my second home for the last five years. I liked their simple honesty. I knew what I was going to get. A clean room, a fairly comfortable bed and a car park. I stretched out on the bed with a stiff gin. I needed to flush the day through before trying for sleep. What was left of the night was going to be difficult if I couldn't quiet the demons. I probably needed out of this game. What had started as a last quest for meaning had long since turned into a vendetta against the charlatans and con artists who plied their trade at the expense of the bereaved and lost.

I ran through the day's events in an attempt to clear my mind. My unnecessary reaction to the stage show. The road closures that sent me spiralling into the path of some doped-up hippy who then wanders in front of my car. And now I have to play nicely and act as taxi driver to a fruitcake. The gin started to take effect and the day slipped into neutral. I showered and readied for bed then watched television until sleep took me.

Chapter Two

I reported at the Police Station at ten o'clock precisely, the time it opened. It seemed Police Stations in Somerset have an arrangement with the local criminal community not to commit crimes before ten o'clock on Saturdays and not at all on Sundays. The Civilian Support Auxiliary Assistant behind the counter took my statement again and informed me it would be reviewed by an actual police officer when one became available. In the meantime I was free to continue my journey. I returned to the hospital to enquire after Mervyn and had to wait an hour to be told he'd already gone.

"He just disappeared," a young nurse said. "I went to take his readings at six and his bed was empty. Clothes gone and everything."

"Was he okay?" I asked.

"Well Mister Perkins, the on-duty psychiatrist, wanted to keep him in. Thought he was suffering from a Dissociative Episode caused by trauma to the prefrontal cortex."

"Huh?"

"Sorry, he was behaving oddly due to a bump on the head."

"Oh, I see." I felt slightly guilty. "But he will be alright? I mean he's not about to drop down dead or anything is he?"

"No, physically he's fine. They gave him a brain scan. He's just a bit confused."

"Oh, good. I'll be off then. Thank you. You're all... um... wonderful." I started for the door.

"You not going to take his things?" she asked.

"Things? What things? He had nothing. Well, apart from Harold." I noticed her expression and added, "His stick. He called it Harold."

"Oh, Harold. Okay. No he didn't leave a stick. Just some stuff they took from his pockets as the E.R. staff attended him." She picked up a small cardboard box from the table. "There you go, give that to him when you see him. And if he starts behaving strangely, bring him straight back in." She didn't wait to hear my protestations and slipped through the door. I pondered for a moment as to what to do. I wanted to head back to London. I'd had enough of Somerset already. Last night's exposé in the theatre had left me with a bad taste. I'd been unnecessarily cruel and I probably needed to stop this now and find something else to do. Freefall skydiving or rock climbing or something else constructive and slightly more life affirming than dealing with nutjobs who claim to see dead people. I certainly didn't want to be searching for a stoned hippy with a dissociative thingy. And anyway, he'd probably be already talking to Injury-Parasite-Lawyer-Monkeys-For-You about now and that was something best avoided. I took the box to the Admissions Counter in Reception.

"This belongs to somebody called Mervyn." I placed it on the counter.

"You can't leave it here," the harassed looking middle-aged woman said from behind the bullet proof glass.

"He was brought in last night. An emergency."

"Oh, I see. Which ward is he on?" She tapped at her keyboard.

"He's not. He's gone now."

"Why do you want to leave that here then?"

"Because it's not mine."

"And what makes you think we're a repository for everything which isn't yours? This is a hospital not a bring-and-buy sale." She flapped her hand towards me indicating that I should stop wasting her time now and leave with the box which wasn't mine and make room for real casualties.

I headed for my car and plonked the box on the passenger seat. What to do? I contemplated just lobbing it out of the window on my way back to London. It wasn't my problem. He'd stepped out in front of me, probably high on pot or whatever it was they smoke these days. I can't be responsible him. I picked the box up and placed it on my lap. On the other hand there may be something valuable in there. Possibly a wallet with an address. Maybe I should just check. I opened the box. It was immediately obvious there was nothing either of value or anything which would assist in locating him. A small rock with a slight blue vein threading through it, a piece of wood about the size of a large pencil, a tattered map of Somerset, a piece of string, half a Cornish pasty and a copy of Fifty Shades of Grey. I closed the lid and placed it back on the passenger seat. That decided it. I scanned the immediate area looking for a rubbish bin large enough to take the box. Nothing. Of course, we don't do rubbish bins any more, not since the IRA took to depositing their political opinions inside them. Never mind. I'd dump it somewhere on the way home.

I headed for the M5 motorway and satnav announced the route was clear of dead caravans or military convoys. As I approached the junction to join the motorway I noticed a sign pointing the way to Glastonbury. I hesitated at the junction until a car behind me tooted impatiently. I drove off the roundabout and towards the Glastonbury road before I'd realised what I was doing. Well, not to worry. I could go through Glastonbury then pick up the A303 as I'd intended last night. If I spotted Mervyn on the way then that was fate deciding he should have his box of little treasures back and if not, well then I dump it at the next rubbish bin I see. That was fair. As I drove, I wondered how one comes to a point in life where all one's worldly possessions amount to a copy of Fifty Shades of Grey and a half eaten Cornish pasty. Drugs probably.

I purposefully drove slowly through Glastonbury, slowing further each time I saw a hippy. Given the demographics of the town this resulted in lots of slowing to an almost standstill, much to the annoyance of following vehicles. Eventually I cleared the town and met the open road again. That was decided then. Mervyn was probably busy getting stoned in a yurt somewhere and I was doubtful he'd even miss his few meagre possessions. I pulled into a lay-by and switched off the engine. What was left of my conscience was poking at me and I didn't like it. What if this really was all he had in the world? Maybe the stone belonged to somebody he'd loved once. I could relate to that. I found myself turning the plain silver wedding ring on my finger. Perhaps he was starving and he was making the pasty last another day? Perhaps Fifty Shades of Grey had been... No, that was taking sentimentality too far. As I reached for the key to restart the engine I heard, and felt, a banging on the rear of the car. I twisted in my seat. Staring at me through the rear window was the face of Mervyn. He held his stick in his hand and beat the back of the car once more. He was shouting something but I couldn't make it out. I started to open the door to get out then paused. What if he was dangerous? Goodness knows what he'd been taking and he *was* armed and looking fairly pissed with me. No, he'd be alright and anyway, I felt partly responsible. I approached him but retained a respectful distance, just in case.

"Mervyn, you alright? They were worried about you in the hospital."

"Mervyn?" he replied. "Nonsense cockenpoop." He rapped his stick against the rear of my car again. "Thieves and brigands! Stealing a man's things then steal a man's name. You'll not stop me. It's time." He still wore the same clothes from last night. Tatty jeans and a thick cotton shirt that had probably once been white. The only difference was that the whole ensemble was now topped off with a hospital gown.

"I've got your stuff," I said. "You left it behind in the hospital." I picked the box from the passenger seat. "Look." I held the box towards him and opened the lid. "It's got your... lump of rock... and your... your... other stuff."

He came closer and peered into the box.

"Ah, I wondered where that had gone." He pulled the half Cornish pasty from the box and broke it in two. "Here, halfsies," he said, passing me a handful of crumbling pasty.

I declined and he shrugged, replacing my halfsy back into the box.

"Where's the book?" he asked accusingly. "It won't do you any good."

"It's in the box, look." I pointed at the paperback.

"Not that, idiot, that's The Prophecy. My book. The one I write in." He stared at me from under the biggest set of pure white eyebrows I'd ever seen. "It must be here." He waved his stick around the verge. "Come along now, you have to help me find it." He turned and patted his stick at patches of grass along the banks of the rhyne.

It was then that I realised we were at the exact spot where

he'd walked out in front of my car last night. I cast my eyes around the scene. The grass was still trampled and squashed where I'd driven onto the verge. More flattened grass pointed the way that Mervyn had fallen into the rhyne. I followed the trail down and just at the water's edge I saw a leather-bound book. The bank was muddy and slippery so I bent carefully to retrieve it. It was about the size of a paperback and the worn leather cover bore no markings other than the scuffs of years.

"Is this it?" I called as I scrambled up the bank.

"Ah, good." Mervyn took it from me and thumbed it open to check it was intact. "Now we can go."

"We? I have to go back to Camden. You're supposed to be going back to the hospital. They wanted to check you for... brain stuff."

"Where's Camden?"

I waved my hand east. "That way. About a hundred miles. London, you do know where London is?"

Mervyn stared at me as if not understanding anything I was saying. I should really take him back to hospital myself. He pulled the tatty map of Somerset from the cardboard box and thrust it towards me. "Show me Camden," he demanded.

I took the map and unfolded it on the bonnet of the car. "This map just covers Somerset," I said. "Look it only goes as far as Wincanton."

"Where's Camden?"

"That's what I'm trying to explain. It's off the map. By a long way." I waved my hand a half metre to the left. "It's over here, this way."

"Off the map?" he questioned.

"Yes. Way off the map."

"That's good then. We'll go there, off the map. They won't find us there. Not if it's not on the map. Excellent plan." He dropped the map back in the box and climbed into the back seat of the car.

I contemplated asking him to get out. I also thought about driving him to the nearest Police Station. In the end I just thought sod it and climbed in the car. I had a passenger to London. I started the car and once more resumed my journey home.

"What's there?" he asked from behind me.

"Camden? Well, it's in London so everything really. You know, the London Eye, the West End, Houses of Parliament, the Queen."

"The Queen?"

"Yes, and Big Ben, red busses –"

"The Queen, ah of course. Why is the Queen in London?"

This was going to be a long drive. I turned the radio on and heard a muttering from the back seat. I ignored it.

After about an hour I stopped for petrol. Mervyn was asleep on the back seat. I paid for the petrol and bought a couple of packs of cheese sandwiches.

"You hungry?" I asked as I set off. There was no answer so I guessed he was still asleep. After about twenty minutes there was still no sign of him waking and I began to worry that maybe he'd slipped into a coma or something. I adjusted the mirror to see if he was alright. The back seat was empty. I stopped in the next lay-by and double checked the back seat just in case he was hiding. He wasn't. I closed and opened the door again as if somehow that would make him reappear. It didn't. Oh well, problem solved.

I set off once more, grateful for my own company. I hadn't covered more than ten miles when I swung round the next roundabout and headed back towards the petrol station. He might have collapsed in the toilets or something. Not that it should be my problem if he had but no doubt some parasitic lawyer gremlin would make it so. I'd insist he goes to hospital.

I hadn't enough left in me to be dealing with a stoned hippy who lacked the road sense of a sleepwalking hedgehog.

I found him in the cafe. A young waitress was trying to persuade him to leave.

As I approached she looked at me with pleading eyes. "Is he with you?"

"Not really but I'll take him."

"He's demanding to see the Queen. Isn't it a bit early in the day for this?"

"He's a bit... special." I took Mervyn by the arm. "Come on."

He looked at me with that puzzled expression he was so good at and said, "Is this London? Not much is it? I was expecting something bigger."

I guided him to the car. "Front seat this time, so I can keep an eye on you. You should be in hospital."

"Not hospital. Where are we going now?" he asked as we pulled into the traffic.

"Camden," I said.

"Oh. A different one?"

We drove in silence for a while. Mervyn seemed fascinated with the passing countryside.

"I can't believe you've never been to London," I said. No answer. I glanced to my left. He seemed to be dozing. I hoped. "Mervyn?" I nudged his arm. "Mervyn?"

"Huh?" He struggled into consciousness. "Who?"

"Mervyn, you alright?"

"Who? Who's Mervyn?"

"You," I said. "You're Mervyn." I was worried he was

24

slipping into that dissociative whatsit that nurse had been talking about.

"Not Mervyn." He sounded angry. "Who's Mervyn? Not me. Mervyn this and Mervyn that. Where's Mervyn? Nonsense talk."

I slowed the car, worried that if he kicked off it could be dangerous. "Okay," I said. "What is your name?"

"Merlin!" he said loudly, twisting in his seat to stare at me with wild eyes that resembled two full moons under a pair of white ostrich feathers. "My name is Merlin."

Chapter Three

"So, erm... Merlin, how did you come to be in the wilds of Somerset in the middle of the night?" I eased the car onto the M3 slip road. Grateful the A303 was now behind us. Soon be home.

"It's in the book," he said. "Or not. I don't remember. Where's Somerset?" He fumbled through his pockets. "My book, where's my book?"

"Look on the back seat," I suggested.

He leaned across me to reach the back seat. "My book, my book."

I lost sight of the road as he wriggled further in an effort to climb in the back. We drifted across two lanes of the motorway as I pushed him away with one arm in an attempt to clear a line of sight. Fortunately traffic was light.

"Ah, here you are," he said and settled back in his seat. "What was the question?"

"Um... why were you in Somerset?"

Merlin leafed through his book. "Here it is. No... that's Avalon. Where's Avalon?"

"I don't know," I said. "I thought it was mythical. Something to do with King Arthur."

"Arthur... Arthur." He thumbed through the tattered leaves of the book. "Ah, yes. That's why I was there in... in... what was the place?"

26

"Somerset."

"Yes. No, not the Somerset. Not that place, the other place."

I felt this conversation was in danger of occupying the rest of my life. "What other place? Or do you mean Glastonbury?"

"Glastonbury, yes. That's the one. I remember now, I wrote it down. I have to go to Glastonbury."

"We're going to Camden."

"Ah yes, Camden. Is that in Glastonbury?"

"No. It's in London. Just London. Not Glastonbury, not Somerset. London. London is where I live and I'm going home. To London."

Merlin fell silent. At last. I was just nudging the car onto the slip road for the M25 when I heard a loud noise and the car started buffeting. *What the hell?* A quick glance to my left and I saw Merlin trying to force open the door.

"What are you doing?" I yelled above the wind roar. "You'll kill yourself. Probably both of us." I tried to reach the door across him but the car lurched as I shifted.

"I have to go to Glastonbury. You have to take me there." He pushed at the door but fortunately the wind rush was too powerful for him. He slumped back in his seat, defeated.

"Look, Mervyn... Merlin, whoever you think you are; I'll drop you at Paddington station. That's the best I can do. The trains go in that direction from there so you can go to-and-fro to your heart's content."

I navigated the M25 and threaded my way through the city traffic. Merlin remained quiet, just giving the odd incoherent mumble as he leafed through his notebook. Every so often he would open the paperback novel to read a passage in there before returning to his notebook. I had to cruise round the Paddington area three times before I found somewhere to pull over. Even then it was only a vacant taxi rank so I would need to be quick.

"Here you go." I reached across him to open the door.

"Is this Glastonbury?" he asked, staring at me with the eyes of a sad puppy.

"No, this is still London. You can get a train in there to Glastonbury. I think. Or somewhere close anyway."

"Where's the Queen?"

"The Queen? Buckingham Palace I suppose." I waved my hand vaguely eastwards.

"I need to talk to Guinevere."

"You need to get out of my car," I said. "I'm going to get a ticket. Come on, out." I jumped out of the car and hurried round to his side. A bit of hurried cajoling and then he was standing on the pavement with his box under his arm. He looked completely bewildered.

"Are you coming back for me?" he asked.

"No." I ran back round the car. I'd spotted a yellow jacketed traffic warden making a beeline for us. "I have to go." I indicated the approaching menace. "If I stay here any longer I'll get shot."

His eyebrows disappeared underneath his white hair. "I will protect you." He hefted his stick high above his head and started towards the closing warden. "Stop," he yelled to the startled man.

I jumped back in the car. I sat for the briefest of moments as I tried to deal with a strange feeling of guilt that had suddenly overtaken me. Not my problem. He should be in a secure home somewhere. He'd probably scrambled his brains with some chemical or other and it's his own fault. I started the car and drove off casting a glance in the mirror as I left. Merlin and the traffic warden were engaged in a heated dialogue that seemed to involve much waving of sticks and pens. They disappeared behind me as I eased into the traffic. I couldn't take responsibility for every fruit-loop that crossed my path.

I slid the car into my designated space in the car park below the apartment building. The lift took me to the foyer where I collected my mail and I nodded a hello to Joe, the concierge, as I passed through. I took the stairs to the fourth floor and my flat welcomed me with the familiar smells of a space too long closed up. I opened the balcony doors and the first orange of the sunset spread into the room. The curtains drifted in the slight breeze. I settled in my chair with a large gin and an equally large pile of mail. Most of it was rubbish. After I'd discarded the offers of double glazing and credit cards I was left with a rates demand and my copy of The Stage. I glanced through it without really seeing anything. I didn't know why I continued with it. Just habit. I hadn't performed for five years now, not since...

I pressed the button on my remote and the television sprang to life, filling my lounge with chatty people and noise which dampened down my thoughts. I channel hopped for a while then finally settled on a nature documentary.

I was woken by the door intercom.

"Got a copper down here for you," Joe's tinny voice informed me.

"Okay," I said into the box. "Send him up."

I wondered what this was about. Complaint from the Weston theatre? Wouldn't be the first time I'd had an injunction served. The hazards of my crusade. I really should call it a day now.

The doorbell rang and I opened the door. A tall police officer stood back from my doorway. Just behind him to one side stood Merlin.

"Mister Barker? Mister John Barker?"

"Yes," I said.

"I think this person is with you?" He indicated Merlin, who was currently occupied banging his stick against the smoke detector in the ceiling.

"No."

"We picked him up trying to climb onto the tracks of the ten-fifty to Yeovil. He thinks he's Gandalf."

"Merlin actually. Gandalf was in... Never mind. How did you come to bring him here?"

"We simply rewound the CCTV from outside the station and there you were; vehicle BN24 6NR. That is your car, isn't it, sir?"

I nodded.

"Just in case it escaped your notice while you were holidaying on planet Mars, Paddington station is now the most surveilled point on Earth. More cameras are watching the habits of the commuters on the eight-twenty from Bristol Parkway than are watching Kim Kardashian on a topless beach in Monte Carlo."

"Ah. Sorry, who?"

"You can't just go around leaving dipsy relatives about the capital whenever you've had enough of them. We have enough trouble with stray dogs without people dropping off their bewildered uncles at the nation's arterial hubs."

"He's not my relative. He's just somebody I... I..." I stopped myself just before admitting I'd run him over. That probably wouldn't have helped my case any. "He's just somebody I was giving a lift to."

There was a loud clatter and we both turned to witness the smoke alarm descend from the ceiling in several pieces. Merlin poked them around the floor with his stick. "Glow spiders," he explained.

"You need to get that fixed," the police officer said. "Contravenes Health and Safety legislation not having one of those in a fully functioning condition."

"Thank you for pointing that out. I'll be sure to raise it at the next resident's committee meeting."

I tugged at Merlin's sleeve, guiding him into the room and then closed the door on the policeman.

"What happened?" I asked. "I thought you were going back to Glastonbury?"

"These aren't the caves of Trewar Venydh," he said, taking in his surroundings.

"No, this is my flat in Camden. You'd better leave Harold by the door." I pointed at his stick. "Don't want any more accidents."

He put Harold in the corner and went to the window. "Good viewpoint. I can see why you chose it."

"You can't stay here, you know. I don't do house guests. Just one night, that's all."

"We can go to Avalon together at first light. He's there somewhere."

"Who?"

"Arthur, of course. The King."

Chapter Four

I set up the sofa bed in my office and found some suitable bedding. Merlin had a shower while I tried to find some old clothes that would fit. He was a good six inches taller than me and somewhat leaner. In the end I gave him a tracksuit I found at the back of the wardrobe, it had always been too big for me anyway. That would do for now, I'd sort out something different in the morning and send him on his way.

I telephoned out for pizza and presented one of the boxes to him.

"What's this?"

"Pizza. You must have had pizza before?"

Merlin opened the box and studied the contents. "I don't know this. What was it before it was pizza?"

"It's always been pizza. That's how they're made."

"But it's all squashed." He picked up one of the pieces by the edge and held it in front of his eyes. "And severed."

"They make them like that." I took a bite from one of my pieces to show him it was safe.

He observed me cautiously from under his eyebrows then held his head back, opened his mouth and dropped the piece in.

After a moment of chewing he said, "Pizza, you say?"

"Pizza," I agreed.

"Pizza," he played with the word as he chewed. "It's good. You must show me where they live."

We ate from the boxes on our laps. Merlin seemed hungry and finished off the slices of mine I couldn't manage.

Merlin threw his empty pizza box to the floor. "Can we go now?"

"Where?" I gathered the boxes and took them to the bin.

"Arthur, he waits. I have to find him."

"King Arthur? You mean the medieval construct created to teach chivalry and honour to uneducated peasants during the renaissance? That Arthur?"

He looked at me as if I were a stupid child then gave a little shrug. "You must take me back to Glastonbury. His tomb is there."

"No chance. Firstly, Arthur doesn't exist. He's made up, there *is* no tomb. And secondly... secondly... actually there is no secondly, that's it. He doesn't exist. Never has, just myths and fairy tales." I took the tops from a pair of Budweisers and handed one to Merlin.

"What's this?" He sniffed at the bottle.

"Beer," I said.

"It suffices," Merlin dismissed. "Arthur, it's in the book. It's The Prophecy." He held up his copy of Fifty Shades of Grey.

I ignored him and picked up my copy of The Stage. I scanned the events section more out of curiosity, idly noting appearances by somebody called Madame Mysteria. No, give it a rest, John.

I made us both a coffee while I mentally chastised myself for getting cross with Merlin. It wasn't his fault. He was clearly away in his own reality and meant no harm.

"Where did you come from?" I tried a switch to light conversational. "Where's your home?"

He pulled his notepad from the pocket of his coat on the

33

chair. "Hmm, it doesn't say," he mumbled as he leafed through the book.

"You don't remember where you came from?"

"Where does anybody come from? I forget things. Then I remember things. When I remember important things I write them in here." He tapped his leather bound book. "Sometimes I remember different things. I remember being hit on the head and thrown in a ditch."

"Look, that wasn't my fault. You just—"

He snapped the book shut. "Can we go now?"

"No."

I put the television on. Loud, drum based music and people running around in a dark building, all badly illuminated by fake green-tinted night-vision effects heralded another episode of 'Mystic Morgan - Spook Hunter'. A so-called reality show in which leather clad femme fatale Morgan the Huntress conjures up the spirits of the dead from famous buildings or a celebrity's home. It always amazed me why people continued to watch this rubbish yet it was one of the most popular shows on television at the moment, enticing the gullible with its populist mix of celebrity and the supernatural. Although its popularity was probably due in no small part to the frequent and gratuitous views of Morgan's leather-clad backside as she raced through so-called haunted buildings and landscapes.

Merlin sat quietly and thumbed through his paperback and every so often, scribbled in his notebook. He seemed oblivious to the television.

***

The following morning I took Merlin down to the market to find some more suitable clothes. We settled on some jeans and a couple of multi-coloured shirts. Merlin also insisted on a green hat. We sat in a snack bar in Camden market. I always enjoyed relaxing amidst the bustle; it stopped my mind going places I'd rather it didn't. I ordered baked potatoes with tuna mayo for each of us but Merlin announced he wasn't going to eat campfire food and demanded squashed pizza.

"Okay," I said. "I'll give you enough money for some food on the journey and for a ticket to somewhere that isn't here and then you really need to be off. I have things to do."

"What things? What things do you do?" he asked.

"I err... Um..." Truth was I wasn't quite sure what I did anymore. "I used to be a magician."

He looked at me with suspicion. "You don't look much like a magician to me."

"No, not the sort of magician you are... believe you are. A stage magician." I rummaged in my wallet and eventually found one of my old cards. I gave it to him. "The Great Xando. Illusionist and mentalist. I used to be quite big."

He studied the card then placed it carefully in the pages of the novel. "And now you aren't big anymore."

"Now? Now I'm a debunker. I'm a destroyer of fakes and frauds. The scourge of the make-believe mystics and the money-grabbing mediums that prey on the vulnerable."

"What happened?"

"Huh?"

"Why did you lose the magic?"

I was slightly stunned by his direct question and especially the words he'd chosen. It took a moment to gather my thoughts.

"What do you mean?" I stalled.

"You let the world take you. Why did you lose the magic?"

That question again. I turned my wedding band. "Long

story, one for another day. So how come you don't remember where you came from?" A not very subtle change the subject.

He smiled and nodded as if recognising my diversion. "The big stones. I remember the big stone, in a circle. They tried to make me think I was somebody else but they are idiots and weak. I remember being in a cave and a dragon opened it for me. Or that bit might have been a dream. Or a film. I like films; they showed me lots of films. I didn't come from here."

"You mean not here as in not from London? Or not here as in..." *Be kind, I cautioned myself.* "As in a different spiritual plane?" Part of me hated myself for even saying the words.

"I was given The Book and now I must follow the messages."

"Your notebook? That tells you what to do?"

"No. Not that book, idiot. This one!" He pulled the battered copy of Fifty Shades of Grey from his pocket and slapped it on the table. "This one," he repeated. "The Fey gave it to me."

"The Fey? How did they give it to you?"

"On a bus. I was on a bus and I reached down behind the seat. Sometimes there's some money there you know. I found a hearing aid once, didn't work. Or it might have been the chewing gum; it was very difficult to get out of my ear."

"The book?" I reminded him.

"Yes, The Book. There it was, down the back of the seat. The Fey are clever, they knew I would look there."

I looked at the book on the table in front of me. Fifty Shades of Grey. I tried to understand how this poor, bewildered soul had come to believe this book was somehow magical. What had happened to him?

We finished our lunch and I took him to Paddington station. This time I parked properly and took him into the station.

I decided to give as little room as possible for cock-ups and bought the ticket for him. "Here's a ticket to Castle Carey," I said. "The train leaves in fifteen minutes and takes about two hours."

He nodded at me as he took the ticket. "Who is the lord?"

That was a left-field question. I thought for a moment then, "Well, some people say he's God, others think—"

"The lord of the castle, you dim-witted arse of a donkey."

"What castle?"

"You said. Castle Carey, you said. So, who's the lord?"

"Oh, I see. No, it's not that sort of castle. Just a place name, like Newcastle. There's no castle there either. I think."

"Why call something a castle if it's not a castle?"

"I don't know. Maybe you can ask them when you get there. Here, this will help." I gave him a twenty pound note. "Castle Carey is just down the road from Glastonbury. I'm sure you'll get a lift."

"Where do I find pizza?"

"They will have pizza in Castle Carey." I didn't know that for sure but it would be a rare town that didn't have a pizza bar.

I wasn't convinced he was going to get on the train and half expected him to start demanding the Queen again at any moment. I took him to the right train and sat in the carriage with him until the last moment. I didn't want to risk him turning up with another policeman in tow. I hopped off just as we started to move and watched the train pull away with him still firmly on board. He looked slightly forlorn and for a moment, I felt sorry for him. But only for a moment. For now, he was gone, job done. I can get back to normal.

I headed back to my flat and cleaned up the evidence of my visitor. With order returned once more I went down to the Green Dragon for my early evening drink. Tim, the landlord, greeted me with a pint of Speckled Hen on the bar before I reached it.

"You're early," he said.

"Difficult day. Difficult couple of days in fact."

The bar was empty so Tim stayed with me. "What's up? Get in a fight with a witch doctor?"

"Not quite," I laughed. "Probably overdue though. No, I ran over a nutter down near Glastonbury and couldn't get rid of him." I supped deep on the beer. "Thinks he's Merlin. You know; the wizard?"

"They're all barking down that way," he said. "Went to the festival once. Only went to see Dolly Parton. Place is full of nutters. All high as kites on crackpot."

Tim was the perfect barman and let me unload on him.

"Have you thought that it's perhaps time to give up this crusade of yours and find something else to do?" he asked, once I'd eventually slowed in my outpourings.

"Frequently." I put the empty glass on the bar and Tim refilled it without being asked.

"How long's it been now? Three years?"

"Nearly five," I said.

"That's probably enough. She wouldn't have wanted you to carry on like this."

"I have a feeling you might be right," I said. "Trouble is I'm not quite sure what else to do now. Give me a gin will you? It's been a bad couple of days."

I wandered back to my flat around midnight. I hadn't had a session like that in some while and the pavement felt strangely soft. It took three attempts to get the key in the lock but only two to find the light switch. I congratulated myself and collapsed in my armchair. The flat felt cold. Not cold as in needing the heating on, but cold as in empty, devoid of warmth. Over the last few years the place had become more functional rather than a home. I'd gradually put away more and more of Amy's bits and pieces, almost without thinking about it. I think I'd probably rationalised that I didn't want them to get damaged. Just a few memories remained on display. My eyes caught the small silver 'Rabbit in the Hat' ornament. She'd found it in an antique store in the market and had it engraved for my birthday. Although neither of us had known it at the time, it was to be her last gift to me. I couldn't bring myself to put that one away. I didn't need to lift it to read the inscription. The words engraved in my heart would far outlast the tiny lettering in the silver base. *'The magic is real, never lose it, never let the world take you'.*

Chapter Five

The next morning I awoke with a strange sense that something had changed. Something was out of whack but I couldn't place it. I scanned my copy of The Stage looking for adverts for mediums and spiritualist shows. A few caught my eye but somehow I didn't feel quite the same anger. Certainly not the usual sense of righteous indignation at the misuse of conjuring skills that would drive me to travel hundreds of miles just to expose them.

Perhaps Tim was right; I needed to find something else to do. I'd been chasing charlatans and flimflam artists for long enough. And what was the point anyway? For each one I'd exposed another two would pop up. They were like 'Whack-A-Mole'. Maybe I'd write a book.

The telephone broke my ruminations.

"Mr Barker?" the voice asked. It sounded official.

"Yes," I replied with a sense of foreboding.

"Sergeant Halliday, Taunton Police. We've just picked up a friend of yours and he's asking for you."

"Who's that?" I knew perfectly well who it was but I needed time to think.

"Says his name's Merlin and that he needs to see you."

"How did you get my number?"

"He had a card of yours, no other identification. Is he supposed to be on medication? Only we don't think he's safe."

"No. I don't know. I don't really know him. He's just somebody I bumped into... I mean somebody I met the other day. Have you arrested him? What's he done?"

"He was digging a hole in the grounds of Glastonbury Abbey."

"Ah, I see. But he's not really anything to do with me. I don't know why he would want me?"

"No idea, but if you can't take him into safe care the FME wants to apply a Section Four order."

"What's that?"

"He'll be taken into a secure unit for his own safety while they assess his mental condition."

I thought for a moment then said, "It's probably for the best. I only knew him for a couple of days. He's certainly not right."

"Well, sorry to trouble you, sir. We'll take care of it now. Thank you for your help." The phone went dead.

I took a walk down to the market. Camden Market is a huge affair that spreads through the streets with a mixture of temporary stalls, permanent outlets or fly-pitchers. It's always busy and always a good place to lose oneself for a few hours. I particularly liked the little shops that crammed the Under-Arches section of the market. I resisted all offers of Chinese rugs and Tibetan prayer wheels as I browsed the stalls with their strange mix of modern, ancient and ethnic. I eventually found myself in the antiques section and one shop in particular drew my attention with its original theatre posters spanning the glory years of Music Hall. There, nestling between Charlie Chaplin and Arthur Askey was a poster announcing a performance by the great master himself, Robert Houdin. He was the magician whom fledgling escapologist Erik Weisz had so admired that he'd appropriated the Master's name and called himself Harry Houdini.

I haggled weakly but I'd have paid any price for that poster and the trader knew it. I took my prize back to the flat to find a suitable wall on which to mount it. In the end I removed the triple split woodblock print of the Grand Canyon. Robert Houdin filled the gap perfectly. The poster announced a performance at Drury Lane with the words, *"Robert Houdin, French conjuror Extraordinaire - Never Lose The Magic."*

Never lose the magic. The words stirred something. Merlin had been right, I'd lost the magic. What had started as a desperate attempt to reach across the River Styx had turned into a witch hunt. My need to hold on to some thread of our love had rotted and putrefied until all I'd had left was a burning hatred for all those who peddled false hope.

I looked around the room; traces of Amy had slowly disappeared over the years. The odd breakage, a move to a more secure place, or just making room for something new. Like the Robert Houdin poster replacing the picture we'd bought together in the market. I turned the silver 'Rabbit in Hat' in my hand and read the words I knew so well yet this time felt like the first time I'd seen them. Really seen them. *'The magic is real, never lose it, never let the world take you'.*

I packed a bag and secured the flat.

"Keep an eye on the place for me, Joe," I said as I stopped off in the foyer to check my mail.

"Be gone long?" he asked.

"Don't know. Could be a while this time."

"More ghost-busting?"

"Not this time, Joe. Got a wizard to find."

***

The road to the West Country ran freely and I reached Taunton just after six. Of course, the Police Station was closed for the night so I found the Travel Lodge in which I'd stayed the last time. The sparse functionality welcomed me like an old friend and I settled in my room with a couple of beers, a cheese sandwich from a nearby garage and a film from the in-house movie channel. Sleep overtook me before the end of the movie. I woke at midnight, just long enough to get undressed and into bed properly and then I didn't surface again until just gone eight. I hadn't done that for a long time. Not sober anyway.

I arrived at the Police Station just after ten. I'd figured that would give them time to deal with the night's criminals and drunks. I was wrong. I was fourth in the queue behind a lost dog, a bad tempered man presenting his driving licence and a bleached blonde woman in a pink fluffy dressing gown trying to report her neighbour for calling her a slag.

"I mean, 'ow would she know? Huh?" the woman complained. "Bitch can't keep her knees together for more'n twenty minutes. Bleeding queue up the stairs most of the time. It's the kids I feel sorry for."

The female Civilian Police Customer Liaison Support Colleague did her best and to her credit, even remained calm when the Pink Dressing Gowned termagant squished her McDonald's 'Breakfast in a Bun' against the glass in protest at not getting the S.A.S. out to arrest her neighbour.

Eventually it was my turn and I peered through the ketchup smeared bullet proof glass as I explained I'd come to see Mervyn. I'd chosen not to refer to him as Merlin in public.

"Sarge," she called towards the back of the office. "Man here to see the Wizard of Oz."

"He's not the Wizard of Oz," I heard a voice call back. "It's Gandalf."

"Not Gandalf," I tried to correct the Support Colleague. "It's Merlin. He thinks he's Merlin, Gandalf was in—"

"Well he's not here anyway," the sergeant said as he appeared. "Bloody Mary Poppins for all I care. Damned druggies with their alphabetty pills. XT wotsits and PSPs."

"PSP is a Play Station, Sarge," the Support Colleague corrected. "I think you mean PCP."

He glared at her and she resumed writing up notes.

The sergeant looked at me. "You Mr. Magic then?"

"John Barker," I said. "Yes, my card says The Great Xando but I've retired."

"Well if you're here to see Gandalf you're out of luck, he's not here. They've taken him to a secure unit. He's a hoot that one. We had Darth Vader in here last week but he wasn't a patch on your mate."

"He's not my mate," I said. "Just somebody I... What secure unit? Where?"

"Just off Cheddon Road, here." He pulled a plastic covered map from behind the counter and slid it through the gap under the glass. "You're here." He indicated a blue cross with writing underneath it that said, 'You are here', so I guessed he was probably right. "You need to go here." He showed a point across the other side of town.

"Do you have the postcode?" I asked. "I have satnav."

He scribbled the address and postcode on a piece of paper for me. "He has to stay in there now, you know."

"How long for?"

"Seventy-two hours," he said. "After that, if they think he's still a danger they can apply for a Section Three. Then he'll be there six months at least. 'Ere, you don't happen to know anything about a little contretemps up at the Weston Pavilion Theatre a few nights back, do you?"

"No."

"Only some Spooky Mary got her knickers all in a twist when somebody called her a fraud in front of five hundred punters." He gazed at me from over his glasses. "Answers your description."

"Never been there," I lied.

"That's alright then." He turned and disappeared into the back office.

Rydon House Secure Unit was laid out like any other NHS secure facility that was trying hard not to look like an NHS secure facility. Neat lawns and flower beds attempted a sense of peace and tranquillity. I explained through an intercom the purpose of my visit and the door lock buzzed, allowing me access to the foyer. Once inside the building the combined aromas of industrial disinfectant and mashed potatoes greeted me.

I explained again to the girl behind the glass screen and she told me to wait while she checked with a nurse. After a moment a young man in jeans and sweatshirt escorted me inside and showed me a small reception room.

"I'm just going to fetch him, have a seat," he said.

The room was institutional but comfortable. A variety of out of date magazines were neatly stacked on one corner of a small coffee table.

Merlin entered ahead of the nurse who hovered near the doorway until satisfied that his charge seemed calm.

"Ah, can we go now?" Merlin asked when he saw me.

"No, you have to stay here a while. Didn't they explain?"

"Oh." He deflated into a chair.

"What were you doing? They say you were digging a hole in Glastonbury Abbey grounds."

"I have to take Arthur back to the Caves of Trewar

Venydh," he said with an air of total reasonableness. I wondered why I'd come down there. One of my more rash decisions.

"And what makes you think Arthur's tomb is in Glastonbury Abbey?" If I could just reason with him...

"The sign, of course."

"Ah, in the book?"

"What? No, well yes, but not that sign. The other sign."

"A different sign? More Fey?"

"No." He looked at me as though I should be the one locked in there, not him. "The little sign on the grass that says, *'Site of King Arthur's Tomb'*. That sign."

I wondered what it was he'd actually seen, probably some graffiti by another fantasy dweller.

"Just because somebody writes something like that doesn't make it true, you know," I said. "Or that you should dig up a historical site."

"But it *is* all true." He waved the battered Fifty Shades at me. "It's all in The Book."

"Show me," I said. Perhaps with reason and logic I could disabuse him of his delusions.

He studied me from under those huge white eyebrows for a brief moment as if trying to judge whether I was serious. He gave a little harrumphing sound as if to say, "Whatever" then came round the table to sit next to me. He opened the book on the table where we could both see it. The pages were crumpled and stained, some words were underlined and many individual letters neatly circled.

"Here. Look." He fumbled through the well-worn pages. "This is the key." His weathered finger pointed to a sentence in the book that read, *'I assign it mythical, Arthurian legend, Lost City of Atlantis status'*.

I read the section twice then said, "But the character in the book is just referring to something as mythical and using Arthur as an example."

"No, don't you see?" He stabbed at the page. "It's the first part of chapter six." He looked at me as if that explained everything. My blank expression obviously convinced him I needed help so he continued. "Six! Number six."

"Sorry, I still don't understand."

"Number six," he repeated. "It's the universal number of truth and enlightenment."

"But the character in the book *says* it's a myth?"

"Cockenpoop! You have the understanding of a flea on the arse of an eagle. It's code, The Prophet has written a very clever code."

"The Prophet?"

"James!" He stabbed the author's name on the cover. "He has written that passage in code, like all of it."

"She," I corrected.

"Huh?"

"James, E. L. James is a she, not a he."

"What? Nonsense stuff. The prophet speaks of Atlantis which is the clue. Very clever, because we know that Atlantis is real, so when he speaks of Arthur alongside Atlantis we know he means they are both real. You see? It's the number six that tells us this. The number of truth."

I was about to question his assumptions about the truth of Atlantis but he'd only paused for breath.

"Look." He opened the book at page one. "Here, where it says *'And support'*, count every two hundred and thirteen letter, which of course numerologically becomes six again, and it spells out Arthur."

"Yes but—"

"And there, in the middle of that, right inside the name Arthur." He stabbed at the page. "Starting at word one hundred and six, which is the first six of the second century, and count every fifth letter, five the number of adventure and journey, every fifth letter spells John." He stared at me, his eyes wide and slightly scary.

"What?"

"It's you, John," he said. "You, you're in The Book next to Arthur. Bound together within the numbers of Truth and Adventure."

"Don't be ridiculous." I took the book from him to see what he was talking about. On page one of the book, beginning in the acknowledgements, he'd circled various letters. They did seem to spell out the names John and Arthur and without going to the bother of counting, they did all appear to be equidistant. "Well, that's just coincidence. You could do that with any book."

I picked up a copy of 'Horse and Hound' from the coffee table. "It's just random. See, if I count every fifth letter from here I get..." I counted carefully. "I get um... HGYF. Okay, so that was a bad example. Wait a minute." I tried a few more sequences but failed to find my name or Arthur's or indeed any word longer than three letters and even that was only 'yak'.

Merlin sat, watching impassively as I struggled to find anything meaningful.

"Okay," I said, conceding defeat. "It's a bit odd, I'll give you that. But it's just chance, it doesn't really mean anything."

He seized on my weakness. "And then in chapter four, which represents home." He thumbed through the book to show me more circled letters. "Here, it spells out Avalon."

The door opened and the nurse came in.

"I think we should let him rest now," he said, nodding

towards Merlin. "He's starting to get overexcited again." He took Merlin by the elbow.

"No, wait," Merlin protested. "I need to explain about Modred. He's in the emails."

"Come on, it's time for your rest. Vivienne will fetch your medicine."

"I'll come back later," I said.

"Just use the buzzer by the door," the nurse told me. "Sandra will let you into reception." They disappeared down the corridor, Merlin protesting loudly as they went.

I pressed the intercom and a bored face in the glass fronted office glanced briefly in my direction and then I heard the buzzing of the door lock, indicating its new, unlocked status.

I let myself through into the foyer and headed for the main door.

I heard a tapping and, "Mr Barker?" from behind me. I turned to see a woman's face behind the toughened glass of the reception office.

"Can you just hang on a moment? We need some details." She motioned that she was coming round. She disappeared out of the rear of the office and a moment later entered the foyer from the door I'd just used.

"Sorry, won't keep you long," she said. "My name's Elaine, I'm one of the nurses helping your friend." She held her hand out and we shook. She was tall, only a few inches shorter than me. She wore faded jeans and a white shirt that flattered her slim figure. A nametag pinned to the shirt confirmed her name was indeed Elaine. I'd noticed the lack of official nursing attire there; everybody seemed to be wearing casual clothes.

"He's not really my friend," I said. "Just somebody I ran into... I mean ... met. I don't know anything about him."

She smiled. "That's okay; we have his notes from the

hospital. Can we check his name? The hospital has him down as Mervyn but he keeps insisting his name is Merlin, like the magician?"

"Yes, that's about it. I think the hospital decided he was confused so they stuck with Mervyn."

"Okay, I see." She made some notes on her clipboard. "We'll stay with Mervyn. I just wondered if you had any other information." Her eyes were a striking shade of green and I felt slightly uncomfortable under their interrogative gaze. "Did he say anything that might help us find a carer or relative?"

"No, sorry. He just carries on about King Arthur. I think he's a bit bonkers." I caught her look. "Sorry... I mean... um... mentally handicapped... or whatever we're supposed to say these days."

A mischievous smile danced across her eyes. "That's okay. Though you could try saying 'learning difficulties'. But I agree it's not quite as succinct as bonkers."

"What will you do with him?"

"Don't know yet, it's a bit early to tell. The consultant psychiatrist is seeing him this afternoon. We'll probably know more then."

A loud buzzing sound erupted from the corridor behind us.

"Oh hell," she said. "That's the alarm. I'd best go. Sandra will buzz you out." She indicated the bored looking girl in the glass fronted office.

The air outside smelled fresh and clean; I breathed it in deeply. The visit to that place had disturbed me. It brought back unpleasant memories of a few years ago; the rounds of hospital visits, waiting rooms and small, windowless offices. People with caring expressions etched into place by years of dealing with the traumatised and scared. I'd grown to hate those places. No doubt the staff would care for him well but the look on his face as he'd been led away had been one of complete bewilderment.

I needed to clear my head. For want of something better to do I decided to take a drive to Glastonbury, to see it in daylight.

After parking in the central car park I bought a ticket for the Abbey. I might as well see what the fuss was all about. The grounds were immaculately kept with neat lawns and flowerbeds giving sharp contrast to the crumbling ruins of the Abbey itself. I followed the recommended path and read the little placards as I passed. At one point I saw freshly turned earth in the middle of a beautifully manicured lawn. Ah, that would be Merlin. The gardeners had clearly been busy repairing the damage to the grass but it would take a while to settle back to a nice even lawn. Red tape had been strung around the area in an attempt to deter more footprints in the fresh mud. Just behind the tape another of the ubiquitous little plaques was staked to the grass. I leaned forwards to read it.

'*The site of King Arthur's Tomb*'. The plaque described how the remains of King Arthur and Queen Guinevere had been found in 1191 and later moved to this position.

Chapter Six

I reasoned that a good place to dig into a little local history would be a pub. And as that coincided with it being nearly lunchtime my idea gained initiative. The barman behind the counter in 'The King George' welcomed me and I took little persuading to sample the local ale. It was a rich and full bodied beer that had a slightly fruity taste.

"Lady of the Lake." The barman pointed to the placard on the pump. "Brewed just down the road."

"It's very good." I studied the picture, a silhouette of Glastonbury Tor with mysterious blue skies above. "That's an Arthurian thing isn't it? The Lady of the Lake?"

"All Arthur round here. It's his island."

"Island? Glastonbury's not an island."

"Not now it ain't. But it was, back in his day. Isle of Avalon they called it. All under water as far as the eye could see. Only Avalon rose. The island of apples. Now the place is full of bloody hippies looking for nirvana, or some such bollocks. Don't know why they think he's gonna give them nirvana. By all accounts he was a bloodthirsty warlord but I suppose it takes all sorts." He disappeared to the other end of the bar to serve an elderly couple.

I settled at a table by the window. Seeing the sign and hearing the barman talk about Arthur as if he were real had confused me. I distinctly remembered my history classes at school and how we'd been drilled with the names and dates of all England's monarchs and I was sure there'd never been any Arthurs. I probably needed a book. I supped my beer and watched the people passing by in the street outside. A strange mixture of new age hippies, business types and what appeared to be a coach load of German tourists.

The sun refracted through the leaded glass of the window causing coloured lights to dance on the table. I slid my glass of beer under the light and watched as the glass caught the colours. An outbreak of confused chattering drew my attention to the door. We were being invaded by the German tourists who had obviously settled on The George as their lunchtime rest break. My tranquillity disrupted, I headed back out to the main street in search of a bookshop.

Glastonbury is an eclectic town with the usual mix of High Street regulars such as chemists, banks and estate agents rubbing shoulders with shops selling magic crystals and other pagan paraphernalia. For a small town there was a surprisingly good selection of bookshops, both new and second-hand. I went into what appeared to be the largest and it didn't take me long to find the Arthurian section. It nearly covered a whole wall. As a stage magician, I'd had a passing interest in the English myths but only in so far as I could use them to steal material for my act. I once had an act which featured the Sword in the Stone. I used to challenge strong men to come onto the stage to try to draw it, which of course they couldn't, and then I'd invite a child up who would be able to free it. That had been the extent of my Arthurian foray, preferring instead to plunder the rich vein of Eastern mythology. Much showier.

Apart from the expected Malory or Geoffrey of Monmouth versions there were countless other versions detailing both the fanciful and the supposed historical biographies. There was also a plethora of new fictional adventures and graphic novels. Various works attempted to present him as either a space alien or an angel with one even claiming he was the second coming of Christ.

Merlin was well represented with a complete set of shelves given over to him. So-called historical studies claiming he was a real character sat alongside a series of novels presenting him as a sort of medieval Batman. There was even a set of Merlin's Tarot cards. The sceptical me bristled. I pulled out one very small volume, about the size of a matchbox, entitled 'Merlin's Little Book of Calm'. Each page carried an illustration of an ancient bearded man in various scenes along with a pithy quote supposedly attributed to the wizard. My favourite was, "When feeling stressed, sit under an ancient oak tree for an hour." Great advice for when you're stuck in a traffic jam on the M25. I slid the book back in the shelf.

"He's my spirit guide, you know," an American voice to my left announced.

I turned to see a rotund woman in her fifties. Her hair was bleached almost white and contrasted sharply with the slightly orange colour of her skin. She wore a brown feather on a leather thong around her neck; it dangled just inside the clearly augmented cleavage.

"Sorry, what?"

"Merlin, he's my spirit guide. He came to me in a dream."

"Oh good." I continued browsing the books, hoping she would go away. She didn't.

"He told me to take up yoga to help cleanse my colon."

"That was very helpful of him."

"I've always been a victim to my colon," she continued. "I think it's too long and things hang around longer than they should."

"How very inconvenient for you." I picked up a book which explained Merlin as an interdimensional being sent to watch over humanity. There was a whole industry here about which I was completely unaware.

"He's not a Brit, you know."

"Who?" I thought I must have lost a chapter of this conversation.

"Merlin. He's not a Brit. Everybody thinks he's a Brit but he's not."

"Okay," I said, still studiously avoiding eye contact.

"He's a Native American Indian. Hopi tribe."

"Really?" I turned to face her. "Merlin? An American Indian?"

"Yeah, of course, most people don't know that. He gave me this." She tugged the feather free from her bosom. "Well, not personally of course." She laughed and pushed my arm in what I guessed she thought was a playful, conspiratorial manner. "No, he uncovered it for me while I was at an Angel seminar in Wisconsin. He sent it to bring me inner peace."

"That's nice. I'll see if he's got one for me next time I see him," I said. "I could use some peace. Inner or outer, not fussy. Now I really must get on, it's been a pleasure meeting you and your feather."

I turned back to the bookshelves and chose one which seemed to be making a reasonable attempt at deconstructing the Arthurian myths and headed to the pay counter.

"That's an awesome book," said the young man behind the counter. "Read bits of it once. Really makes you think. Like, there's some dudes who don't even think he was real, know what I mean? That's fucked up, man."

I took the book and headed back to Taunton. I wanted to stop by the unit again to see how Merlin was doing but when I entered the foyer, instead of buzzing me through like before, the girl asked me to wait. I settled into one of the soft chairs and idly thumbed through the book while I waited.

Elaine, the nurse with whom I'd spoken earlier, arrived after about ten minutes. She sat down in the chair next to me.

"Sorry to keep you waiting," she said. "We have two new clients in and they're feeling a bit lost."

"No problem. I was just wondering if it was possible to see Mervyn?"

She shifted in her seat. "He's resting at the moment. He's feeling a bit tired after his meeting with the Psych evaluation team."

"What happened? What did they decide is wrong with him?"

She gave me that look again; the one that intimated I'd just said something dreadful. "I mean... right with him..." I struggled. "I mean his difficulty thing, challenging. His differently abled potential."

"Nice try," she said with a smile. "I'm afraid I can't divulge that information. You're not family or carer. Sorry."

"But he doesn't seem to have any family," I said. "Unless of course you count Harold."

"Harold?"

"His stick, he calls it Harold."

"Ah, yes, I remember. Perhaps you could come by tomorrow? He might be feeling better then."

***

The Travel Lodge was sited almost alongside a large pub. I stopped in there for supper and a couple of beers. The place was full, mostly young people gearing up for a night out. The smells of cheap aftershave and sickly vaping fumes overwhelmed me. I ate quickly then retired to my room with the book.

I skimmed the chapters and found the section on Merlin. The book was a well-balanced treatise and gave what appeared to be good historical references along with the fictional sources. No real attempt had been made to come down on one side or the other although the feel of the narrative was that there had been a real character in sixth century Wales called Myrddin Wyllt. He'd been known either as a prophet or a madman depending on the differing views of his contemporaries. Five hundred years later, Geoffrey of Monmouth had blended the character with his Tales of King Arthur and changed his name to Merlin. I tracked through the references to Arthur which again proved inconclusive. As with Merlin, there appeared to be a real character in sixth century Wales who might have been called Arthur. A brave warlord who protected his environs and people from enemies and monsters.

Okay, so nobody was going to say categorically whether or not either character actually existed. I remembered the grave I'd seen at Glastonbury and scanned the book until I found mention of the Abbey. Surely as a real historical and religious site of some importance they must have a reasoned view. Once again though ambiguity reigned as historical facts became embellished with myth and hearsay. The Abbey cleverly avoided making any definitive statements and just detailed the movement of some bones until they'd finally disappeared when the Abbey was destroyed. One theory the book posited was that the monks had hijacked the Arthurian myths in order to bolster their flagging pilgrim trade. That was probably as valid as any other opinion.

I threw the book to one side. What I'd thought would be a very simple yes or no answer dissolved the more I looked into it. Everybody had an opinion and the trouble was that most of these opinions were driven by profit motives. Books to sell, religions to promote, tourist currency to attract or pilgrims to rob. Nothing changes.

I settled to bed and my dreams were invaded by Arthur and Merlin. In the morning I showered and

enjoyed a full English breakfast in the pub next door before setting off for Rydon House.

I was told to wait in the foyer as somebody wanted to talk to me before I saw Mervyn. I had to wait nearly twenty minutes before Elaine appeared.

"Sorry," she said. "We're a bit stretched at the moment. We had several new clients in last night and one of them is extremely disturbed."

"That's okay," I said. "It can't be easy. How's Mervyn?"

"I need to talk to you about him. He had a really bad episode yesterday after you left. Vivien was trying to give him his medicine and he became quite violent."

"But... but... He's never showed any signs of that. That's not like him. What happened?"

"We're not sure but something set him off. That's the trouble with schizophrenia, it's often impossible to anticipate the trigger."

I thought for a moment. "Is that what he's got then? Schizophrenia?"

"Interim diagnosis but yes, that's what Mr. Kashani thinks. He's the consultant. We see this more and more these days unfortunately. Usually the result of skunk weed."

"Skunk weed?" I'd heard it mentioned but wasn't quite sure what it was.

"It's a genetically modified version of cannabis. Extremely dangerous and usually smoked by people who spend most of their time protesting about GM crops. Ironic really."

"Oh, I see."

"We've had to apply a Section Three order."

"What's that? Sounds serious."

"Sort of, yes. It's so that we can keep him safe and see he gets his meds."

"Oh. How long's he likely to be here?"

"Probably at least six months. The difficulty is that we can't release him into anybody's care. If we can't find a responsible family member to look after him after his release, it makes it difficult."

"Can I see him?"

"Of course but don't expect too much." Her green eyes danced across my face as if searching for something. "I'm sorry," she added.

Elaine was right to warn me. The person waiting in the Family Room was not the Merlin I'd come to know over the last few days. He sat slumped in the high backed chair, eyes staring sightlessly ahead.

"Merlin? It's me, John."

He shifted his gaze in my direction. "Who? Oh, yes, John, John John. I remember John. Who's John?"

"How are you feeling? You're looking good," I lied.

"John?"

"Yes."

His eyes brightened momentarily. "Can we go now?"

"No, sorry, they say you need to stay a bit longer."

"Did you bring any pizza?"

"No, I'll come back with some later if you want."

"They keep giving me squashed potatoes. Squashed meat

with squashed potatoes on top. Why do they keep squashing all the food here?"

"It's just temporary," I said.

His eyes fell. "They took my book," he said quietly, more to himself than to me.

"Why would they do that?"

He suddenly grabbed my arm as if trying to crush my bones. "Vivien," he said, his eyes suddenly alive. "She tried to poison me." He looked genuinely afraid. "I'm not going in the cave." He released my arm and slumped back into the chair.

"Why would she try and poison you?" I asked. But he'd gone away.

I waited a moment but he seemed to have nodded off. I headed for the door and just as my hand touched the handle I heard him say, "John?"

I turned but he still seemed to be asleep. I slipped out of the room.

Once in the foyer Elaine reappeared.

"What have you done to him? He looks dreadful."

"It's just the medication he's on. He'll get used to it, you'll see. It often takes them time to adjust."

"I'll take him," I said. I was shocked at my own words as they left my mouth.

"What?" Clearly they shocked Elaine as well.

I considered what I'd just said for a moment then added, "I can look after him. He's not that bad. I had him for a couple of days. Okay yes, he did drive me nuts... I mean learning difficulties... um... you know what I mean."

She sighed. "Even if he were able to be released, we couldn't release him into your care anyway. You're not a relative, or a registered carer. Your only connection with him is that you knocked him over with your car. Hardly qualifies you really. Sorry." She did her best caring nurse smile.

"Why did you take his book?"

"It seemed to be exciting him too much. He's a bit calmer now; I'll see he gets it back."

I drove back to the hotel and packed my bags. I'd done my best. I wasn't quite sure what I'd hoped to achieve by racing down there and leaving him in an institution certainly wasn't the plan. But it was probably for the best, he was clearly disturbed and he needed help. I settled the bill, threw my bag in the back of the car and drove straight back to Rydon House. It was only when I pulled up in the car park that I even consciously considered what I was about to do. Merlin may be away with the pixies but he didn't deserve that. He wasn't dangerous, he was just different. But there was also something else about him I couldn't fathom and it intrigued me.

The girl in the office buzzed me through without any thought and I waited in the foyer for somebody to let me through into the residential section. Elaine arrived after a few moments.

"Did you forget something?"

"Sort of," I said. "Can I have another few words with him?"

"We can't keep letting you through like this," she said. "We have official visiting hours. We make exceptions for new clients but we can't keep doing it."

"Last time, I promise."

She gave me a slightly puzzled, slightly knowing look then tapped in the security code on the door lock to let me through.

I waited in the Family Room until a male nurse brought Merlin through.

He sat in the same chair as before. He clutched his notebook and battered copy of Fifty Shades of Grey.

"I see they gave you back your book," I said.

"John?"

"Yes, it's me."

"Can we go now?"

"Yes, Merlin. We can go now."

I opened the door a crack and peered through. The corridor was empty. I turned back to Merlin. "Come on but you have to do what I say and be very quiet."

"Quiet, yes. Shhh."

"And small," I said. "You have to be quiet and small."

I led him to the door to the foyer and made him get down on all fours. I pressed the intercom and the bored office girl gave a cursory glance in my direction. Merlin was below her line of vision so she just pressed the remote door lock and returned to Facebook or whatever else it was that was occupying her interest on her phone.

I walked slowly to the main door with Merlin crawling on all fours alongside me like some shaggy Labrador. He was still below the eye line of anybody in the office so as long as nobody actually entered the foyer from the residential area he'd remain hidden. I reached the front door and turned the handle. There was no lock on this side so the door swung open under my hand. We continued our strange walk until we were out of sight.

"Okay, you can stand now." I helped him to his feet and we made our way unsteadily to my car. He slumped into the seat as if the effort had taken the last from him.

I started the engine and breathed out slowly. Calm.

"Where's Harold?"

"What?"

"Harold, I can't go without Harold."

"You're going to have to. We were lucky to get out."

Merlin pushed open the door and attempted to get out. He collapsed into a lump on the pavement.

"Get in!" I yelled. "We need to go now."

"Got to get Harold."

"They'll lock you up again if we get caught. For good next time, and me with you most like."

He started crawling along the path. "Quiet and small. Shhh."

"Damn it!" I thumped the steering wheel. "Get in. I'll get Harold."

I strode up to the door with all the false confidence I could find. Bored girl buzzed me in once with a slight expression of surprise. No alarm bells yet. I marched up to her window and she slid the glass to one side.

"You planning on moving in here?" she asked with a small grin.

"No," I said. "I forgot something."

"Just go through." She indicated the interior door and slid the glass shut.

"No, it's not there."

"What?" The glass opened again.

"It's Merlin's... Mervyn's stick. It was taken from him when he arrived."

"A stick? They're not allowed sticks in here."

"Yes I know." I glanced around me. The longer this conversation continued the more chance of Merlin being missed. "I assume that's why it was taken from him."

"They could hit each other with sticks."

"I can understand that. It's probably in a cupboard or wherever you keep your inmate's stuff. The stuff they're not allowed to have."

"Can you describe the stick?" She pulled a clipboard from under the desk.

"Describe it? How many sticks have you got back there?"

"I don't know until I go to look." She raised her eyes with a flick as if I should understand stick cupboard protocol.

"It's about five feet long and—"

"What's that in metres?" she interrupted.

"Huh? I don't know. Two? Nearly."

"Any distinguishing features?"

"Really? Can't you just go and see what sticks you have? I could point to the right one."

"But you might point to one that's not yours."

"Why on Earth would I do that? Do I look like a stick thief?"

"Any distinguishing features?" she repeated.

I glanced around once more. I was really pushing my luck. I should really make a run for it.

"It's got some feathers tied to it and it goes by the name of Harold."

The interior door opened and Elaine came in. "John?" she said. "Is everything alright?"

"Oh, yes. Fine." I looked around, no burly guards coming yet. No alarms. "It's Mervyn's stick."

"I told him the inmates aren't allowed sticks, Nurse," the girl in the glass box said.

"They're not inmates remember, Sandra? They're clients." Elaine turned to me, her eyebrow raised in a questioning manner. "Stick?"

"Yes. It's about five feet long with feathers."

"I remember," she said. "Harold isn't it?"

"Yes, he's concerned about it. Wants me to look after it for him."

"He thinks we're going to lose his stick?"

"Hum..."

64

Elaine turned to Sandra. "Go fetch the stick."

"But I haven't filled out the form."

"Just get the stick, Sandra."

The girl disappeared through the back.

I turned to Elaine. "Thank you," I said. "It's important to him."

"I can see that," she said. "He wouldn't want to leave it behind would he?" Those green eyes lanced through mine.

"Um, no," I said.

Sandra emerged complete with Harold and slid it through the glass hatch.

"Thank you," I said.

"You should really go now, John," said Elaine.

Chapter Seven

I hurried out of the doors and dived in the car. Merlin was asleep in the passenger seat.

I needed to go somewhere where we wouldn't be noticed. That might prove tricky as Merlin was hardly a forgettable character. Another Travel Lodge was probably the best bet. Anonymous and simple but it would need to be well clear of Taunton. I headed east on the A303 for no other reason than it just seemed like an anonymous type of road. As I drove the full impact of what I'd just done began to spread over me. That had certainly been one of those life changing decisions, right up there with Napoleon's bright idea to visit Moscow for his summer holidays. I was not usually given to great acts of impulsiveness and certainly not ones which involved the potential for arrest and imprisonment. I glanced over at Merlin; he was still fast asleep.

After a few more miles I pulled into a motel. It wasn't a Travel Lodge but seemed to be of the same type. It was out of the way and unremarkable. The disinterested desk clerk took my cash as prepayment then handed me the keys. I bundled Merlin through to the room without anybody seeing and he collapsed on the bed to resume his sleep. I tried watching the television for a while but it was either Jeremy Kyle or some celebrities spending four hours striking a bargain over a second hand teapot worth fifty pence.

I picked up Merlin's copy of Fifty Shades of Grey. The pages were tatty with many in danger of falling out. Scribbled notes covered many of the pages, completely obscuring the text in places. Hundreds of letters had been circled with different coloured ink and lines and arrows connected the circles. Names were scrawled in the margins, some I recognised from the Arthurian book, but most I didn't. I put the book down and took a peep into his notebook. That seemed filled with random letters and more circles and lines. There were many hand drawn maps with lines across them, diagrams with strange symbols and lists and lists of numbers. I heard Merlin stir and quickly replaced the book.

"Who moved the cakes?" he said.

"You alright?" I asked.

"Where's Harold?"

"He's over there." I nodded towards the corner of the room.

Merlin slipped back into sleep and didn't awake fully for another two hours. I plied him with coffee and we went in search of food. A nearby fast food place provided an acceptable burger and chips although Merlin didn't seem to notice what he was eating. I kept the caffeine intake going. I didn't know what they'd given him or how to counteract it or even if it was dangerous to stop the treatment suddenly. But Merlin survived and gradually became his usual self, if anything about him could ever be deemed usual.

"Where are we?" he asked eventually round a mouthful of chips.

"Somewhere near Salisbury."

"I can't be here."

"Why not?"

"I don't know. Where are we going?"

"Ah, to be honest I haven't the faintest idea. Can't go back to London, that's for sure."

"Avalon. I have to go to Avalon." His eyes had taken on a wild, slightly manic look and I figured I'd probably overdone the coffee.

"Avalon, that's Glastonbury isn't it?" I was proud of the bit of knowledge I'd gleaned.

He paused for a moment, contemplating my assertion then, "Ah, the glimmerings of reason. We go there."

"I don't think it's a good idea going back there. They're probably looking for you... us."

"I need to find Arthur."

"He's not in Glastonbury you know," I said. "If he ever was."

"Where's he gone?"

"Nobody knows. The placard in Glastonbury Abbey says the bones were moved to somewhere else. But there are definitely no bones in the bit you were trying to dig up. I checked."

"Oh," said Merlin. "Then I need Cynbel. Cynbel will find him."

"Where's Cynbel?"

"I don't know."

"I thought you were a wizard. Shouldn't you know everything?"

"Of course I don't know everything. For example, I don't know..." He paused, clearly trying to think of something he didn't know. "I don't know what's behind me."

"Okay."

"What's behind me?"

"Huh?"

"What's behind me? I'm worried now."

My phone rang; I didn't recognise the number so I just pressed 'Ignore' and left it on the table. It rang again.

"Your little box seems very angry." Merlin pointed at my phone.

The phone carried on ringing so I took a chance and answered it.

"Mr Barker?" a male voice enquired.

"Yes."

"Sergeant Halliday, Taunton Police."

"Oh, yes. I remember."

"We're looking for a missing person and wondered if you might drop by the station to lend your assistance, as it were."

"Sorry that won't be possible." I was watching Merlin trying to use his spoon to see what was behind him. "I'm on my way back to London."

"Well that's somewhat inconvenient."

"Who's missing?" I asked.

"Your friend Mervyn. The fellow you were enquiring about at the enquiry desk."

"Who?" I played dumb for effect. "Oh, that guy who was digging in the church or something. I remember. He's not my friend though, just somebody I bumped into. How can I help?"

"He's done a bunk from the nuthouse. We were wondering if you had seen him."

I watched Merlin empty little piles of salt onto the table.

"No, not seen him. Is he dangerous?"

A long pause at the other end indicated doubt. I followed up quickly to drive home my advantage. "Do you think he's coming for me? It was only an accident. Shouldn't I have police protection or something?"

"No, sir. I doubt he's looking for you. Probably long gone now. Sorry to trouble you."

"Okay, as long as you're sure." I hung up. "Merlin, what the hell are you doing?" Little piles of salt spread all over the table.

"Salt runes." He poured another little pile. "How else am I supposed to find Cynbel?"

"What are salt runes?"

He studied me carefully as if in deep thought then pointed at the little piles of salt and said, "These are."

I sighed. "Okay, but what are they supposed to do?"

"I just told you." His tone was scolding. "I have to find Cynbel. Pfah! You have the ears of a stubborn ox and your memory is more slippery than an eel in mud."

"But you never—"

"Shush now. Enough of your jibber-jabber. I need quiet or the runes won't speak."

He lowered his head to the table and viewed each little pile of salt carefully from different angles. "Ah," he said after about a minute. "It is clearing. I can see—"

A waitress's napkin swept across the table, scooting the piles of salt into a little pan.

Merlin gave a high-pitched squeal of horror as his runes disappeared in front of his nose.

"Sorry," said the waitress. "Some of the salt pots have loose lids. At least it didn't go all over your food." She finished cleaning up the salt. "I'll get you a fresh one."

"Yeaow!" Merlin yelled.

"Shush," I said. "People are watching. I'll buy you a whole bag of salt to play with if you want."

He stared at me, his eyes seeming to grow into two moons. "I saw the lines. I know where Cynbel is. We have to go." He stood and marched out of the restaurant.

I paid the bill and caught him up next to the car.

"Map," he demanded as we got in.

70

I fished out my large scale road atlas of Britain and handed it to him.

"Pen."

I found a pen in the glove box then started the car.

Merlin grabbed my hand. "Wait," he said. He scrabbled through the pages of the atlas and settled on the full page map of southern England. He drew a line straight across the map from the most easterly point of Great Yarmouth through to the far west point of Land's End. "Show me Avalon," he demanded.

I found Glastonbury and pointed it out to him. Oddly, it lay exactly on his line.

"The big stone circle. Where's the big stone circle?"

I assumed he meant Stonehenge and indicated it on the map. He drew another line from there to Glastonbury and then one dropping south from somewhere near Clevedon to somewhere a few miles south of Glastonbury. The end point of each line settled on a 'Site of Antiquity' according to the key on the margin of the map. I guessed these were the so-called ley lines that the fairy chasers and UFO spotters get all excited about.

"Here," Merlin said, stabbing at the point where the three lines intersected. "Here is where we will find Cynbel."

"Who is Cynbel?"

"Not who. Cynbel is... Well maybe a who. Where's my map?" he demanded.

I opened up the large scale section of Somerset and compared it with his lines on the small scale page. The lines appeared to intersect at Glastonbury but the scale was still too small to determine precisely where. I wasn't excited about heading back to Glastonbury. Far too close to Taunton and I was probably on some most wanted list of kidnappers and jail breakers.

"Isn't there something of more interest at the other end of the line?" I pointed to Great Yarmouth. "This place looks promising. It's still on our line and I happen to know they have a nice theatre."

He stared at me and scowled. "Here," he said, poking at Glastonbury. "We go here."

Chapter Eight

As we approached Glastonbury I spent more time watching my rear view mirror than looking forwards. Each time a car stayed behind me for any longer than a few minutes I would either slow right down to see if they passed or I'd turn off and do a loop. The things one can learn after years of being force-fed American cop shows in hotel rooms. Merlin took no notice of my paranoia and spent the whole journey either underlining or crossing things out in both books.

"I need a stone," he said as I struggled with Glastonbury's narrow streets.

"I wish you'd said earlier. We passed some fields a few miles back, bound to have been some there."

"Fields?" He seemed to have a think about that. "No, that would take too long. Could take years."

"Years? To find a stone in a field?"

"The right one," Merlin snapped. "It has to be the right one, in tune with my vibrations. Any old stone nonsense people. Pfaf!"

I hadn't the faintest idea what he was talking about but I knew that once he had one of these strange ideas fixated in his head there would be no deterring him. I remembered Glastonbury's collection of shops.

"I know where you might find one," I said.

We parked up and headed up the High Street. Almost every

other shop offered a selection of stones and crystals. The first shop we entered had dozens of racks of little boxes with hundreds of different coloured rocks and semi-precious gems. I idly ran my fingers through a little box of shiny blue stones. They felt smooth and pleasant to the touch. I picked up a large piece of quartz that had been polished smooth on one side. The colours shifted as I moved it in the light. Some green pebble shaped things caught my eye and I picked one up for a closer look. It had speckles of black in it. Quite odd.

"Whoa, man," I heard a voice behind me. I turned to see a man with long dreadlocks and green coat that skimmed just above the floor. "You're mixing the energies, man."

"What?" I said.

"The energies, man. You keep taking energies from different crystals and muddling them. Not cool. Bad energy syncing."

"Sorry," I said. "I'm still not sure what you're talking about."

"Talking nonsense words. Farmyard babble. " Merlin approached us, looking at the man.

"What do you mean?" the man asked.

"Cockerel noise! The nonsense sounds a cockerel makes in the morning when it can't think of anything to say to the sun. Cockerel noise."

The man thought about that for a moment then shook his head and said, "But he's mixing the energies." The man pointed at me. "You can't mix the energies."

"Him?" Merlin said, pointing in my direction. "He can't mix his own porridge. He certainly can't mix energies from a crystal as old as time itself and neither can you." He pointed his stick at the man. "Numwit."

"Thank you, Merlin. I think."

"Merlin?" the man said.

A woman emerged from the rear of the shop. "What's happening?" she asked, glancing at the three of us as if we were naughty children.

"It's Merlin!" the man said, pointing at Merlin.

Oh bugger. "Mervyn. I didn't say Merlin; that would be silly. His name is Mervyn, not Merlin. Whatever next." I gave a little forced laugh to show the humour of the mistake.

"It's Merlin," the man said again. "Look, he's got a wand. It must be Merlin."

"What? That's not a wand," I said. "It's a walking stick. His name's Mervyn and that's a stick. Look, anybody can have a stick." I picked up a stick from a nearby rack of sticks. "See, now I've got a stick."

The woman touched my shoulder and carefully took the stick from my hand. "Actually, that is a wand as well," she said. "We don't sell sticks."

"Well, it still doesn't—"

My phone rang, interrupting my hole digging.

"Your little box is angry again," said Merlin.

I answered the phone as an escape.

"John?" a female voice said.

"Yes." I watched as Merlin poked the man in the chest with Harold.

"It's Elaine. From the Rydon House Unit."

"Who? Oh, yes. How are you?" Inane comment, I realised as soon as the words left my lips but I was preoccupied watching Merlin as he picked a stone from a box and held it to his forehead.

"Can we meet?" Elaine asked.

"Um? Oh, yes. Can you hang on a moment?" I put my hand across the phone to shield the sound and said to Merlin, "What are you doing with that? Put it back."

"He's divining his companion," offered the man.

Merlin tossed the stone on the floor proclaiming, "Worthless trinket," and reached for another.

"John? John?" the phone squeaked from under my hand.

"Oh, yes, sorry. What did you say?"

The woman shopkeeper chased after the stone as it scuttered under a book rack.

"Can we meet? It's important."

"Yes," I said. The man offered a green stone to Merlin who poked at it with the feathered end of Harold and then dropped it to the floor and batted it across the shop like a seasoned golfer.

"Where are you?"

"Glastonbury. Look I've got to go. Little bit of a crisis going on here."

"I'll meet you in an hour. In the King George. Do you know the George?"

The shopkeeper tried to position herself between Merlin and the rack of wooden boxes.

"Yes," I said. "The George. One hour." I killed the phone call and took Merlin by the arm. "Come on, we need to go."

"Worthless rubble," he said as I guided him out of the shop. "Shiny rubbish for shiny minds."

"Sorry," I said over my shoulder to the shopkeeper. "He's a bit... learning difficulties. Sorry."

"I need a stone," said Merlin. "How do you expect me to find Cynbel without a good stone?"

"I know where you can get a stone," the man with the Rasta hair said. I hadn't noticed he'd followed us out.

"Who are you?" Merlin tapped the man on the chest with his stick.

"Casio," he said. "But my mates call me Cas."

"Casio?" I said. "Like the digital watch?"

76

"Yes, my parents were children of the seventies."

"Then lead on, Cas of the seventies children," said Merlin. "We have a stone to find."

"No, wait..." I started but they were already in full mission mode heading up the High Street.

I followed them down a narrow alley which bristled with small shops along its sides until they disappeared into one called 'Total Majyk'. The shop was crowded with the three of us. The shopkeeper sat behind a small desk in the corner. He had long blond hair that tumbled in tangles over a multi coloured shirt. He tried to stand when he saw Cas but the location of his desk under the staircase meant he could only stand into a crouch.

"Hey, Cas," the shopkeeper greeted. "Cool. You still on Community Service?"

"No, just finished. But I got to go back to court again next week. They found some weed on me when I went into the Police Station to sign off."

"That's bad, man. You don't expect to be searched when you go into a Police Station. They're getting tricky."

"I know; you can't trust 'em. This is my mate, Merlin." He indicated Merlin. "He needs a stone."

The man extracted himself from his corner and hugged Merlin. "Merlin, I'm Baz, it's been a long time," he said.

"I have to find Cynbel," said Merlin once he'd freed himself from Baz's embrace.

"Cynbel is real?" asked Baz. "I thought it was just legend."

"Of course Cynbel is real," Merlin said. "Why would I need a stone to find something that isn't real? What sort of idiot son of a barn door do you think of me?"

"Who's Cynbel?" I asked.

"Come, come," said Baz, tugging at Merlin's sleeve. "I have some special companions here."

I turned to Cas. "Who's Cynbel?"

He shrugged. "Beats me."

Merlin and Baz were hunched over a selection of plastic boxes in the corner of the shop with much mumbling and stone examining. Suddenly Merlin held up a small rock and said loudly, "Aha, here you are." He marched out of the shop clutching his prize followed closely by Cas.

I turned to Baz. "Sorry, he forgot to pay. He's a bit... um... differently challenged. How much is that bit of stone?" I took some change from my pocket.

"It was his all along," Baz said. "I was just caring for it."

I thought for a moment then said, "You do know he's not *really* Merlin, don't you?"

Baz looked at me as if I'd just told him the sky was made of pink jelly. "The time is coming." He returned to his corner and pulled a book from a shelf.

I stood for a moment, still holding the money but he ignored me. I went in search of the others.

"Have we done now?" I asked Merlin. "Only Glastonbury is probably not the best place to be for either of us."

"I need somewhere quiet to find Cynbel," Merlin said.

I looked around. The town was a bustle of activity with hippies, shoppers and tourists all fighting for pavement space.

"How about driving out of town and finding a field?" I suggested hopefully.

Merlin glared at me. "What is your fascination with fields?"

We walked up the street a while until Merlin found a peaceful courtyard behind a church.

"Acceptable," he announced and settled himself on a wooden bench.

I suddenly remembered the phone call and checked my watch.

"I have to go," I said. "Are you okay here for a while?"

"I need some string," said Merlin.

Cas searched his pockets and shrugged. "Nothing."

Merlin looked at me expectantly.

"I haven't got any," I said.

"Wait here," said Cas and darted across the courtyard to intercept a pair of hippies as they passed by. The man was very tall, slim with sun-bleached hair whilst his companion was a willowy woman who appeared to be totally dressed in an assortment of coloured scraps of cloth and feathers. An animated exchange followed of which I could hear nothing but involved much pointing in Merlin's direction then all three came over to us.

"See," said Cas indicating Merlin's stick. "I told you."

"Wow, cool," said one of the hippies. "Can I touch it?"

Merlin glared at the man and snapped, "String?"

The hippie pulled a roll of string from his pocket and handed it to Merlin.

"I have to go," I said. "You'll stay here?"

Merlin ignored me.

I turned to Cas. "Keep an eye on him. Please?" I knew it was a futile request but they seemed to be busy with stones and string so that might keep them amused for a short while.

I hurried along to the George and found Elaine already there.

"Sorry, got held up. Can I get you a drink?"

"I'll have small cider, thank you." She wore jeans and a plain white tee shirt, her hair was loose and tumbled across her shoulders.

I bought the drinks and we found a discreet table in a corner.

I took a long sup on my beer. That was much needed. "So, what's the panic?"

"It's about Mervyn."

"Ah, what's happened? Is he alright?"

"John, don't take me for a fool. I know you helped him escape."

"Hum..."

"I've been suspended."

"What? No, hell. That's not right. You didn't do anything."

"He got out on my watch. That's quite a big no-no in social care."

"Okay, look, I'll get him back."

She reached across the table and covered my hand with hers. "It's alright. It's just procedure. They'll do their inquiry then reinstate me. Take them a couple of weeks, lots of interviews and forms to keep the scorekeepers happy then I'll be back to mopping up vomit or fighting off violent junkies in no time. Whoopee."

"I see. Sorry. So, why the urgent meeting?"

"We had some more information come through about him. Look, I don't know why you feel the need to help him but I just wanted you to know what you're getting yourself into. It might make you think again about what you're doing."

I drank the last of my beer and pointed to her glass. "Another one?"

"Why not?"

I returned a moment later with the refills and faced her across the table. "Okay, what's the story?"

"It took a while to track him back as we had no real name or I.D. Anyway, after a general query through the system we had a result from Shapwick Lodge in Salisbury. It's another secure psychiatric unit; he was there about two weeks ago. He was picked up by the police after a disturbance at Stonehenge."

"Digging?" I asked.

"No, he was just wandering around inside the stones but as you know they're fenced off. Nobody has any idea how he got in there in the first place, it's got more fences than Buckingham Palace. The English Heritage staff tried to control him but in the end they were worried he'd turn violent and called the police. Eventually he was sectioned and sent to Shapwick Lodge."

"How do they know it's the same person?"

"He claimed he was Merlin and demanded somebody take him to King Arthur's grave. Sound familiar?"

"Ah, I see."

"Anyway, he managed to escape, goodness knows how. Next time he was spotted, he was on a bus to Glastonbury where he started shouting at the other passengers. He was described as a wild man in a long dressing gown in the back of the bus waving a book and shouting about the prophet. Can you imagine the panic that caused? Of course by the time the bomb squad arrived he'd long gone and nobody saw him again until you brought him in to Taunton General."

"Bit of a character then."

"That's one way of describing him. I just wanted you to know. He's quite ill; he really should be somewhere secure. For his own safety."

I thought for a moment and supped slowly at my beer. "Why are you telling me and not calling the police?" I asked.

"I'm not really sure. He needs help but I'm not sure we can give him the help he needs. Yes, we can keep him safe and subdued but he shouldn't really be locked up. The trouble is, the mental health system is struggling for funds and that doesn't leave us with many options, especially when there's no relative to offer a safe place."

"He'll go mad if he's locked up again." I realised what I'd just said. "Sorry, I meant... no, I really don't have another word for it."

"That's alright. Sometimes that's just the right word. What is he to you? Why do you feel the need to save him?"

I studied my empty glass. "It's a very long story and I'm not sure you want me to bore you with all the details."

She sat back in her chair and tipped her head to one side. "Try me. I'm told I'm a very good listener."

I smiled. "I'm sure you are." I thought for a moment. "He said something once—"

I glanced out of the window to see Merlin, Cas and the two other hippies passing by. Merlin had a spade across his shoulder and the whole group seemed to be moving with great purpose. That wasn't going to end well.

"Oh, hell," I said.

"What is it?"

"I've got to dash." I stood up and headed for the door. "We might be about to lose another national monument."

"I'll come with you. He might listen to me."

Chapter Nine

We caught up with the group halfway up the main road.

"Merlin!" I called. "Where do you think you're going?"

He didn't answer and just carried on at full march.

"Merlin," I repeated. "Whatever it is you think you're doing, don't. You're going to end up in a police cell again."

"He's right," Elaine said. "You won't escape again. They'll see to that."

He stopped and turned to Elaine. "Ah, the Lady Gaoler. Come with more of your poison no doubt."

"Nobody was trying to poison you, Mervyn. Merlin." She turned to me. "Merlin? Really?"

"Yes, sorry."

"Cynbel is this way," Merlin said and continued his mission. The little group followed.

"Who is Cynbel?" Elaine asked me.

"Funny that. I've been asking the same question and can't seem to get an answer. I guess we follow and see."

We followed the road as it twisted at the brow of the High Street and wound through a more residential area. At least this was less conspicuous. I moved alongside Cas as we walked.

"Do you know where we're going?" I asked.

"To find Cynbel," he said.

"Who is? Sorry forgot, you don't know either. Where then? Where does this idiot think he's going?"

"To the Tor. The stone showed him."

"The stone?"

"His divining stone. The one we got from Baz. Really, it's all very simple really."

"Why are those two coming along?" I indicated the two hippies.

"That's Sebastian and Tree," he said as if that answered the question.

"Tree?"

"She's an angel channeller."

He moved away from me to walk next to them.

"We're going to the Tor," I told Elaine. "With an angel channeller."

"Oh good," she said. "That will be nice."

***

The Tor is a fairly taxing climb and by the time we'd reached the top I was quite out of breath. The sun was just setting over the Somerset levels, spreading shafts of colour across the fields. It was a spectacular view. Despite the climb and the late hour there were still a good number of visitors milling around although the demographics of Glastonbury being what they were our strange group attracted little attention. That was until Merlin pulled his stone out, which now dangled off a piece of string. He drifted around the hilltop holding it out in front of him and muttering under his breath. In my role as a professional debunker I'd never paid much attention to diviners. They'd always seemed to be just a harmless bunch of crackpots and never appeared on my radar as scam artists or fraudsters. That was until some scammers created a modern version of the divining sticks which they claimed would detect bombs then sold them to governments around the world. I'd been called as one of the expert witnesses to testify as to the trickery involved.

However, the one thing I did know for sure was that Merlin wasn't a scammer. I didn't know what he was but he had no intent to lure anybody, quite the contrary in fact, and it was that which I found most intriguing.

It wasn't long before we had a little group following us around. Each time Merlin stopped to examine the tiny undulations of his pendulum a hush descended only to be broken again by excited jabbering when he started moving again.

Eventually he stopped at a spot just outside of the tower and announced, "Cynbel is here." He swung the spade from his shoulder and set to digging.

I ran over and grabbed his arm. "You can't dig here. It's a historical site."

"Nonsense, this is Arthur's land." He threw the spade into the ground and turned a square of turf to one side.

"You have to stop him," Elaine said. "He's starting to attract attention."

She was right; a little group had started to gather.

"Do you want to try? Because he never listens to me," I said. "I'm just hoping he gets bored before the police come."

Merlin continued to dig with a fury which belied his physical build. We gradually collected more interest from the tourists.

One man sidled over to me. He wore brown corduroy trousers and a navy blue jumper. "He's not allowed to do that," he said. "This is National Trust property. They don't allow detectorists to dig. Not on National Trust property. They're a funny lot."

"He's not a detector—"

"Detectorist," the man corrected. "It's a criminal offence you know, metal detecting on Scheduled Monuments."

"He's not metal detecting." I watched as Merlin dug deeper.

"Only I'm the branch secretary of the Central Somerset Metal Detectorists. We do try to maintain a spirit of Entente Cordiale with the National Trust."

"I'm sure you do, but he's not detectoristing or whatever you call it."

Merlin threw the spade to one side and started scrabbling in the hole with his hands. "Aha!" he yelled. "Cynbel, here you are." He stood and brushed dirt from a small object he held.

"Oh dear," said the detectorist. "That's going to cause friction at the next committee meeting."

I moved a step closer to see what Merlin held. It looked like a ring of some sort, with a large stone but it was still caked in dirt so it was difficult to see.

"Merlin, we need to go."

"I need to find Arthur," Merlin said. "Now I have Cynbel I can find him."

"Merlin, if we don't go now—" I was interrupted by somebody behind me pushing me to one side. I turned, ready to snap but stemmed my tirade when I noticed a pair of blue uniforms.

"What's going on here?" one of them asked as he pushed his way past me.

Merlin gave a high-pitched squeal and yelled, "Vagabonds and footpads." He stepped backwards and tripped into his hole. The ring tumbled from his grasp and landed about a metre in front of me. As the policemen started towards Merlin I knelt to retrieve it, hoping nobody would notice.

Cas grabbed Merlin's arm and helped him to his feet and

then the pair of them sped down the hill. The policemen started to follow but Sebastian and Tree interposed themselves, giving time for the others to disappear. One of the policemen span in my direction before I was able to pocket the ring.

"Not so fast," he said. "What have you got there then?"

His colleague turned to assist and grabbed my wrist before I had chance to do anything. He took the ring and held it up to the fading sunset in a hope of better discerning what had caused all the fuss.

"This looks like a ring to me," he said to his colleague. "We'd best take this one with us."

They took an arm each and I was guided down the path. They seemed contented that they had at least one culprit and they weren't about to give me the option to slip away. We continued down the path to the fading cries of, "Police Brutality," and "Fascists." I guessed that was Sebastian and Tree giving their considered opinions on the proceedings.

I was bundled into the back of the police car and driven to Taunton Police Station where I was relieved of my belt and shoelaces, finger printed, photographed, processed and deposited in a cell all within the space of thirty minutes.

"You'll be interviewed shortly," said the duty sergeant as the cell door closed on me.

I looked around my new home for the next few hours. It was small, barely two metres wide with a built in bed taking up the whole of the end wall. Glass bricks high above the bed would provide light during daylight. It was slightly longer than wide with a stainless steel toilet and washbasin halfway along the tiled wall. Not quite up to Travel Lodge comfort standards.

Had I come prepared I could probably have picked the lock, escapology had always been a big feature of my stage show. However, I hadn't brought a pick and there was nothing to hand with which I could create one. And even if I did, I would still have to get past the front desk. No, that idea was a non-starter. I also didn't want to spend the rest of my life being a wanted fugitive. I needed a better way out of this, a way where I could walk clear. I contemplated hypnotism; I used to do some quite spectacular shows involving hypnotism. But of course hypnotism's never quite as easy as the professionals make it seem. It's not possible to hypnotise somebody by just putting your hand on their forehead and saying 'sleep'. That's just clever editing for television. It takes one-to-one preparation time. It also needs a responsive subject. Although the popular belief that one can only hypnotise the weak minded is completely unfounded, there are still only certain types of people that respond well and quickly. Oddly, police officers and military personnel are generally very receptive as they are conditioned to respond to orders. But even so, hypnotising the desk sergeant to let me walk free wasn't going to happen. Even the most responsive subjects will not do anything out of character or against prior training.

I settled onto the hard bed and wondered just how much trouble I might be in. If the metal detectorist had been right and metal detecting on National Trust was actually a criminal offence rather than just a civil one then it could be quite serious. On the other hand, nobody had actually been in possession of a metal detector. I wondered if I should demand a solicitor.

The cell door opened and the desk sergeant came in and handed me a small carrier bag.

"Just in case you're hungry," he said.

"Thanks." I peeped inside the bag. A plastic wrapped sandwich, a plastic bottle of Coke and a chocolate biscuit. Clearly a 'Meal Deal' or something from a local petrol station.

"The arresting officer will be along shortly, he's just been out on a burglary."

"Is he supposed to be doing that?"

"What? Oh I see, humour. You'll go down a storm in Wandsworth."

"Wandsworth?" I felt a moment of panic.

"See, I can do humour too. Don't worry, he'll take your statement then we'll have you up in front of the magistrate in the morning. You'll be out there on the steps of the Town Hall with your broom doing your community service by tomorrow afternoon."

"But I'm innocent."

"Of course you are. We only ever lock up innocent people; don't you read the Daily Mail?" He closed the door gently but it still sounded like a slam.

I sat for a while contemplating my situation. I'd only caught a quick glance of the ring. It had a large stone and could well be silver under the dirt and if that was the case, I'd been caught in possession of an item of potential value or even historical significance. I could argue I'd just found it but Merlin's hole probably wasn't going to help that plea.

I munched at the sandwich; the label suggested it contained cheese and onion. Possibly. It might also have been cardboard and potato peelings.

It was whilst I was unwrapping the chocolate biscuit that I began to formulate an idea. I put the biscuit to one side and carefully spread out the silver paper. The thing about hypnosis is that, excluding the extroverts on stage shows, most people will only do those things that are normal to them. I folded the silver paper until I had a strip about six inches long and a quarter inch wide. The art of the hypnotist is to convince somebody that the abnormal is actually perfectly normal. I twisted the silver paper strip into a small loop around my finger. The hypnotist also needs time alone with the subject, free of distraction. I took the plastic bottle top and twisted it into the silver paper ring. Passable. I slipped it into my shirt pocket then ate the biscuit.

I had to wait another hour before the officer who'd arrested me finally made an appearance.

"John Barker?" he asked, somewhat unnecessarily as he'd originally taken my details.

"Yes," I confirmed.

"Follow me," he said and headed off up the corridor, leaving me to follow. I wondered if I should feel slighted at his obvious disregard for my escape potential.

I followed him into a side office and he indicated I should sit opposite him at a plain metal table. A large mirror took up most of the facing wall and I assumed that was a sort of two way glass. I also assumed that the severity of my crime probably didn't justify a team of detectives on the other side of it observing my every move.

He switched on a recording machine and clearly announced his name as Police Constable Eric Ambledon. He went on to give a formal preamble which included basic details of the arrest.

When he'd finished he pushed a plastic bag across the table towards me. "Recognise this?"

I examined the bag. It held the ring, in a slightly cleaner state than when I'd last seen it. It certainly looked silver. The stone was black, large and of a rough cut. It appeared to have hints of a sparkle in there somewhere. So this was supposed to be Cynbel. Probably just junk jewellery lost by some kid.

"I think so," I said with a deliberately quiet voice. I glanced upwards as if looking at something on the ceiling. I noted his eyes followed mine as if trying to make out what I was looking at. That was promising.

"My recollection is a bit vague," I continued. "I'd been out walking. It was a very warm day, relaxing, very relaxing." I looked up at the ceiling again and once again he raised his eyes to follow.

I slowed my voice and dropped my tone. "I remember feeling a bit tired. You know, sleepy. You know how it is after a busy day when you're tired and warm?"

He nodded and relaxed noticeably. "Is this going anywhere?"

"Sorry," I said. "It's just my way of making sure I remember everything. I find it helps when you're feeling stressed and need to relax..." I continued in this way for several minutes making sure to include as many trigger words as I could. Each time I raised my eyes to the ceiling he followed and I noticed his eye movements were slowing.

After ten minutes he was in a fully hypnotic suggestible state.

Time to test. "Can I see your watch?" I asked.

He took it off and slid it over the table. Good, nicely receptive. I held it for a moment then gave it back to him. "It's very kind of you to let me relax and to remember," I said and slowly opened the plastic bag which held the ring. He made no reaction.

"You know how things can be confused when we don't look closely?"

He didn't answer but nodded slowly. I raised my eyes to the ceiling once more and as soon as his followed I did the switch. A neat little trick I'd performed on stage probably ten thousand times. The switch of one object for another. In the instant his eyes left my hands I'd replaced the ring in the bag for my own homemade silver paper and bottle top version.

"I'm sorry," I said. "I'm very tired now. Can we do this later?" I slid the bag back towards him. If I had done my job right, he would see in that bag precisely what he expected to see. A dirt encrusted silver and stone ring.

He took the bag without checking it. "Come on. I'll take you back to your cell. Sergeant Halliday can deal with you tomorrow. I've had enough for today." He stood with a slight wobble and led me back to my cell.

Just before he closed the door I said, "Remember to tell Sergeant Halliday that you've not been drinking."

He looked at me with a puzzled frown, gave a slight harrumph and closed the cell door on me.

I sat on the bed. PC Ambledon may well be in a very relaxed state but I certainly wasn't. My calm exterior and relaxing voice had been a charade which was actually very stressful for me to maintain. The swan, calm on the surface and pedalling like hell underneath. I breathed slowly and deliberately to control my racing heartbeat.

I'd planted enough trigger words to create an air of confusion in his memory. I was certain he wouldn't remember the switch and he'd probably struggle to remember the events of the arrest. I relaxed on the bed and tried to settle into sleep.

Chapter Ten

I was awoken by my cell door banging open. Sergeant Halliday filled the doorway.

"Up you get," he said. "Don't think you're going to spend all day sleeping in my cells. Got a football match on later so we'll be needing your bed." He stood back and waved me out.

We headed back to the interview room and he indicated I was to sit. He went through the same formalities as PC Ambledon of the previous evening.

"Right," he said. "It falls on me to clean up the mess created by that dopey PC last night."

"Is he alright?" I asked with my best serious and caring voice. "Only he seemed a bit... sort of wobbly."

"Wobbly is it? Kept telling me he hadn't been drinking then fell asleep on the floor. I suppose you could call that wobbly."

"Why am I here?" I asked. "Only I'm still not sure what I'm supposed to have done."

He banged both huge palms flat on the table. "Well, we'll start with metal detecting within the grounds of a Scheduled Monument, that's a criminal offence, then we'll probably move on to removing Treasure Trove without informing the relevant authorities and if I can make it stick I might add theft from National Trust property. That do you for starters or do you want me find some more? Only I have a feeling you're probably something to do with the escape of Harry bloody Potter from the local nuthouse as well."

"I wasn't digging," I said. "I was just watching somebody else digging. Don't know who it was, some hippy type."

He scanned the notes and mumbled to himself. He pushed the notes to one side and said, "Perhaps you'd like to tell me in your own words what happened then?"

"I was just stood watching somebody digging. I thought it might be Time Team or something."

"Time Team is it? What about the ring? Would you like to explain what you were doing with an item of Treasure Trove removed without correct permissions or authorisation?" He looked down at PC Ambledon's notes. "Namely one silver ring with large unidentified stone."

"What ring?" I asked. "All I had was some rubbish I'd accidently dropped then picked up."

He stood and headed to the door. "Wait here," he said and closed the door behind him. He returned a few minutes later with the evidence bag in his hand, he tossed it onto the table.

"Recognise that?"

"Yes," I said. "That's the rubbish I dropped which I then picked up again. That's when the officer grabbed me."

He examined the silver paper ring and bottle top in the bag. "Get out of my Police Station," he ordered. "And take your rubbish with you." He tossed the bag at me and left the room.

I followed nervously. When I reached the front desk Sergeant Halliday was already in flow down the telephone. "I don't care if he's still feeling wobbly; just tell him to get his incompetent backside in here now." He slammed the phone down and turned to see me. "You still here? If you don't bugger off now I'll charge you with loitering."

I needed no further telling.

As my car was still in Glastonbury I had no option but to ring Elaine and beg a lift. She was instantly obliging and ten minutes later we were headed to Glastonbury once more.

"I really appreciate this," I told her.

"No problem. I had to go to Glastonbury anyway."

"Oh, why's that?"

"A friend of mine needs a lift." She grinned.

We chatted as we drove. Elaine wanted to know how I'd managed to avoid being charged and she laughed when I relayed the sergeant's anger.

"Serves him right," she said. "He was very rude when he interviewed me about Merlin's escape."

We found the car park where I'd left my car.

"I need coffee and breakfast," I said. "Can I buy you one? Just to say thanks."

"Coffee would be good but I'll pass on the breakfast."

The only eatery open that early was a vegan Asian Fusion cafe so my choice was restricted to tofu sausage, noodles and alfalfa sprouts. Hardly the fry-up I'd been hoping for but at least the coffee was good and strong.

"What happened to Merlin after I was arrested?" I asked.

"I didn't see. He just ran off down the Tor and disappeared. What will you do now? Back to London?"

"I thought about it but I have the ring Merlin was after so he'll only hunt me down if I try to run. The man's relentless."

"Can I see it?"

"Of course." I placed it on a paper serviette on the table.

Elaine picked it up and studied it. "Could be silver, I suppose."

"It could also be a cheap trinket from a Christmas cracker."

"Don't you think it's a coincidence that it was exactly where he was digging?"

"Not really. Glastonbury Tor attracts tens of thousands of tourists every year. I should imagine if one were to dig anywhere round there something would turn up."

She polished the stone on the serviette. It had a dull shine to its irregular surface. "So why is this so important to him?"

"From what I can gather, he's got it into his head that he has to find the bones of King Arthur and take them to the caves of wendy-wondy or something."

"Wendy-wondy?"

"That's what it sounded like. He thought Arthur was in Glastonbury Abbey and I'd rather hoped that when I'd proved he wasn't there, he'd give up. No, now he needs a divining stone to find Cynbel, which I assume is what he thinks this thing is, and now, somehow this trinket is going to lead him to a secret grave or something."

"And you don't believe any of this?"

"Do you? I mean, you see these fruitloops every day... sorry... umm... differently challenged learning people. You see them all the time, what do you think?"

"Well, Merlin is certainly a new one to me. Mostly we get messiahs and aliens. Although we did have a Tony Blair once. He kept apologising for the war, which was how we spotted he wasn't the real Tony Blair." She paused thoughtfully and took a sip of coffee. "That and the fact he was five-foot two and as bald as an egg. But I try not to make judgements on their reality. My job is to help them come to a position where they can function outside in the world."

"I've spent my life in the world of make-believe and illusion," I said. "Either creating illusions or destroying them but I've yet to see anything which can't be explained rationally."

"How does David Blaine levitate?"

"Huh?" The random question caught me off-side.

"That street magician, David Blaine. He levitates himself, how does he do that?"

"Really? Oh for goodness sake, that's just tricky camera work and a bunch of kids getting paid by the number of times they can squeal 'OMG'."

"Oh." She seemed almost crestfallen. "What is it with his obsession with Fifty Shades of Grey?"

"David Blaine?"

"No, you idiot." She thumped my arm playfully. "Merlin, he spent all day reading it and making notes."

"He believes it's a prophecy book." The waitress came over to clear the table and I ordered more coffee.

"A prophecy book? Fifty Shades of Grey? How on Earth does he see that?"

"He's found a code within the text. There are words in the book like 'Arthur' and 'Avalon' and so on, that are spelled out when one counts different sequences of letters. For example, the name Arthur is spelled out in the first paragraph of the book, every so many letters, can't remember how many, and then straight after that is your name. You count every... erm, I think it was every thirty fifth letter or something."

"My name?" She seemed shocked.

"Yes. He made a point of showing me that one, all marked out in little red circles in the book."

"That's very strange." She shifted uncomfortably in her seat and toyed with her coffee cup.

"Hmm, I have to admit it is a bit odd."

The door of the cafe burst open and Merlin breezed in followed by a small group.

"Where's Cynbel?" he demanded.

"Good morning, Merlin," I said. "Nice to see you too." I turned to Elaine. "See, I told you he would hunt me down."

97

"Who is this?" Merlin pointed towards Elaine.

"That's Elaine. You remember? From Rydon House?"

"Ah, the fair Lady Elaine. She knows not what the curse may be, and so she weaveth steadily."

"Thank you," said Elaine. "I think."

"I have more remembering today." Merlin turned to me "Cynbel?"

I pulled the ring from my pocket and gave it to him. He snatched it from my hand and held it up to the light.

"Yes," he announced to his entourage, "this is Cynbel."

"Thank you, John," I said. "How was your night in a prison cell? Really? Oh I am sorry to hear that. Must have been dreadful for you."

Merlin stared at me. "What nonsense are you speaking now? You look like you've found the last toad in the box." He looked around the café. "Do they keep pizza in here?"

"It's vegan, so probably not," I said.

He moved my coffee to a different table then pulled my road atlas from his shoulder bag and spread it out on the table. He tied a piece of string to Cynbel and dangled it over the map. His group gathered round in rapt interest. In addition to Cas, Sebastian and Tree, he now also had in tow the metal detectorist from last night. I squeezed out of the crush and moved to the table to follow my coffee.

The waitress hovered to see if any of this strange group was actually going to order anything or just clutter up her tables.

Tree put her hands to the sides of her head, closed her eyes and made small moaning noises while Merlin scrutinised the dangling ring. I guessed this was an example of her famed skills with the angel channelling although she might have been having an orgasm.

"What are they doing?" asked Elaine.

"I think Merlin is using the ring to divine his next assault on some unsuspecting ancient monument and the..." I just stopped myself before the word '*Nutcase*' left my lips. "The lady with the beads and ribbons in her hair is probably trying to call down the Angelic Hosts to help with the digging."

"You don't have much time for the spiritual, do you?"

I cupped her hand in both of mine. "Trust me; I've wasted far too much time on people claiming they can talk to fairies, aliens or the dead. Most of them are just scam artists trying to fleece the bereaved and the rest of them... Well, I suppose they're mostly harmless. Until the point where they turn up on your doorstep wearing a tinfoil hat and holding a cucumber."

She gave me the threatening eyes and looked as though she was about to say something cutting but I was saved by Merlin.

"Here," he shouted. "This is where we go." His finger stabbed repeatedly at my road atlas. I watched the pages rumpling under his attack and wondered which particular site of ancient antiquity was about to fall victim to his enthusiasm.

I stretched towards the map to risk a peek then turned back to Elaine. "How do you feel about a day trip to Salisbury Plain?"

Chapter Eleven

My car wouldn't take the full ensemble so Sebastian, Tree and Cas followed in Sebastian's yellow Volkswagen bus. Elaine and I took my car with Merlin and Colin, the metal detectorist, in the back seat. We had to stop first at Colin's house to collect his metal detecting kit which turned out to be far more substantial than I would have thought and resembled a home fracking outfit. The traffic was kind and soon we were heading up the A303.

Colin explained to Merlin in great detail the benefits of his Minelab GPX5000 detector and why it was far superior to the previous model while Merlin mostly ignored him and continued to count letters in Fifty Shades of Grey. Both seemed contented each time I glanced in the mirror.

"You were going to tell me a long story," said Elaine.

"I was?"

"Back in Glastonbury, you were about to tell me why you felt a need to look after Merlin. You said it was a long story."

"As I said; if I try to lose him he'll just hunt me down. He's like a Patriot missile, relentless. And prone to explosions if you don't pay attention." I pulled out to overtake a line of military vehicles.

"That's not a very long story."

"I lied."

"What's eating at you, John Barker? Why are you so angry at the world?"

"Because it's a shit world, full of lies and deception and those who take advantage of the weak. The politicians make noises about protecting the vulnerable then use them as sacrificial pawns to their own ambitions while the snake oil salesmen of the afterlife gather the bewildered like sheep and tease them with dreams of eternal smileyness and calorie free chocolate cake."

"I see," Elaine said after a slight pause.

The line of military traffic seemed endless and a pair of caravans cluttering up the overtaking lane weren't helping.

I heard a loud thwack from the back seat followed by an affronted, "Ow!" I glanced in the mirror. Merlin was beating Colin about the head with Fifty Shades of Grey.

"Merlin," I called. "What's going on?"

"Will you tell this bumble-headed flea brain here to keep his mindless gibbering to the inside of his head only?"

"I was only explaining how the coil on the Minelab is tuned... Ow!"

Another loud thwack announced a further collision of book and head.

"I have no need of any Minelabs, even if I had the slightest idea what one was, and your interminable dribble of words is muddling my numbers."

"Will you two pack it up," I yelled into the back seat. "Or I'll stop the car and you can both walk."

I heard Elaine giggling to my side.

"Don't you start," I scolded.

I felt her hand rest on my arm and give a slight squeeze. It felt nice.

***

We stopped at a roadside services just outside Warminster. The yellow Volkswagen pulled up alongside and the other three piled out.

"I'm not sure where we're going from here," I told the others. "We'll get a bite to eat and stretch our legs a bit while Merlin talks to his precious."

The car park to the restaurant was large and meandered from gravel to the moorland of Salisbury Plain at its edges. I strolled across the grass to give my head some space. The expanse of the countryside spread out before me with drifts of grass and wooded areas sharing the land as far as the haze heavy horizon.

I felt, rather than heard Elaine slide alongside me.

"I don't believe you, you know," she said as I continued to stare out across the gently rolling plain.

I said nothing.

"You're attracted to his spirit," she continued. "He's so alive; he has purpose and a mission. Something you've forgotten. Yes, he's as mad as a box of frogs but he's alive."

"I thought you weren't allowed to say stuff like that?" I still refused to catch her eye.

"I'm on suspension so it doesn't count." She was close by my side. I could feel her warmth. "He has the magic you seem to have lost somewhere."

Her choice of words startled me. I stiffened and fixed my gaze on a far tree.

"What happened?" she asked.

I stayed silent, not trusting myself to speak but the words climbed to be heard. I had kept these boxes closed and hidden for so long I wasn't sure what would happen should I reply.

I felt her hand take mine. "Talk to me, John."

I took a deep breath. "Her name was Amy." I hadn't spoken

her name out loud for so long the sound was unfamiliar on my voice. "Sixty-two days from diagnosis to..."

I felt her hand squeeze mine.

"We met at university. While the lecturers taught me the names of the galaxies, she taught me how they looked on a cold winter's night from the top of a hill. She taught me the meanings of the constellations and I taught her card tricks." I kept my eyes focused on the tree. It looked like an oak from here, could well have been there for a hundred years and with grace, it may well last a hundred more. "She went on to be my assistant in my stage show when I turned professional. We were never more than fifty feet apart for twenty-five years. And then... Do you know the names of all the characters in Alice's Adventures in Wonderland or the complete twenty-third psalm?"

I turned to face her and she kept my eyes. She shook her head.

"I do. Amy taught them to me, along with the names of all the chakras and the language of trees. She believed in the magic. While I created clever illusions for the stages of Europe she talked to the plants and they grew magically under her hands. That's the magic she held. She believed in the persistence of the spirit and the unbreakable bond between two souls locked together across eternity."

Elaine's eyes searched mine. "And you don't?"

"I did. I believed in the magic. When the medicines failed her, we tried everything. We had the faith healers and snake oil salesmen queueing at our door. And yet... When the end came of course it was all my fault. They told me I hadn't had enough faith." I held my breath for a moment to quell the rising anger. "In those last days, she made me a promise. She promised to come back and connect with me. She wasn't sure how or when

103

but we agreed a code. A phrase that only the two of us would know, so there could be no doubt. So the tricksters could not deceive us... me."

I drew a deep breath and exhaled slowly until my eyes could see again through the film that had started to gather.

"What happened?" Elaine asked.

"Just lies and trickery. Thieves who make their promises and tempt with their flimflam games. The trouble was I knew all the tricks. I knew all about cold readings, rigged decks and Barnum phrases, I knew how easy it was to trick those who desperately wanted to believe. No matter where I looked, all I found were liars and cheats ready to rob the heart-broken."

She held both my hands and scanned my face trying to see beyond my words.

"What did you do?"

"I exposed them. Every one of them I met. I took them down and showed their lies to the world. There is no magic; it's all just tricks and illusion. There's no better place waiting, no souls reaching out to each other through the void. There is only the void."

I turned away from her and found my tree again. "And do you know the worst thing?" I asked when I had regained control of my voice.

"Go on," she said.

"The worst thing is that we never said goodbye properly. She was so convinced we would connect again she refused to say goodbye. She just said to me, 'The magic is real, never lose it'. Those were her last words to me. Don't ever lose the magic." I felt Elaine's arm slip through mine and her body pressed close. We stood for a while saying nothing, just watching my tree.

After a few minutes, with my breathing under control, my

eyes clear and the lid firmly back on the box we went into the restaurant to catch up with the others.

**

We ate burgers, pizzas and chips around my now dismantled atlas of Britain. Merlin had drawn straight lines across it which I assumed were ley lines. We appeared to be sitting right on top of one he'd marked with a big red cross. It ran directly between Glastonbury and Stonehenge. Merlin was dangling Cynbel from a piece of string into the centre of a triangle formed by the intersection of three lines. I craned between the others who were studying his efforts as if he were a surgeon embarking on open heart surgery. The focus of his attention appeared to be a large area mostly marked in green on my map and mostly devoid of sensible roads.

"I hope you brought your wellies," I said to Elaine.

Merlin moved his pendulum to the east where it immediately came to a slightly unnerving dead stop. It was poised halfway along one of his lines which seemed to join Avebury with Stonehenge.

"That's a really powerful Ley," said Sebastian. "Do we really have to dig there? We might disturb some deep, powerful forces."

"What's so special about that?" asked Elaine.

"Don't encourage them," I whispered to her.

"It runs from Stonehenge and it goes up to Silbury Hill." Sebastian looked at Elaine for signs of understanding. "Silbury Hill? Surely you know about Silbury Hill? Huge, massive and really old, like really old, man-made hill. It's about the size and shape of the pyramids. Did I say it was old? 'Cus it is. There've been a mega load of alien crop circles there, even a

Mayan symbol once. Not a good place. It's full of tunnels that go nowhere."

"I warned you," I said.

"How long is this line?" Merlin demanded, stabbing at the map.

I took it from him and compared the line to the scale in the corner. "Looks about thirteen and a bit miles," I said.

"Thirteen, thirteen." Merlin stared at his hands. He had a slice of pizza in one hand and Cynbel still dangling from the other. He glanced at his copy of Fifty Shades of Grey as if wishing he had a third hand. After a small but anguished hesitation, he placed Cynbel on the table and picked up the book. "The number of evil. Aha, here." He poked his slice of pizza at a point on the page. "Thirteen and a bit?"

"A bit," I repeated. "Difficult to tell accurately. Call it thirteen, near enough."

"Thirteen and a bit." Merlin's pizza slice followed the words down the page, leaving a slight orange coloured stain in its wake. "Here," he announced.

We grouped around the book. Two sets of letter sequences were circled, one set marked in red and the other in black. The words clearly spelled out 'Modred Keep'.

"What's that mean?" I asked and immediately regretted it as all eyes turned to me. Each set shared the same expression of incredulity as if I'd just asked who Father Christmas was.

"Modred, Arthur's undoing. Mordred, Medraut, Medrod. Many names for one demon. Arthur's final nemesis." Merlin glared at me. "Brains of a cabbage and the sense of a pig on a plate. Modred killed Arthur. We will find Arthur at Modred's Keep. It's here." He pointed at the circled words. "It's all written in the prophecy, see? Doubting halfwit son of a dimble head."

Muted, drawn breaths circled the group.

Finally Sebastian broke the reverence. "I told you, it's a bad place. Modred's Keep, that's too heavy."

I looked at the map where Merlin had now planted a big orange pizza stain. There was nothing there and certainly nowhere called Modred's Keep.

"So, just to recap," I said. "We go here, in the middle of lost, where we will find somewhere called Modred's Keep and that is where we will dig up the body of King Arthur?"

"Cool, isn't it?" said Cas with a big grin.

"You've got to be kidding me."

"Look at it this way," said Elaine. "When we get there and find nothing but cows, you can put all this to rest with a great big 'Told You So' and we can all go home."

***

**MOD
REDS
KEEP**

The wooden sign stood proud and displayed the words, 'MODREDS KEEP'.

"Seriously?" I said as I stared at the sign. Elaine sniggered.

We had followed Merlin's convoluted directions through narrow lanes and across country tracks. We'd had to stop frequently for Cynbel dangling and angel chanting in between several U-turns when we had found either impassable fields or fences. It had taken three hours of to-ing and fro-ing before we'd finally come to a barbed wire fence where the sign heralded the impossible. MODREDS KEEP.

"This is some sort of joke." I moved closer to the sign to

examine it. A wooden post about two metres high supported the sign itself, also made of wood. The age of the timber on both sign and post indicated it had been there for some time and not just thrown up yesterday to pull some stunt. The right hand side of the sign looked like it had rotted or broken away leaving a ragged edge. I pulled at the post; it was solidly installed further indicating it had been there for some time.

"I don't understand it," I said. "This is just insane. I mean, look." I pointed at the words in case Elaine hadn't seen them. "Modred, it says. Modred's Keep. Only he's a minor mythical bit-part in a larger mythical book of made-up stories and yet here we have a sign to his Keep in the middle of Wiltshire. Real Wiltshire that is, not made-up mythical Wiltshire."

"Yes, I can see that," said Elaine.

"It's ridiculous, it can't be right."

"Yet here it is, exactly where Merlin said it would be. Just the same as the ring appeared yesterday."

"He knew. He knew it was here all along. In fact I wouldn't mind betting he put it here in the first place. There has to be a rational explanation."

"Other than the one which says he might just be who says he is?"

I studied her face to see if she was making a joke. She wasn't. "I think you've been too long in The Happy Palace; they're starting to get to you."

She stooped to pick up a stray stick. "If I thought you were being serious I'd beat you with this." She waved the stick at me in a mock threatening manner.

"If I thought *you* were serious about the offer, I'd let you."

She returned an ambiguous grin.

The others were gathered around the barbed wire fence amid much discussion. I moved closer to examine the fence. It was around one and a half metres high with five strands of rusting barbed wire stretched taut. It was clearly designed to deter entry rather than offer total impenetrability. Certainly more than was necessary to keep animals either in or out. It stretched off into the distance in both directions with what appeared to be further signs placed every few hundred metres. Off in the distance a small construction nestled close to the fence. From here it was impossible to make out what it was but it was clearly man-made.

Merlin was trying to push at the fence in an attempt to find a weak spot.

"We could cut the wire," suggested Sebastian. "I've some wire cutters in my van."

"We can't do that," said Colin. "It looks like private property. We could always ask the owner for permission to dig."

"I wonder if it's electrified." Cas tapped at a barb with the tip of his finger.

"There's something over there." I indicated the structure. "It might be a gate."

"Yeow!" yelled Merlin as he sought to extract his coat from the barbed wire which now entangled him.

"I'm sure we could pull this post down if we all work together," suggested Sebastian. "It looks quite old."

Tree was walking in gentle circles, her eyes apparently closed; she was making low humming sounds.

"Shall I get my detector?" said Colin, to nobody in particular. "Only we might find something of interest here outside the fence rather than destroying somebody's private property."

"You won't get through here." Sebastian pulled at Merlin's coat but as fast as he disentangled one set of barbs another strand caught hold.

"Over there." I pointed at the construction in the distance again. "Might be somebody we could ask."

I heard a thump and a very un-angelic expletive from behind me. I turned to see Tree sitting on the ground rubbing her ankle. Probably the victim of the rabbit hole next to her.

I looked at Elaine and nodded towards the construction. "Fancy a walk?"

We picked our way along the edge of the fence, rabbit holes providing a persistent hazard. As we approached, the structure came more into view revealing a small collection of make-shift shacks and tents. They looked like they had been abandoned for a very long time.

"No way in here," I said.

"Look." Elaine pointed to another of the signs. This one was complete and the words read,

MOD FIRING RANGE
RED SECTION 7
KEEP OUT - DANGER

"Ah," I said. "*Not* Modred's Keep then."

"The other sign must have been broken," suggested Elaine. She chuckled. "It's quite funny when you think about it though."

A clattering noise from one of the shacks caught my attention. A bearded man emerged; he wore army surplus fatigues, a camouflage cap and clutched a broom handle with a vicious looking hunting knife duck taped to the end of it. He aimed it at my midriff.

"You'll not move me," he said. "I have rights enshrined in the Magna Carta and I'm not going until Trident leaves."

"Who's Trident?" I asked.

"I think he means the missiles," Elaine said. "Trident, the nuclear missiles."

"Here? In the middle of Wiltshire?" I said. "I never knew Trident was based here."

"That's what they want you to think." The man relaxed slightly. "They convinced all the others." He waved his spear round the empty shacks and tents. "They believed the propaganda and lies. Not me. I can see through their spin doctors and corrupt politicos." He held his hand out to me. "I'm the General."

"General?"

"I was elected general of the People's Rebellion Against Trident. Only they all went, so it's just me now."

"How long have you been here?" I asked.

He counted on his fingers. "Seventeen years. Ever since they brought them here. They snuck them in on millennium night while everybody was busy in their street parties watching the fireworks."

"How did you know?" I knew I was going to regret the question as soon as it left my lips.

He studied my face as if trying to decide if I was being serious or if I was just plain stupid. "It was on the internet," he said finally and with a tone that said that should have been self-evident.

"And you've lived here for seventeen years?" Elaine's eyes scanned the site.

"I've everything I need. Supporters bring me food, the occasional beer or sometimes a small financial contribution for the struggle." He looked hopefully at me for a moment then carried on. "Although I am running out of firewood. I've had to start burning their signs." He indicated a pile of wood just to one side. Much of it appeared to be bits of the warning signs.

111

That would explain why the one we'd first encountered was incomplete.

"Why only take part of each sign?" I'd noticed there were no complete signs in the pile.

"I don't want them to know it's me," he said. "If I only take a bit of each they'll probably put it down to the rabbits."

"The rabbits?"

"There's lots of them round here. They get into everything."

"What about this one?" Elaine asked pointing at the still complete sign on the fence. "Why did you leave this one?"

He tapped his nose. "Ah, that's to throw them off the track."

"The rabbits?" I asked.

"No, the fascist military. Clever, huh?"

I looked through the fence. Salisbury Plain drifted off into the distance. Rolling low hills, earthy mounds and small wooded areas but not much of anything else. Certainly no buildings or anything to indicate a Trident nuclear base.

"You do know that Trident is a submarine based missile?" I said, staring across the fields.

The General looked at me for a moment, and then said, "That's what's so clever."

I gave up on that conversation and turned to Elaine. "I think we should point out the real sign to Merlin and see if we can persuade him to give this up. There's nothing in there."

"Good luck with that," Elaine said. She turned to the bearded man. "Do you ever see anybody in there?"

"They run around out there in their little tanks and Jeeps, I think they're chasing aliens. They've been doing more since the crash. Sometimes they come over to me to talk to me, the soldier ones are alright but it's the generals who want me gone. But usually it's the drones. They keep buzzing me, taking pictures and trying their mind control rays on me. They disguise them as birds now you know. But I see them, I know."

I pressed a twenty pound note into the man's hand. "You take care."

We walked slowly back to the others while keeping an eye on the landscape the other side of the fence.

"He's a bit of a character," Elaine said.

"That's one word for him but at least we've cleared up this nonsense about Modred's Keep. I must confess that had me going for a minute there."

"I noticed." She smiled. "Still a bit odd though, don't you think?"

We arrived back to find the others in a state of confusion and panic. Merlin had finally managed to fight his way through the barbed wire and was walking up and down, holding Cynbel out on the piece of string. Tree was still chanting and Sebastian yelled left-a-bit, right-a-bit instructions to Merlin. Cas appeared to be trying to persuade Colin to part with his metal detector.

"You can't just chuck it through the fence," Colin said. "It's a piece of precision equipment. He wouldn't be able to use it anyway, bones aren't metal."

"What's happening?" I asked as we joined them.

"Tree has picked up the ley energy field and Merlin is trying to follow it," explained Cas.

"He needs to be quick," said Sebastian. "I think there's something coming."

I listened and could clearly make out the sound of an approaching vehicle. It sounded big and lumbering and came from the other side of the fence.

"We need to go." I spotted a dust cloud drifting towards us that a moment later materialised into an army truck. "Merlin! Quick!"

He looked up at me and I pointed at the approaching truck. He waved back at me and returned to his dowsing.

"Elaine, get the others into the cars. I'm going to have to get him back."

"They'll lock you both up if you're not quick."

I fought my way through the barbed wire, picking up scratches and cuts with each movement. At one point my shirt became so ensnared I had to shrug myself out of it and leave it behind. I stumbled into the clear and ran towards Merlin.

"Ah, there you are," he said. "Be a good fellow and put your foot just here." He indicated a little dip in the ground.

"No, we have to go, look." I pointed at the truck, now clearly visible as an armoured troop carrier. "They're going to catch us, Merlin."

He shrugged me away and continued his dowsing.

"You'll never find Arthur if they lock you up again," I tried. "I won't be able to get you out next time."

He paused whilst he considered this for a moment and then said, "Spawn of cur hounds with their infernal war machines." He shook Harold towards the truck then ran for the fence with remarkable speed.

We scrambled back through the wire just as the troop carrier neared. I gave a tug at my shirt on the way through but it was too entangled. Gathering more cuts and scratches we finally broke free as the truck pulled to a halt.

A soldier jumped clear, he bore the marks of a sergeant on his arm.

"Hey, you," he yelled. "Come back here."

We decided to ignore his request and piled into our vehicles and raced off up the rough track.

"That was close," Elaine said.

"Way too close," I agreed. "Are we finished with this

nonsense now, Merlin? I mean, it's nothing to do with Modred's Keep or Arthur."

"It's in the Prophecy and the signs were there," he said.

"But the sign was wrong. It's not what it said at all." I swerved to almost avoid a large pothole. "It was an M.O.D. warning sign. Just broken, that's all."

"The sign was there, just where The Book said it would be. It matters not how it was created only that it was."

"But it's only... Oh never mind."

"You might as well give up," said Elaine.

"It's what he's got planned next that's worrying me."

"What's that?"

"I haven't a clue, that's the worrying bit. I don't do well with surprises."

Chapter Twelve

We found a remote pub that also had some rooms available for the night. Not quite enough rooms though, so some negotiating was going to be needed but for the moment, I was hungry and the only decision that concerned me now was the menu.

The Highwayman's menu was typical of any traditional English country pub and offered a choice of pizzas, lasagne, burgers, chilli con carne, fry-ups or curry. I chose an All-Day Breakfast which promised a 'Satisfying meal at any time of day or night' and a pint of whatever local ale was available.

No matter how much I tried to head it off, the conversation soon turned to the problems of accessing the area where Merlin remained convinced he would find Arthur's grave.

"Cynbel knows." Merlin carefully picked bits of pineapple off his pizza and stacked them on the table. "What are these things?"

"Pineapple," Elaine said.

"What idiot puts this on a pizza? They should leave them natural. A pizza is no place for apples."

"It's a Hawaiian," she said. "You didn't specify what type of pizza you wanted. You should have said."

"I need to say what I *don't* want them to put on a pizza? What nonsense is that? I would be talking all day. Nobody should put things on a pizza that don't belong. And those things." He poked the pineapple chunks with his knife. "They don't belong anywhere. They're not like any apples I know."

Cas picked up one of the chunks and popped it in his mouth. "We could dig a tunnel."

"We can't go in there at all," I said. "Not with a tunnel, a helicopter or even a set of batwings. Remember how quickly they found us?"

"That's only because they could see us," said Cas.

"What does that mean?" I had a horrible feeling I knew exactly what that meant.

"We need to go in under cover of darkness."

"Right, this is madness. I'm now officially calling time on this lunacy. Just how much crazy is too much for you lot? We've already desecrated a sacred site and dug holes in a national monument and I'm not breaking into an M.O.D. firing range in the middle of the night. We could get run over by a tank or anything. That's even if we don't get locked up and executed under the Official Secrets Act or something first."

Elaine touched my arm.

"Well, I'm right. It's madness, isn't it?"

"Probably," she said. "But what else were you planning on doing with your weekend? It will be an adventure."

"Adventure? My idea of an adventure these days is going out without an umbrella, not breaking into a top secret army base."

The waitress brought my meal and I studied my All Day Breakfast. A couple of eggs, a sausage, some hash browns, fried potatoes, beans and tomatoes.

"No bacon?" I asked when she returned with some cutlery.

"Sorry, we're out, love. Had a football coach pass through earlier, they all wanted bacon sandwiches. You can have a burger if you like, make up for it?"

"No thanks. I'll make do. Just another one of these please."
I pushed my empty glass towards her.

We were the only customers of The Highwayman which was probably for the best as most of our conversation concerned breaking into a military compound.

"We really should get official permission first," said Colin. "We're supposed to have signed consent to dig on government property."

"We're not digging," said Cas. "Just investigating... with spades."

The door swung open and a couple made their way to the bar. They appeared dressed for outdoor pursuits and carried binoculars and cameras. Bird-watchers I assumed.

"We don't even know anything is there," I said. "We can't dig up the whole of Salisbury Plain."

"Merlin will find it," Cas assured me. "He's got the gift, he's magic."

"Magic? There's no magic. Not in this world or the next. Trust me, I've seen the best."

"Show him, Merlin. Show him some magic."

Merlin glowered at Cas. "I don't do tricks. You take me for a jester? Tricks and conjuring to order belong in the sideshows at fairs. I have the power of the ages and the blood of the druids."

"There you go." I stuck my fork in my sausage. "Told you, no magic."

"What about the ring?" asked Cas.

"And the sign," said Sebastian.

"Don't forget the names in the book," said Elaine.

I turned to her and waved the sausage at her. "Et tu, Brute."

She grabbed my arm and took a bite off the end of the sausage. A mischievous grin fluttered across her face.

"Ouch!"

"Show him, Merlin," persisted Cas.

"Bacon." I pointed at my plate. "There you go, that's a challenge. A scientific experiment under laboratory conditions. Magic me up some bacon." I tapped my fork on the plate.

Merlin shouted some mumbo-jumbo words and banged Harold on the floor. I wasn't sure whether he was rising to the challenge or swearing at me in ancient Celtic or it could even have been Russian. The bird-watchers paused in their chatter and drinking to watch us.

I made a great show of looking at my plate. "Oh dear, no bacon. Can we all go home now?"

Cas pulled out my increasingly battered road atlas and pieced it together amongst the plates and glasses. "This ley line cuts straight north from Stonehenge and runs across near the area we looked at." He picked up a tablemat to use as a straight edge. "See? Only we were a bit too far east by the looks of it."

They weren't going to give up. I should choose to leave them all to it, go home to London. To... to what? More séance hunting? Travel Lodge nights? They'd only go and get themselves arrested, Elaine along with them no doubt. She didn't deserve that. Neither did Merlin. I was going to regret this but it would be interesting to find out by how much.

"That looks to run about where the General lives, the Trident protester," I said.

Elaine looked at me and smiled, her eyes said uncomfortable things to my soul and I had to turn away from her look.

"So, we go through the fence where he is?" said Cas.

"That's the Silbury Ley," a voice from over my shoulder announced with a note of authority.

I turned to see one of the bird-watchers staring at the map from behind me.

"Told you," said Sebastian. He turned to the newcomers. "I told them that's what it was."

"It's the most powerful ley line in the world," the man said. "Silbury Hill is one of the largest man-made monuments on the planet yet nobody talks about it. You have to wonder why."

"I'd have thought Brian Cox would have done a thing on it if was that big," I said.

"That's because officially, it doesn't exist. It would raise too many questions." He turned to his companion still at the bar. "Stevie, they're doing the Silbury Ley."

Stevie came over to join us. "That's amazing," she said. "Eric and me are spotting on that one tonight."

"Spotting?" I asked. "Birds?"

"No, we're not bird-watchers." Eric said it with such distaste I could well have accused them of being Barbie doll collectors. "We're Friends of the Siriuns."

I was confused. "What, like town twinning with Damascus?"

Eric looked at me then grinned. "No, not Syrians, Siriuns. The planet. The Dog Star. We're friends with the visitors from there."

"Oh, sorry."

Eric flapped his hand dismissively. "Don't worry, happens all the time."

"I'm still not sure what you mean," I said. "What visitors?"

The door swung open and a middle-aged couple came in, a small animal at their heels. It looked like an overweight Pug but it was difficult to see from there.

"The Siriuns," said Stevie. "They've been coming here for centuries. They follow the lines of power around the world.

They left a massive crop circle at Silbury a few years ago; it was even on the BBC."

"That was the Mayan symbol," added Eric. "The one which warned of the end of the world."

"But it didn't end," I said. "In fact, I distinctly remember it *not* ending." I heard a kerfuffle coming from the bar and a high-pitched squeal. I didn't know Pugs made that sort of noise.

"No, of course it didn't end," said Eric. "That's why the Siriuns left the symbol at Silbury, to show us they'd helped us avoid the end of the world."

"Of course," I said. "I was wondering how we'd managed to miss that one."

"I went up to see that one," said Cas. "We had a happening. I didn't know it had been made by the Siriuns. That sort of blows your mind when you think about it. It's like, cosmic."

The kerfuffle by the bar exploded into shouts and more squeals. I looked over. The woman was trying to climb onto the bar stool which was wobbling dangerously under her weight. I looked at the floor near the stool to see the source of her terror. What I'd thought was a Pug was actually a piglet. Who the hell takes a piglet out for a drink? The man kicked out at it but the animal was too fast and ran across the bar straight under our table. We all jumped.

"Is that your pig?" yelled the landlord from behind the bar. "Only we don't allow pigs in here. It's a brewery rule not to allow pigs."

"No, not ours," I said. "I thought it came in with them?" I indicted the couple at the bar. The woman sat with her knees tucked up under her. A neat trick on a bar stool.

"Why on Earth would we bring a pig in here?" shouted the man accusingly. "It must have followed us in."

I felt a nudge under the table and watched as the piglet tried to squeeze itself under my seat. It looked terrified.

"You can't have a pig in here," repeated the barman. "It's not hygienic."

Elaine reached down and tickled its nose. "It's cute. He seems to have taken to you."

"I'm so glad," I said.

She straightened and looked me in the eye, and a huge grin sparkled across her face. "You know what this is, don't you?"

"No. Go on, surprise me."

"It's your bacon. Merlin's magic. You asked for bacon." She held her hand towards the piglet. "And here it is. Magic."

"Don't be absurd. It's clearly escaped from a local piggery or whatever they are. It's just a —"

"Coincidence?" she intercepted my word. "Like the sign and the ring? The messages in the book?"

"Oh, wow!" exclaimed Cas. "See, I told you. Merlin, he's the dude."

"You'll have to take your pig outside," said the barman. "I'll lose my licence if anybody sees that in here."

"It's not my pig," I repeated.

"Try telling him that," said Elaine, pointing to the baby porker trying to make itself invisible under my feet.

"Did you say Merlin?" Eric asked looking at Cas. "Like the wizard?"

"Not *like* the wizard, this *is* the wizard, the real Merlin," Cas said.

"Oh cool," said Eric.

"Cool?" I said. "A stranger tells you this is Merlin and all you say is cool? You immediately believe him?"

"Why wouldn't I?" Eric looked puzzled at my question. "I've never met him before, why would he lie to me?"

"The pig?" the barman said loudly.

"You'd better take your friend outside," said Elaine.

"It's not mine." I gathered up the surprisingly heavy little piglet and carried it outside. I quite expected to see a forlorn looking farmer desperate to be reunited with his pig. But no. Just the night closing in, four cars in the car park and not a sign of anybody else. I put the pig down on the gravel of the car park. "There you go, little buddy. Freedom, run, piggy, flee while you can."

The pig nudged at my feet and refused to run free. I felt rather than heard Elaine join me.

"Looks like you have a new friend," she said.

"Not my friend. Not magic. Just a lost pig. Come on, time for a nightcap."

"You can't leave it here."

"Why not? It's a wild animal."

"A pig? You don't know much about farming do you."

"What do you expect me to do with it? I'm fairly sure the residents' committee of my apartment block have a rule about pigs. They get funny about goldfish."

"Tell you what, leave it here and if it goes away it was never meant to be yours but if it's still here in an hour you'll look after it? At least until we can find it a home. How's that sound?"

It sounded like a set-up but I was confident the pig would wander off again as soon as it was on its own.

"Deal."

Back in the bar plans were being formed for the evening's excursion. It seemed we had adopted the Friends of the Siriuns as they were helping plan the routes of ingress. Apparently they'd done it once before when they'd been trying to locate a Siriun UFO that had crash landed in the military zone. Unfortunately, the military had got there first and taken the machine to a secret base and dissected the aliens. The balance of opinion had it that the best time for the attempt was around one o'clock, when the shifts were changing and the spy planes were refuelling. We had several hours to kill. We went to check on the pig.

"Well, what are you going to call him?" asked Elaine looking down at the little creature as it nuzzled at my legs.

"How about Breakfast?" I suggested.

She hit my shoulder. "Don't be mean. Look at him, he loves you."

We left him outside and returned to the pub to collect the keys for the room.

Room sharing negotiations had been fraught but I'd stuck to my guns to share with Elaine. Not for any reasons of impropriety but simply because to share with any of the others would likely have resulted in bloodshed.

Elaine gave me a slightly coy look as we entered the room to find only one double bed.

"I'll take the chair." I looked around the room for a chair. Only a high backed dining car sat in the corner. "Or the floor. We're not likely to get much sleep anyway, got to go in a couple of hours."

Elaine flopped onto the bed. It bounced deeply and for far too long. "Come on." She patted the space next to her. "You might as well make yourself comfortable until we go. I promise not to molest you."

I joined her on the bed. It was far too soft and even if sleep had been an option I'd never get comfortable on that.

"Sorry to involve you in all this," I said. "He's not your responsibility."

"Nor yours."

"Hmm."

"The world can have magic, you know." She propped herself on one elbow, half turning towards me. "Look at the trees or the stars, there's much we know but even more we don't. The scientists claim they know everything but then brush over the gaps. Even quantum physics has large areas marked, *'Here be dragons'* and we can still only guess at what goes on inside the mind."

I stared at the ceiling. "Are you trying to tell me you think he's really Merlin?"

"No, but I'm also not trying to say he isn't. I've seen enough people who believe deeply in a personae they've created. Sometimes they end up in institutions, other times they end up running giant corporations or even countries. I gave up long ago trying to see the lines between real, perceived or simply delusional."

Her words echoed to a different time. I didn't trust myself to speak.

"You follow Merlin because he reminds you of what you've lost," she continued. "The magic."

She reached across and traced a finger along the line of my cheekbone and I felt a slight wetness under her fingertip as she neared my eye. Her touch was at once caring, sensual yet oddly familiar. I was in a different place, a different time.

A loud banging at the door shook me back to the room above The Highwayman.

"Your bloody pig's digging up my wife's begonias," a voice shouted from outside the room. "She's won prizes for those."

"Sorry," I yelled. "We'll sort it."

The moment thankfully broken, we went downstairs to find the piglet. He was covered in mud with some half chewed flowers hanging from the side of his mouth. I assumed they were examples of prize begonias.

Against my better judgement we put Breakfast in the back of my car on an old blanket then returned to the room. We made coffee to keep us awake then drank gin to calm the nerves. An old movie on the television held a diversion for a while.

"Better think about getting ready I suppose," I said.

"What's to get ready? I'm not sure what one needs for an evening breaking and entering a top secret military base. Ski masks and crowbars?"

"Forgot to pack either I'm afraid. This wasn't in my diary."

We joined the others who were already gathered in the car park. We were a motley assortment. A pair of UFO hunters, a metal detectorist, a handful of hippies, one wizard and a pig. We set off to the M.O.D. enclosure in convoy with me leading the convoy. Merlin complained all the way about having to share a seat with Breakfast.

"You'll just have to put up with it," I said. "You conjured him up."

I heard a loud squeal from the back which I guessed was the pig although it might equally have been Colin.

We tried to drive on sidelights to avoid being seen which turned out to be a big mistake as it took us twenty minutes to extract Sebastian's VW bus from a ditch. After that we used headlights. We found the fence then headed west towards the shacks. The General leaped out of his shack as we approached, blinking into the glare of three sets of headlights and holding his spear forward like a Zulu warrior. He shouted something we couldn't hear but was probably some sort of threat or a battle cry about not taking his freedom.

I parked up and went over to him. "It's okay, it's me, John. From earlier?"

"Oh," he said. "What do you want?"

"I've brought some food and beer." I pulled a box from the boot which we'd prepared earlier for him. "Here, help you out a bit."

"I'm not leaving."

"I know. These are my friends, Elaine, Cas... um... Merlin and some others. We want to go look around the other side of the fence."

"You're mad," he said. "The drones will spot you in a flash."

"Drones?" said Colin. "Nobody told me about drones."

"They're not real," I said quietly. "He's a bit... well, he's a bit... you know."

"They'll probe your mind. Wait here a moment." He disappeared inside his shed and returned a moment later with three beanie hats. They were each covered in tinfoil which was held in place by brown parcel tape. "They're all I've got but they'll help."

"Thank you," I said.

We left Breakfast with the General and joined the others near the fence. Merlin was already busy with his string-dangling and Tree had gone into an early trance. Cas and Sebastian were busy at the fence with torch and wire cutters.

"Better get your kit," I said to Colin. "Looks like we're going through."

Twenty minutes later and after much scrambling we all emerged inside the perimeter fence. The General offered to stand guard outside the gap and looked suitably alert as he stood with his back to the fence, pig on a piece of string in one hand and his spear in the other. Ready to hold the world at bay.

The moon provided a mean light in the clear sky and we were able to avoid most of the rabbit holes and other nature traps. Merlin, Tree and Colin set to work searching with the assistance of ring-dangling, angel helpers and modern technology. I didn't hold a lot of hope for the project but I contributed by scanning the weak beam of my torch around looking for anything that might resemble a medieval tomb. Much to the detriment of my worsening paranoia, the group were far from discreet. With Merlin's grumblings, Tree's chanting and the strange whistling noises emanating from Colin's machine all drifting into the night, we wouldn't need mind-probing drones to alert the authorities. A semi-conscious octogenarian would probably ask us to keep the noise down.

Chapter Thirteen

We wandered up and down for a while, did a little bit of round and round and quite a lot of to-and-fro. Eventually hi-tech electronics, medieval string-dangling and ethereal angels all finally agreed on the perfect spot to commence digging. To me, it looked just the same as every other bit of grass we'd been traipsing across for the last hour but the group were convinced they'd finally found the location of King Arthur's grave. Cas offered to start the digging and threw the spade deep into the soft earth. Two minutes later we were the proud owners of a beer can. Not to be deterred, the group spread their search pattern and we gathered a delightful collection of bottle tops and miscellaneous unidentifiable lumps of metal. The moon drifted behind a cloud bank and against our rising paranoia we had to use more torches. Eric and Stevie seemed more interested in the sky rather than the earth as they wandered slightly separate from the rest.

The field was beginning to look like a family of oversized moles had recently moved in. Little holes and piles of earth accumulated at an alarming rate. I glanced back at the fence; it seemed a very long way away. We had wandered further away from the perimeter fence than I'd anticipated and easy escape was no longer looking quite so easy.

"How long do you think they'll keep this up before they realise it's a fool's errand?" I said to Elaine.

"I don't think any time soon. Look at them; they're having a lovely time. Bit like a bunch of children on Blackpool beach!"

Colin's machine gave a particularly loud squeal and much excited chattering signalled another potential find.

"What do you reckon?" I said. "Another beer can? Or we haven't had a pram yet, probably overdue for one of those."

The group gathered around the latest hole as Cas went to work. The earth pile grew as he dug deeper, stopping every few spadefuls to allow a bit more detecting or Cynbel dangling. Then Sebastian pushed his way into the group and shone his torch into the hole. He scrabbled with his fingers and came out with something small. Probably another bottle top. We wandered over to join them.

Sebastian held the object in the palm of his hand while Colin squirted water at it from a squeegee bottle. It turned out to be a coin.

"It's late Roman," said Colin as he squinted closely. "That's Emperor Constantine, puts it third or fourth centuries. How exciting, I wonder if there's more down there." He aimed his torch into the hole.

I heard Elaine's unspoken words. "Doesn't mean anything," I said. "People are forever digging up Roman stuff. They were notoriously careless with their things, probably because they never invented pockets."

"Idiot," she teased. "Bit of a coincidence though."

Digging resumed with increased enthusiasm and holes continued to accumulate. Sebastian offered to take over the digging but Cas was on a mission. He wanted to be the one to make the find. He threw the spade into the ground again at a fresh point agreed by the trio. A loud clunk this time instead of the usual soft thud. He froze.

"Something big here," he announced and continued to make probing strikes into the earth.

Sebastian reached into the earth and brushed the loose dirt away. "It could be metal." He cleared more earth away with his hands. "It's sort of round. Could be a shield."

Cas set to work with his spade clearing a trench around the object. The object gradually revealed itself under the collected torchlight to be a ridged metal object around twenty centimetres diameter. The surface contained a series of concentric circles. They looked machined.

"Looks like a car hubcap," I suggested.

"It's a shield," said Cas. "They used to bury shields with ancient kings; I saw a programme on the Discovery channel."

"That's not a shield," I said. "Look, it's engineered, way too precise."

"Erm," Elaine started. "It looks a bit like—"

"It's a shield," repeated Cas as he edged his spade underneath the object. "They were very skilled at shield making. They used technology we still haven't rediscovered yet."

"Are you sure you should be doing that?" asked Elaine. "Only I'm certain it looks like—"

"Out of the way," blustered Merlin as he pushed his way into the middle of the group. "Let me see." He crouched over the hole. "That's no shield of a king. More like a dinner plate." He stood up and continued his dowsing.

"Might still be worth something," said Colin. "Be careful."

Cas managed to find access underneath the object and started to wriggle it free.

"Please stop," Elaine sounded more urgent.

"What's up?" I asked.

With a final huge effort, Cas lifted the spade clear of the

131

ground with the large disc sat proudly on the blade for all to see. The group gathered and poked.

"Could be a hubcap I suppose."

"Looks more like a frisbee."

"A metal frisbee?"

"Well, they didn't have plastic in Roman days."

Eric suggested it resembled one of the small probe ships they'd recovered from the Roswell crash site in 1948. The group slid backward slightly, leaving Cas and spade in the centre of a circle. He pushed the spade out at arm's length, trying to keep as much distance as the handle allowed.

"Is it radioactive?" asked Stevie.

Elaine pulled at my arm. "John, I'm fairly sure that's a mine," she whispered to me, as if speaking the words loudly would make them true.

"A mine?" I stared at the object still held on Cas's spade. Eric tapped at it with a small trowel and explained it wouldn't be radioactive as the Roswell aliens used a much more sophisticated ion drive propulsion system than decaying uranium.

"I remember seeing pictures of Princess Di somewhere in Africa with one of those." Elaine held my arm in a pincer grip. "It was just like that."

"A mine?" I repeated. "As in landmine, the explosive kind? That sort of mine?"

"I think so."

I stared at the object. It certainly looked possible, the size and shape, with a little raised section in the middle. "Umm, guys," I started. "I think we may have a problem."

They all stopped and looked at me.

"I think that's a landmine."

Open mouths and wide eyes stared back at me.

"Nonsense," said Eric. "This is England not Rwanda. Nobody puts landmines down in England. It's alien technology."

"Remember where we are," I said. "Salisbury Plain? Big fences, warning signs? Very popular with the army."

I should have paid more attention to the signs warning M.O.D. firing range but I'd been so wrapped in delight at them *not* announcing Modred's Keep that I'd not comprehended their real purpose.

"He's right," said Colin. "Oh shit. Oh shit."

The group expanded back leaving more distance between them and Cas. "What do I do?" he yelled.

"Don't make any sudden movements," I said. "It's probably very old and very unstable." That was about the limit of my knowledge of landmines so I looked around to see if anybody else had anything more to offer. Nothing. They all looked at me as if I was now the acknowledged authority. Great.

"Okay, Cas," I said. "Very slowly and without tilting it, lay the spade on the ground."

The group moved away even further. Cas didn't move.

"Just move from your knees, without tipping it, hold your breath and crouch down. Very, very slowly."

Cas gave a loud scream and threw both spade and landmine into the air as far as he could. He was running for the group before the mine had reached its zenith in the night sky.

"Or you could just do that." I watched as the mine and spade tumbled to the ground. We all braced.

A double thud as they landed then silence. Not even the sound of breathing.

"Phew, looks like it was a—"

The explosion slammed into the still night throwing clods of earth upwards in a cloud of fire and dust. The spade circled upwards for the second time before landing in two pieces. My ears rang with the blast so I could only guess at the shouting everybody seemed to be doing. I turned to Elaine; surprisingly she appeared to be laughing.

"You alright?" I said, exaggerating the mouth shapes in case she too was deafened.

"I'm fine," she said into my ear and gave my hand a small squeeze. "Quite a night out."

After a moment's running in aimless circles everybody slowly calmed and discussion turned to the next step. Colin and the Friends of the Siriuns were all for calling it a night and heading back. Merlin rallied his faithful, saying Arthur was never afraid of the tools of war so why should we be.

"Somebody will have heard that," Colin said. "The police will be here any minute. We're trespassing." He picked up his detector and headed towards the perimeter fence.

"Wait!" I shouted as a thought struck me. Everybody stopped to look at me. "Who lays just one mine?"

"Um, one mine layer?" offered Sebastian.

"Listen, John's right," said Elaine. "If there's one, there'll be more. Probably lots more. We could be surrounded by them." She pointed at Tree. "You could be standing on one right now."

"No," said Tree. "I have angels. They'd have told me. Especially something that important."

"We're going to die," said Cas. "We're either going to get blown into a million pieces or we'll starve because we can't move." He slumped to the grass cross-legged with his head in his   arms.

"We need to lie down and make a clear path," said Sebastian. "We probe into the ground ahead and leave markers for the next person to follow."

That sounded remarkably sensible. "Okay, seems like a plan." I said. "What can we use to probe?"

"Bayonets."

"Bayonets?"

"That's what they used on Kelly's Heroes, bayonets. They slid on their stomachs across this field, loads of mines there were. We can do that."

"Kelly's Heroes? Your plan is from a comedy war film?"

"You got a better one?" asked Elaine.

"Well actually... I was thinking we could... No, sorry, I've got nothing."

"We do have a metal detector," said Eric. "And I have night vision binoculars so somebody could use those to find what looks like the best route then creep along using the metal detector and leave stakes."

"It's a metal detector," said Colin. "It's not a mine detector."

"It detected that one." I pointed towards the hole.

"Well here, you have a go." Colin handed me the detector. "Good luck, I'll wait here. Oh, and please be careful with it that cost me three months' wages."

I studied the machine, it had seemed straightforward enough when Colin had been using it but now it resembled the control panel of an F-15 jet fighter. Somehow I'd got the gig. I tried stepping forward a bit with the detector out in front of me and my head tipped back in case of an explosion. I swept it around in a semi-circle and it gave off a high-pitched whistle. Everybody jumped back a bit and I froze.

"It's only the calibration signal," Colin said as if I should have known that. "You need to turn the search mode to general and increase the tracking speed. Might also help if you fine tune the iron reject setting."

I looked at the controls again. "Okay, got it," I lied. I stepped forwards once more and the machine clicked and squeaked. This was hopeless. I had an idea. I extended the handle as far as it would go; including the control section and the plate I had around two metres in length.

"What are you doing?" asked Colin.

"Just making a couple of adjustments." I lay down on the ground, arm stretched out in front of me with the metal detector leading. This put my head a good distance from the end plate. I slid forwards and bounced the plate up and down a bit, waiting for the bang. Nothing. I pushed forward a fraction more and repeated the operation.

"You can't do that," yelled Colin. "That's a Minelab GPX 5000 and you could do that with a six foot stick."

"Have you got a six foot stick?"

"Well, no. But that's not the point."

"Well until you find me a six foot stick I'm using this." I slid forward a bit more and bounced the end. More clicks and squeaks; I had no idea what the thing was trying to tell me. So far so good. Another half metre, more squeaks from the machine and more outraged squeals from Colin.

I'd covered around ten metres when the machine let out a particularly large squeak and a collection of clicks. The others, who'd been following me on all fours, reversed up a bit. Thanks guys. I stayed still for a moment trying to understand the noises. "What's that mean, Colin?"

"It means you haven't calibrated it properly," he yelled back from somewhere behind me.

I bounced the end up and down a bit to see if it made a different noise. It did. It went bang very loudly and covered me in flying dirt and bits of Minelab GPX 5000. Well that's buggered it.

Through the sound of a million tuning forks I heard Elaine asking me if I was alright. I turned and she slid alongside.

"I'm fine," I said. "But I think Colin's detector is going to need a few spare parts." I held up a smoking metal rod which was about all that was left of the device.

"What do we do now?" yelled Cas above the tuning forks.

"We could use Merlin's stick," suggested somebody. Merlin's response was loud and immediate. Even through the noise in my ears.

I tried to adjust my position to peer at the hole in front of me. Logic dictated there wouldn't be another mine for a few feet at least, so we could gain a little more ground. I shuffled forwards. It was fairly pointless but at least it felt as if we were doing something. Something sharp dug into my knee as I passed over the freshly thrown earth. I reached back expecting to find a part of the mine or the metal detector. It was caked in mud and looked at first like a rather large horseshoe. But as I cleared the mud it became apparent this was something different. It was quite a lot larger and very heavy. I pushed more dirt from the surface and rubbed it against my shirt.

"What have you got there?" Elaine asked.

"Not sure." I aimed my torch at the object; bits of it glinted back at me through the mud. It looked like braided rope, about a foot long and twisted into a horseshoe shape with a large knot at each end. Only it was made of some sort of metal. As I cleared more mud the knots turned out to be loops of braided metal, a gold coloured metal. I passed it back to Elaine. "What do you think?"

"Looks very old," she said after a while.

"What's that?" Colin called. We passed the item back to him.

I heard a string of expletives.

"What's up, Colin?" I called.

"It's an Anglo-Saxon torque. I think. Don't know. Fuck. This is huge." He jumped up.

"Steady," I said. "Remember where we are."

"But this is massive. We have to report it."

"What the hell is a torque?" asked Cas.

"Something a king would wear into battle," Merlin said, straightening up. "A noble and powerful king."

"Oh dear," I said. "Merlin's off again." I stood up, carefully treading only the ground I'd already been on.

"He's right," said Colin. "This is the dream find. Most detectorists spend their whole lives never finding anything like this. This is mega huge."

"Are you really telling me this is proper treasure?"

"If this is gold it will be worth a fortune. But it's unlikely to be a single find. There'll be more here. We need to dig."

"Hang on, and before we go poking around anymore in an active minefield, can you just clarify something?"

"What?"

"This torque thing that you both seem to think is old and significant. Just how old and how significant?"

"These come from around the third to fifth centuries. Around the same time as the coin we found. If this was part of a burial it would certainly be an important person."

"How important? Sort of... king type important?"

"Almost certainly," Colin said. "A find like this is probably indicative of an Anglo-Saxon king's burial site."

The lights shafted across the area with blinding fury. Lances of brilliance piercing the night sky.

"They've come," yelled Eric. "It's the Siriuns."

"Demon owls," shouted Merlin and shook Harold skywards.

Two beams criss-crossed the site then eventually both

settled on our position. The glare was immobilising. I put my hands in front of my face but the light still seemed to penetrate.

Then the noise started. At first just a rumbling then it became violent thundering threatening my still delicate eardrums with a low frequency pounding. The brilliance increased and the air around us beat us down.

"What the hell's going on?" Elaine sounded terrified.

"Helicopters," I shouted above the racket. "Probably police. I think we're in a spot of trouble."

The voice came loud and electronic, cutting through the racket. "Do not move," it commanded. "You are standing into danger."

"What's that mean?" Elaine yelled at me.

"Not police." I cupped my hands around her ear. "That's a navy expression. Probably Royal Marines. It means we're in big trouble. Very big trouble."

Chapter Fourteen

The helicopter landed with seemingly little regard for the minefield. I guessed they knew exactly where they were. We had to turn our backs to the dust as the machine settled in a fury of noise, bright lights and hammering wind from the blades. A man in military camouflage jumped down and yelled at us to stay put. We complied. He walked a slightly twisted path to us while placing small red flags every few feet. Once he reached us he introduced himself as Sergeant Maddock.

"You need to follow," he shouted. "Do not go away from the flags unless you like loud noises."

We were ushered into the belly of the machine and instructed to sit on the floor, although Tree and Elaine were offered fold-down seats. Large ear defenders were given to each of us with an accompanying mime as to their use in case we didn't understand.

The machine thundered and rumbled through my body as it lurched into the air. I clung tight to a cargo strap and gave Elaine a weak smile.

"It will be alright," I mouthed.

She nodded in return.

The flight took only a few minutes and we landed with a careless bump. The hatch swung open and we were ushered out with instructions to keep low and to follow the white lines into the building. The silence and light welcomed us into what appeared to be a large briefing room. I looked around the room. Stark military drab was the theme along with touches of functional efficiency and hygienic easy-clean. Sergeant Maddock supervised a brisk but efficient search by two soldiers then indicated a set of chairs arranged around a group of tables. We all sat as instructed and he left the room. He'd neglected to close the door so I wondered if we had just been rescued or arrested. It probably didn't make a lot of difference though as we'd be unable to leave the base.

After about five minutes Elaine was the first to break the silence. "Who wants to play I Spy?"

Suddenly everybody was talking at once.

"We're going to prison."

"Fascists."

"They'll make us disappear; we'll never be seen again."

"I wonder if this is where they're keeping the bodies from the Rendlesham UFO?"

"I'll be thrown out of the Chipping Sodbury Detectorists for this."

"Sons of plague dogs."

"Well, this probably calls a halt to this little adventure," I said to Elaine next to me.

"You think?"

"What will happen to Merlin?"

"I expect he'll be taken back to a secure unit under Section Three; that means they can keep him sedated."

"And you? What happens to you? This is not going to look good at your Disciplinary Review."

"Oh, I'll be alright. I was thinking about a change anyway. Maybe I'll give McDonalds a go. Shouldn't be able to get into too much trouble there."

I covered her hand with mine. I wanted to say something

profound and reassuring but I had nothing so I just gave her hand a gentle squeeze.

"I wonder when breakfast is?" she said.

A man in an officer's uniform walked in and stood in front of our tables. "I'm Captain Bedivere of Her Majesty's Royal Marines," he announced.

A loud but unintelligible grumbling noise emanated from Merlin's direction. The captain glared at him then continued.

"Now, until I am informed otherwise, you lot are terrorists." He aimed a short stick around the group. "And terrorists who are currently knee-deep in doggy-do."

A corporal entered with a pile of paper and distributed a small pile in front of each of us.

"In front of you, you will find a copy of the Official Secrets Act. You are required to sign this."

"And if we don't?" Cas pushed his pile away from him.

"You're quite at liberty to refuse of course. We can't force you. But the problem is military law dictates you cannot enter a military establishment until you have signed it. And if you leave this room, you are de-facto entering a military base. You see the problem?"

"You can't keep us here," Sebastian said. "We have rights."

"You do indeed have rights, you are quite correct. Just not in here." He turned towards the door. "Corporal," he called.

The corporal marched smartly back into the room and snapped to attention in front of the captain.

"Sir." He saluted sharply.

"Do you have any rights, Corporal?"

"No, sir."

"Thank you, Corporal. Dismissed."

The corporal left the room in a brisk march.

"There we go then, that's cleared that up. Now if you'd all

be so good as to sign the papers we can decide what we're going to do with you." He left the room.

We looked at each other.

"Well I'm not signing it," Cas said. "Fascists think they can do what they like. We need to make a stand."

"They've got us whatever." Colin looked as though he were about to break into tears. "Breaking into a military base. What was I thinking? How did I get talked into this?"

Merlin banged his stick three times on the floor. We all froze, half expecting a thunderbolt to appear or the Earth to open. Nothing.

"I don't see we have a lot of choice," Elaine said. "They're never going to let us go if we don't."

"I agree." I leafed through the papers. It was unintelligible legal double speak and ran to around fifty pages. I gave up trying to make any sense of it, signed the boxes marked and filled in my details.

Eventually, and after much protesting, everybody signed the papers apart from Cas. We sat for a while in a mixture of stunned silence and simple exhaustion.

The captain and the corporal eventually returned and gathered the papers. He stopped when he reached Cas. "Ah, a rebellion! Jolly good, we like spirited people. Don't we, Corporal, spirited people? We like spirited people."

"Yes, sir. We like spirited people."

The captain continued, "We like to see how they look on the dissection table. Like the aliens of Rendlesham." He gave a knowing glance in the direction of Eric and Stevie. "Yes we have those here, or we did until we broke them. Pity really, we were only trying to take them apart to see how they worked."

"You can't do this, you're bluffing." Cas's voice didn't quite carry the conviction of his words.

The captain leant his hands on the table in front of Cas and looked him straight in the eye. "I can do whatever I like. Until you sign that paper you don't actually exist. You could just disappear, forgotten. Didn't you know we are twinned with Area 51? We're part of the Bilderburg Group, The Freemasons and the Illuminati and probably the Roman Catholic Church as well, I can't quite remember. Anyway, we can make every trace of you disappear. You're not the first bunch of miscreant hippies to grace our little establishment. The last lot were trying to find Trident, or was it E.T.? We hid them both just in case. You remember Simon Calshaw? The famous anti-nuclear protester?"

Cas looked puzzled and shook his head. "Never heard of him."

"There you go then. My point exactly. Now, are you going to sign that form or would you like to meet him?"

Cas pulled the papers towards him and signed without attempting to read them.

"Excellent, I knew you'd see it my way."

He continued round the tables gathering the forms until he finally reached Merlin. He picked up Merlin's form between the tips of thumb and forefinger as if it was contaminated. "What on Earth have you done with my Official Secrets Act?"

He separated the sheets of paper and held them up, studying each in turn before laying it on the table. "Oh dear, oh dear."

Even from where I sat I could see that Merlin had been very busy. Dozens of individual letters had been circled and lines drawn joining them together. Numbers and notes littered the margins. When he arrived at the signature his eyebrows narrowed.

"Ah, and you are Merlin?"

"And you are a donkey's arse with the brains of last week's chicken stew," Merlin said. "That ridiculous collection of nonsense verse hides the plottings of Modred. If you did but realise it."

"Merlin, huh? Well I suppose it makes a change from Mickey Mouse or Darth Vader. And you've put your address as... The Caves of Tree War Vendy? Corporal, you're Welsh, what on Earth does this say?"

"I don't think it's Welsh, sir. But if I had to guess I'd say Trewar Venydh."

"Merlin from the Caves of Trewar Venydh. I swear this place is a nutter magnet. Why couldn't I have been posted to Baghdad? Take over, Corporal, before I do something which will need even more paperwork. And get this idiot to sign a new copy of this, we can't send that to the Ministry." He threw the pile of scribbled upon paper back to Merlin.

As soon as he left the corporal visibly relaxed.

"Merlin's a bit... special needs, challenged," I said quietly to him.

"Ask me, the lot of you are. What got into you all? Breaking into MOD land and plonking around in a minefield? Bleeding bonkers the lot of you."

"Aren't you supposed to put up signs or something?"

"Well, call us spoilsports but we kind of assume that would spoil the surprise element of a minefield. And anyway, didn't you see those bleeding great wooden signs? MOD firing range? Or are we supposed to give you a list of what particular explosives we're using? World's gone bleeding mad."

"But we could have been killed," complained Cas.

"Not likely. They're only training ordinance, just flash and bang. Only put 'em down this morning for tomorrow's exercise. Hardly enough oomph in those to blow your bollocks

145

off." He looked at Elaine. "Sorry, ma'am. I meant genitalia of the male kind. Got to lay 'em all again now thanks to you lot."

That explained why the captain had been so over the top.

"What happens now?" I asked.

"Up to the Red Caps. You'll probably be kept here for a bit while they check you on the Special Branch Watch Lists. Then, if you're clear, you'll be handed over to the local plod."

We were left to our own devices in the briefing room. Somebody brought in a large coffee pot and a tray of sandwiches and left them on a table without a word. The coffee was good and strong and the sandwiches surprisingly tasty. I felt slightly better. Merlin sat at one of the tables seemingly oblivious to his surroundings while he scribbled notes in his book. He gave little mumbles and occasional curses as he worked.

"Sorry," I said to Elaine. "I shouldn't have involved you in all this."

"Don't worry," she said. "It's quite exciting really. I don't get out much."

"Wonder how long they'll keep us here?"

"Can't you hypnotise them to let us out?"

"Doesn't work like that I'm afraid. Contrary to what people think, you can't be hypnotised to do something intrinsically against your nature. Soldiers can't be hypnotised en masse to let, what they see as dangerous prisoners escape. It worked in the Police Station because I just had to switch the ring, easy trick, and then convince the policeman he was seeing what he expected to see. Not difficult."

"How about your escapology then? You could escape and bring help?"

"I was an escapologist. Not Steve McQueen!"

"Aha!" Merlin waved his mutilated copy of the Official

Secrets Act in the air. "Here it is. Help comes soon. It's written here along with Arthur's name as the pointer."

I looked at his copy of the Act. There in the middle of page eight he had circled four sets of letters, all equidistant, and clearly spelling out the words, Help, Comes, Soon, Arthur.

"This is madness," I said. "It can't be. This is the Official Secrets Act for heaven's sake."

"I expect it's just another silly coincidence," Elaine said with a grin. "You know how these things keep happening."

"Shut up."

Around six o'clock a different sergeant came into the room. He held up the torque which had been taken from us the night before. "Whose is this thing?"

We looked from one to the other. I offered, "We found it. It was buried."

"Looks like a Saxon king's burial site," said Colin. "The area needs to be protected."

"It is protected," said the sergeant. "We've got a bloody great fence around it if you hadn't noticed."

"I meant the burial site. It needs securing and that," Colin pointed at the torque. "That should be sent to the coroner. It's treasure trove. There's probably more stuff there."

"You mean valuable, like gold and stuff?"

"Probably."

"I'll have it looked into. Which one of you is Merlin?"

We all looked towards Merlin; he looked up from his notes. "What?"

"Special Branch can find no trace of you further back than a few weeks. You changed your name?"

"Merlin. I've always been Merlin. I've been Merlin since before your ancestors found their way out of the swamps."

"Can you prove you're who you say you are?"

Merlin thought for a moment and then went over to a window. He studied his reflection in the glass then said, "Yes, that's me." He sat down again and resumed his note writing.

"Do you have a driving licence, passport, credit card? Any papers?"

Merlin ignored him.

"He's been in care," said Elaine. "He has learning difficulties, I'm his carer."

The sergeant thumbed through his sheaf of paper. "Ah, yes. Here you are. You're on suspension from your employer pending disciplinary proceedings."

"Well, yes but—"

He turned to me. "John Barker?"

"Yes," I said.

"You were detained two days ago by Taunton Police following an incident on National Trust property?"

"Yes but—"

"You seem to have a bit of a thing for digging." He turned to Eric and Stevie. "And you two seem to make a habit of breaking into military stations."

"What?" said Eric.

"Woodbridge RAF base, near Rendlesham?"

"Oh that. That was ages ago and they were hiding a crashed UFO there."

He looked at Tree. "Assaulting a police officer?"

"He wasn't a cop; he was possessed by the archangel Michael."

He turned to Cas and read from his papers, "Possession, possession, possession with intent to supply, possession, yada yada. Busy little chap aren't you?" He thumbed his papers again and looked at Sebastian. "Illegal camping outside St Paul's Cathedral? Erecting banners on public buildings? Spray painting Hinkley Point Nuclear Power Station with CND symbols?"

He moved over to Colin and studied his papers. "We don't seem to have anything on you... Oh, hang on... A fine for a late library book in 1986. Quite the rebel, huh?"

"I had tonsillitis and couldn't leave the house."

The sergeant ignored Colin's protestations and left the room.

"Fascist spies," announced Sebastian. "It's the GCHQ and the puppet masters in the NSA. Nothing we do is private. I bet they have cameras and microphones watching us in here."

"No we don't," said a voice from a small speaker high in the corner I'd not noticed before.

Merlin stared at the speaker for a moment then threw a plastic water bottle at it. "Spirit boxes, work of Modred." He returned to his notes.

Apart from Merlin's constant mumblings the rest of us fell to silence.

Just after eight o'clock a corporal and two soldiers marched in and ordered us to gather our things.

"You're being handed over to civvy police," the corporal said.

Chapter Fifteen

The ride to Salisbury Police Station took around thirty minutes and we were handed over to the waiting desk sergeant with a brusque, "You're welcome to this lot, mate. Bunch of nutters, found them playing around in a bloody minefield." He dumped a pile of paper on the sergeant's desk and set off without another word.

The sergeant scanned through the papers. "Ah, yes. Merlin's Merry Men. Been expecting you lot. Your bail's been approved already so we just need some signatures and you can all head off back to Hogwarts or whatever particular corner of insanity you inhabit."

"Bail?" I said. "We never applied for bail."

He looked through a different set of papers and followed his pencil tip down a page. "Signed off just half an hour ago. Posted by..." he squinted at the signature. "Morgan, somebody called Morgan posted it."

He read a bit more. "For and on behalf of Morgan Productions. Never heard of them. Is that who you work for?" He looked up at me.

"No. Don't know them. That's odd."

"Well it stops you lot cluttering up my nice tidy Police Station so that makes me a happy desk sergeant. Just need you all to sign these." He pulled yet another stack of paper from under the desk and pushed it in our direction.

"Who's Morgan Productions?" Elaine took her bail form and signed it without reading.

"It's ringing bells." I scanned the paper but figured there was little point in reading it properly. Sign it and go free, don't sign it and stay in a cell. I'd had enough of cells for the time being. I signed it and dumped it back on the desk just as I remembered who Morgan Productions were.

"Morgan le Fay, sorceress, witch." Merlin threw his form back at the sergeant.

Elaine gathered it up. "I'll sign on his behalf," she said. "I'm his registered carer."

The sergeant looked at her and then shrugged. "Whatever; just get him out of my office."

We left the Police Station and blinked in the sunlight. I needed a shower, food and sleep. Lots of sleep. It wasn't destined to happen. Just as I was wondering how we were going to retrieve our cars, a black Range Rover slid alongside the pavement. The door swung open and the driver leaned over, a striking woman in her mid forties with sharp cheekbones and a distinctive head of purest black hair. Morgan, now I remembered.

"Mister Barker," she said. "Or should I call you the Great Xando?"

"John will do fine. I'm retired."

"So I heard."

"Who's this?" Elaine asked.

"This is Morgan Faylon. Mystic Morgan, spiritualist, medium and genial host to the ghosts of the rich and vacuous."

"I see retirement has brought you peace," Morgan said.

"Why the bail?"

"Why don't you hop in, John." She patted the passenger

seat. "I can give you a lift. We can chat on the way back to your hotel. The Highwayman wasn't it?"

"No thanks. We'll get a cab."

"Oh dear, that's not very sociable. And after I rescued you from the hands of the military legal machine."

"You're from that TV show about ghosts," Elaine said. "What's going on? Was it you that put the bail forward?"

"No way!" Cas said from behind me. "Mystic Morgan. I know a haunted house in Little Chedzoy you should have a look at. It's got this big fireplace with goblin faces. They stare at you like they've got no soul and they want to eat yours."

"Come on, John, don't be churlish." Morgan patted the leather seat once more. "I have an idea that may be profitable to us both."

"What part of 'retired' are you struggling with?"

"Just the time it takes to drive to your hotel. I promise."

"What's to lose, John?" said Elaine. "Saves a taxi bill and I really need a shower."

I gave in. Elaine and I slid into the vehicle along with Merlin and Cas. The others said they'd catch up with us back at the Highwayman.

The Range Rover slipped into the morning traffic as if under its own control. Silent and smooth.

Morgan wasted no time. "I understand you've found a Saxon grave?" It was a statement but phrased as a question. "Possibly even the burial site of King Arthur?"

"Where did you hear that?"

"Researchers, dear. What do you think I pay researchers for?"

"Arthur's not real you know," I said, keeping my voice low to avoid engaging Merlin in this.

"Says who?" Morgan challenged. "The Great Xando,

scourge of the spiritualist world? Let's not squabble, John. And besides, there's more documented evidence of King Arthur than there is of Saint George and yet they name pubs after *him* and Parliament is prepared to send the British Army to war behind his flag."

"Your point?"

"Whatever it is you found, it's big. Even if it's just a run of the mill Saxon burial site the publicity my team can spin up will make us both some big money."

"You're planning on ghost hunting King Arthur's grave?" That time my shock at her suggestion overtook my desire to keep the conversation low key.

Merlin leaned forward and grabbed Morgan around the neck. "Demon witch from the pits of Hades," he yelled. The car slewed across the road and Morgan just managed to bring it back as a coach closed on us from the other side of the road. "You helped kill him once but this time I'll see you burn."

I dragged Merlin's fingers from her neck. Not that I hadn't felt like doing the same on many an occasion but not while driving at speed through Wiltshire lanes.

Morgan pulled the car to a dusty halt in a lay-by. She turned and stared at Merlin. "Despite the coincidence of a name, I can assure you I am nothing whatsoever to do with any Morgana, Mordred, Blofeld or any other literary villain. And if you touch me once more I'll turn you into a hamster and feed you to my pet snake." She turned to face the road ahead, straightened her hair and restarted the car. "Now, where were we?"

By the time we'd reached the Highwayman hotel we'd reluctantly conceded to her ideas. Her alternative offer was the withdrawal of her bail and the peculiar influence which she seemed to hold over Her Majesty's Constabulary.

She left us standing outside the hotel entrance and disappeared in a cloud of gravel dust.

"How are we going to get the car?" asked Elaine.

"Don't know. I do know I need food and a shower."

We went up to the room, threw off our mud-stained clothes and showered, too tired for modesty. We collapsed naked onto the bed. I thought about staying there for just a moment while I gathered my breath. I thought about the chaos of the last twenty-four hours and how it was probably time I left them all to it and slipped back to Camden. I thought about the naked woman at my side. I reached towards her and took her hand, giving a quick squeeze. I thought about trying to stay awake.

**

I awoke with a start.

Elaine was already dressed. "C'mon, sleepy boy. Thought you were hungry?"

"What? Mm, what time is it?"

"Nearly eleven. The others are back, I heard them arrive, that's what woke me."

I stumbled from the bed and dressed in my remaining clean shirt and jeans. Breakfast at the Highwayman was a cardiologist's nightmare. All the expected English breakfast items were present, with the notable exception of bacon. There was a nice selection of cholesterol inducing treats like deep fried pork rinds and fried pork pies, apparently a local delicacy. I heard my veins creaking even as I scanned the selection. I settled for cornflakes with full fat milk, the only milk on offer. Elaine chose muesli and we found a table away from the smell of more culinary creations wafting from the kitchen.

Merlin joined us after a moment and greeted us with, "What's a dildo?"

"Good morning to you too, Merlin." I pushed my bowl away. I couldn't deal with full fat milk this time of the day.

Merlin dumped the battered copy of Fifty Shades on the table. The pages were becoming loose now as the binding began to fail under Merlin's hands. "A dildo. Look, it says it here." He stabbed at the page with a sausage before popping it into his mouth.

"Would you like to field that one?" I asked Elaine.

"What makes you think I know anything about them?"

"Lady business," I said with a grin.

"Thanks. You see, Merlin, when a man keeps falling asleep when he should be attending to his lady." She gave me an accusative look then continued, "That's when a lady might turn to a dildo for comfort."

Merlin grunted then squinted at the page again. "Has that got anything to do with a butt plug?"

A woman at the next table gathered up her two children and hurried them towards the door.

"Sorry," Elaine said to the fleeing trio. "He has Tourette's, he can't help it."

I suppressed a giggle and she glared at me. "Not helping, John."

We hurried Merlin to finish his breakfast, encouraging him to leave the book alone for a while. After breakfast, we met Eric and Stevie outside and they offered to drive us to the General's encampment to collect our cars. Elaine stayed at the hotel with Merlin and Cas. The General came out to challenge us as he heard our approach but when he realised who we were he relaxed.

"I heard them take you," he greeted. "Thought you'd all be

locked in the underground bunkers. They're linked you know, miles of them, go all the way to Porton Down. What happened?"

"They let us go," said Sebastian.

"Have you checked for implants? They wouldn't let you go without implants. It happened to a friend of mine, he only went in there to set the aliens free, that's when they caught him. I told him he should have stuck with chickens."

"Chickens?" I asked.

"Yes, chickens. He led the West Puckington branch of the Chicken Liberation Front but then he heard about the aliens."

"What happened to him?" I noticed Breakfast emerge from the shack; he saw me and raced towards me.

"They put implants in his... well... in a place no man should have an implant then they let him go. Just like you."

"What did these implants do?"

"They could watch everything he did. Who he talked to and everything."

"From an implant in a place where no man should have an implant?" I bent down to greet the piglet.

"Drove him mad in the end," said the General.

"I can imagine." Breakfast snuggled into my arms and promptly fell asleep. I sat on the still damp ground.

"How did he know?" asked Sebastian. "About the implant I mean. How did he know they'd put one in?" He looked uncomfortable.

"He woke up while they were doing it. Bit of a shock he said. It's not something you want to wake up and find, some stranger messin' with your personal places like that."

"I need to get back," I said. "Thanks for looking after the pig."

"No trouble. He was quite a good companion. We had quite a chat. He likes Mahler."

Back at the Highwayman we said our goodbyes to the others and headed off through the twisty lanes of Wiltshire. The roads were unusually quiet and I settled into the drive, it was good to be back to some sort of normality even if I did still have a medieval wizard and a pig in the back of the car.

"What happens now?" asked Elaine.

I tooted my horn to remind a little Fiat that the central white line was not for sightseeing. It pulled in and I accelerated past. "Well, first I suggest we get some proper food, sleep and work out what to do with him." I nodded towards the back seat where Merlin was deeply engrossed in his book.

"Where do we put him?" Elaine asked. "He can't stay with me and we certainly can't take him back to the secure unit that would kill him."

"Yes, I know," I'd already been thinking about that. "I was going to drop you back at your place and then take him back to London with me. He can get lost there and one more fruitcake is not going to attract much attention. Especially around Camden."

"Then why don't I come with you? I can help and I have no particular need to be in Somerset."

"You sure?"

"Of course. You can't manage him on your own, he'll drive you nuts."

"You mean you don't trust me not to lock him in the attic."

"I was thinking a cupboard but I suppose an attic works just as well."

We swung onto the A303 towards London and for a while we made good time but then just as we were driving past Stonehenge the traffic slowed to a crawl and finally, a complete stop. I guessed it was to do with the tunnel or

157

whatever they were putting in there but we were too far back from the source of the jam to see.

"Why are we here?" Merlin asked from the back.

"You mean in a philosophical sense or from the stuck in traffic sense?" I replied.

"The gate, why are we here at the gate? I can't go back there."

I twisted in my seat. Merlin was staring through the window, his eyes wide under the straggly eyebrows.

"Oh, you mean Stonehenge. We're just passing, that's all. Traffic jam."

"Of course," said Elaine. "That's where they picked him up. Wonder how he got in there in the first place?"

"Space time portal to an alternate Loonyverse I expect."

Elaine poked me in the ribs. "Don't give me that. There's something about him that intrigues you. Disturbs you even."

"Disturbs me, yes. My life was relatively peaceful and sorted and then all of a sudden I'm springing a certified nutjob and digging holes in a minefield. Disturbing is an understatement. I was all sorted before he turned up with his stick and soft porn book."

The traffic eased forward three car lengths.

"Sorted? You're carrying more baggage than a Kardashian on a weekend trip to Paris. I know the pain you've suffered but you don't have to be so dismissive of everything that's just a little out of the ordinary. The world is allowed to contain a few mysteries that even John Barker can't explain."

I stared at the rows of brake lights in front of me, stretching into the distance. "The world is full of conmen ready to exploit the misfortunes of others, we need a cull. Every day innocence is abused and the jackals are waiting to tear apart the fallen. We live in a world where Jeremy Kyle is seen as the voice of reason and pictures of dead dogs are used as click-bait on social media to sell telephones which nobody can understand anymore."

"But this doesn't have to be your mission, John. You must have been fairly comfortable as The Great Xando, you did very well. Don't you fancy going back to that?"

"Ah, you've been Googling me."

"I didn't need to. I remember you on your TV specials. That one where you drove the car off Beachy Head. How did you do that?"

"Just your everyday dematerialisation and reappearance in another place. Nothing to it."

"Is it because of Amy? Is that why you quit?"

"No, not straight away at least, but after a while, later. Magic had changed anyway, what with the likes of David Blaine and so on. This so-called Street Magic relying on tricky camera angles and hysterical teenagers, that's not magic. I decided to retire and use my skills chasing down fake mediums instead."

The cars in front moved forwards and we stopped again just five cars back from the source of the trouble. A caravan lay on its side blocking one carriageway. Pieces of spilt caravanning holiday littered the grass verges in amongst the various bits of rescue paraphernalia.

"So now you have a mission to destroy every little bit of magic you come across?"

"No, not really. I just haven't found any."

"What about him?" Elaine flicked her head backwards to indicate our passenger.

"Him? There's nothing magic about him. He's just... um..." I caught Elaine's warning glance. "Special. He's just special."

"You keep telling yourself that if it makes you feel better.

Pay attention, we're moving." She pointed at the cars in front which had started filtering past the overturned holiday.

"Your evil sow has eaten a page of The Book," Merlin said.

"Let's hope it wasn't important," I said.

"I saved a corner but I don't understand. The man is eating her feet, what message is that? Without the full page I can't decipher the meaning. The numbers won't speak. Infernal swine, animal of the demons."

"Trust me," I said. "You probably don't need to know that bit. Some things are best kept a mystery."

"So, what do we do in the Big City? You going to show me the sights?" asked Elaine.

"If you like, although I'm guessing at some point Morgan Faylon is going to demand her pound of flesh for getting us out of the clutches of the Ministry of Defence."

As it happened, we didn't have to wait long. We hadn't driven for more than ten minutes when my mobile rang. I swung onto the side of the road and answered it.

"Ah, John," Morgan's voice. "I've been talking to Martin Springborn and he wants a meeting."

"Martin Springborn? Isn't he that idiot who does that TV show Celebrities With Spades or whatever it is?"

"Celebrity Time Diggers, dear. And it's very popular, you remember popular?"

"Why does he want a meeting with me? There's no way you're getting me on that show. It's the most appalling nonsense."

"Now, now, don't be peevish. You owe me, remember? Anyway, it's not you he wants, it's your wizard."

"Merlin? You can't put him on a TV celebrity show. And he's not my wizard, or anybody's wizard. In fact, he's not a wizard at all; he's just... just confused."

160

"Confused or not, he's a bit of a celebrity at the moment. Perfect fit for the show; ancient reincarnated wizard digging up buried treasures. It's got ratings written all over it."

"Well, it's not happening. He doesn't deserve to be wheeled out and poked fun at. I've seen what they do on that programme. Find yourself another victim."

"Do you really want me to ring Monty?"

"Monty? Who the hell is Monty?"

"Captain Montgomery Bedivere, remember? He was rather keen on locking you up in the Tower of London if I remember. That is until I came along and saved your arse. I'm sure he'd be glad to see you all again. Lovely man, quite delightful really. Just gets a bit touchy over communist spies."

"I'm not a communist spy."

"Look, I know that, dear. But you know how these military types can be. Now, I said to Martin we'd meet him in his office in Wardour Street at ten tomorrow. That good for you? Jolly good." The phone went dead.

"Damn," I said.

"What is it?" Elaine looked concerned.

"It's that bloody woman Morgan Faylon. I knew we'd regret getting tangled up with her. She wants Merlin on Celebrity Time Diggers."

"Oh. That'll be fun. I quite like that programme."

Chapter Sixteen

We pulled up in my parking space beneath the apartment building. I turned off the engine and sat for a moment.

"What's up?" Elaine asked.

"Just wondering how I'm going to smuggle a wizard and a pig past Joe."

"Joe?"

"The doorman. He's ex-SAS or something, so he's bound to notice a wizard and a pig."

"I know these caves," Merlin announced from the back seat.

"Yes, Merlin. We were here two days ago. It's where I live."

"Here, put this on him, like a coat." Elaine handed me a small tartan travel rug.

"That'll never cover him."

"I didn't mean Merlin, idiot. For the pig, cover him in this and we can lead him on a bit of string."

Joe glanced up from his desk as we crossed the foyer towards the lift. "Ah good afternoon, sir. You have a..." He stared at Breakfast. "A pig?"

"It's a dog, my uncle's." Elaine tipped her head towards Merlin. She moved closer to Joe and whispered conspiratorially, "I know it's an ugly dog but Uncle Mervyn loves him, it's all he has left. It's a Japanese Pug."

"Looks like a pig," said Joe. "Pets ain't allowed, is he staying?"

"Only a couple of nights. Uncle's a bit poorly and he'd be heartbroken to be separated from him."

"Well don't let Mrs Chamberlain in number twenty-eight see it. She'll have a fit."

"Nice one," I said to Elaine as we crammed into the lift. "But I really can't keep a pig here. We'll have to do something with him. With both of them."

I put Merlin and Breakfast in the spare room and guided Elaine to my room. "I'll sleep on the couch," I said. "The apartment's not really designed for house guests."

"You don't need to do that," she said. "I'm sure we can work something out." A mischievous smile sparkled across her lips.

"We need to get some food in," I flustered. "I wasn't expecting a house full. What do pigs eat?"

"Don't know. Is there a pet shop nearby?"

"I think there's one in the next street but I'm guessing they're more used to catering for Siamese cats or Chihuahuas than farmyard livestock. This is Camden after all, not Smithfields. I need a walk anyway, coming?"

We left Merlin and Breakfast watching Celebrity Operation and headed off to Camden Market where we found some organic oats, which the assistant convinced me, were perfect for house-pigs, a second-hand army blanket and a dog drinking bowl with a picture of sausages printed inside it.

"I think that's probably in bad taste," Elaine said as I dropped the bowl in my bag.

We wandered the market for a while, just chatting and enjoying each other's company and then headed back as the stalls began closing up for the day.

As I opened the door, something huge rushed at my face. I ducked and pushed Elaine to one side. I turned to watch the creature bouncing from the walls in the corridor. It was a huge bird.

"You let Myrgrath loose," Merlin yelled from inside the apartment.

"It's an owl," said Elaine.

The creature swooped back towards me and I ducked once more. I'd never seen an owl quite that close before, it was huge.

"You sure?" I watched as it collided with the window. "I thought they were cute little things that sat on branches. That thing's a monster."

"Myrgrath!" Merlin yelled once more.

"How did that thing get in? Merlin? What the—" The owl hurtled straight for me and I held my arms over my face, bracing for the collision. It never came, instead I felt the wings brush my arms as it flapped past me and back into the apartment.

I straightened and turned towards the door just as Merlin closed it in my face. "Merlin…"

I turned to Elaine. "There's an owl in my apartment," I said.

"I know," she said flatly.

"Apparently its name's Myrgrath."

"So I believe."

"That's okay then. Just as long as it's not just me." I tried to turn the key in the lock but Merlin had dropped the catch. I banged on the door. "Merlin!" I shouted. "Open this door."

"I can't. Myrgrath has the tremors. You've upset him."

"I've upset…What? Open this door now."

"There's too much darkness in your soul. That's not good for Myrgrath. He needs peace before he'll speak. You can come back later when the darkness is gone."

I looked at Elaine. "Have you any idea what he's talking about?"

"I think he means your anger is disturbing his owl."

"My anger? He's not seen anger yet." I banged on the door with both hands. "Open this bloody door before I knock it down, beat you round the head with it and feed that owl to you a feather at a time."

"There, you see," came the voice through the door. "No good with the darkness."

"Merlin!" I shouted and kicked at the door but the solid Victorian timberwork ignored my assault.

"Having trouble, Mister Barker?" I turned to see a stocky woman in a tweed twinset standing behind me.

"Ah, Mrs Chamberlain. Yes, I appear to have locked myself out."

"Well banging on the door won't help will it now, silly thing. I'll call down for Joe; he can pop up with his pass key. I did the same thing only last week. Left the bath running too, dreadful mess. You haven't left the bath running have you?"

"What? No. No need for that, thank you anyway."

"No trouble." She headed towards her apartment at the end of the corridor. "I'll get him to bring up a mop and a bucket just in case."

"Really, no. I'm fairly sure I haven't left the bath running. It's my uncle... Elaine's uncle... he's..." Mrs Chamberlain disappeared into her door.

"Oh, joy. So much for keeping Merlin under the radar."

A loud squeal from Merlin and a crash of something expensive sounded inside.

"You talk to him," I pleaded to Elaine. "He might listen to you."

Elaine tapped gently on the door. "Merlin? How's Myrgrath?"

"How's Myrgrath?" I hissed.

"Shush, John. Do you want me to help or not?" She turned back to the door. "John's calm now. You can open the door." She must have felt me bristling behind her as she waved a hand towards me to shoo me away.

"Having trouble, sir?" Joe gave me a start. He stood with a mop in one hand and a bucket in the other. "Mrs Chamberlain said you'd gone and locked yourself out with the bath running. Bit of a fool thing to do if you ask me."

"Uh? No, she's got hold of the wrong end of the stick. It's just my uncle... Elaine's uncle, he's... got the door stuck. Silly old... whatsit."

"Can't he turn the bath off then?"

I stared at Joe trying to work out how to end this nightmare when the door eased open. I turned and made to push my way in but Elaine intercepted me with a calming hand against my chest.

The door swung fully open and Merlin stood framed just inside. He was wearing my Champney's white bathrobe which he had failed to tie up in the front. It flapped open.

I heard a squeal from behind and turned to see Mrs Chamberlain's frozen figure, hands covering her eyes, trying to unsee what she'd just witnessed.

"I'll just check the bath," said Joe as he headed for the door. He never made it through.

A large owl fluttered from the dining room behind Merlin and settled calmly on the top of the wizard's straggly head. I groped for an explanation to offer Joe but gave up when Breakfast appeared from between Merlin's legs. It stared briefly at Joe, gave a little squeal then hurtled back towards the bedroom.

"Well," I said. "I think that's all okay now then. Come along, Uncle, it's time for your medicine." I encouraged Elaine into the apartment and closed the door to the open mouths of Joe and Mrs Chamberlain. "That could have gone better."

***

"So, this owl, Myrgrath," I said once I'd found a beer and let its soothing effects take hold. "It just flew in through the window and started talking to you? And will you please cover yourself up?"

"Of course he didn't. That's nonsense." Merlin pulled the bathrobe closed. "He talked to me first; I had to invite him in. You have to invite in your familiar, they can't just come in on their own."

"I thought that was vampires. You had to invite vampires in?"

"Vampires? They're just mere creations of fiction. Why are you talking about fairy tales, nonsense designed to scare children?"

"So, familiars have to be invited in but not vampires?"

"Indeed. What anarchistic disorder would seize the world if familiars just came and went as they pleased?"

"Sorry, so this owl spoke to you from outside and you thought it a good idea to open up the window and invite it into my apartment? My apartment where no pets are allowed. The one I've lived in peacefully for many years and from which I am probably about to be evicted. That's if they don't come after me with pitchforks first."

"John, let him talk." Elaine turned to Merlin. "Who is Myrgrath?"

Merlin pointed at the owl but said nothing.

"Okay, but where did he come from?"

Merlin pointed at the window.

"Before that, Merlin. Where does Myrgrath come from? When he's not here."

Merlin pointed to the ceiling. "Here, there." He waved his arms around in an expansive circle. "Other worlds, places not for mortals to see. He came to warn me of danger. Arthur is in danger."

"Arthur?" Elaine asked.

"Arthur's dead," I said. "That's if he ever existed. How can he be in danger?"

"She's going to stop his return. She has plans to scatter his bones for the alchemists to destroy. If she does this he can never return."

"Who, Merlin? Who is she?"

"Morgana of course. The evil one."

"Morgana?" I said. "Look, Merlin—"

My mobile phone rang and I answered it without thinking.

"Bit of a delay, darling," Morgan Faylon's voice chirped through the airwaves. "Can we change the time of our meeting tomorrow until say, midday? Only Martin's arranged for some others to join us and they're going to be late. Good for you? Jolly good."

"What other people?" I asked.

"Got to go, dear. Lovely talking. Catch up tomorrow. Don't be late, there's a love." The phone went dead.

I caught Elaine's quizzical expression. "That bloody woman again, Morgan Faylon. Wants to delay the meeting until twelve. Something about other people coming. It's turning into a circus."

"Morgana!" Merlin jumped up and the bathrobe flapped open again. "Myrgrath knew. He warned me."

The owl circled the room once then settled on Merlin's head.

168

***

Later that evening we ordered a Chinese meal and settled in front of the latest Bond movie on Netflix. Merlin even put his scribbling to one side for a while and became captivated with the action. I wondered about him again, as I did from time to time. He seemed to be settling into our world better now, almost as if he really had come from somewhere else and was learning as he went. He was certainly less fazed by modern living than he had been when I'd found him. It was still highly probable that some trauma or other had caused a sort of soft reset in his brain and was working its way through. Although... I felt Elaine's hand slip into mine and she pushed closer to me on the sofa. I gave a gentle squeeze and she rested her head on my shoulder. It felt comforting.

When the film finished, I carried the dishes into the kitchen. As I filled the sink I felt Elaine press up behind me.

"I've been thinking about the sleeping arrangements," she whispered gently in my ear and pressed closer.

I turned the tap off. "And what conclusions did you come to?" I felt her breath on my neck.

"That the couch looks uncomfortable and that the bed is too big for me. That's as far as I'd got." She turned me round to face her, still pressing close. "Any ideas?"

I scanned her eyes. It had been a long time since I'd been this close to a woman. A very long time. I felt the firmness of her body. "I suddenly seem devoid of ideas," I said.

"Mmm, maybe between us we can come up with a few? What do you say?"

"I say let's go into the bedroom and have another look at that bed, see how big it really is."

As we passed through the lounge, Merlin was deeply engrossed in another movie. Looked like a fantasy film.

The bed welcomed us and seemed just the right size for two. Elaine's arms felt natural and safe as she wrapped them around me. We kissed and I felt a real connection with another human for the first time in many, many years. The feeling was so intense, so sudden that I started and froze.

Elaine noticed my response. "It's okay," she said. "Really. It's time."

I held her tight so she couldn't see my face. We lay there like that for a while. Me, unable to move or speak, Elaine just being there.

Eventually the warmth of her body, her smell, her breath, all moved to stir me and desire took hold. We fumbled with each other's clothes like a pair of teenagers and tumbled across the bed in a tangle of half removed clothes and desperate bodies.

Chapter Seventeen

The following morning we took a cab to Wardour Street. Merlin insisted we took Myrgrath who sat patiently on Merlin's right shoulder like a giant parrot. I went along with the idea in the vain hope that the thing would fly off as soon as it took the scent of open air. It didn't.

Martin Springborn's office occupied a corner position on the second floor and gave views over the midday traffic chaos below. Leather and oak presented the dominant themes. He stood from behind his oversized desk as we entered.

"Ah, you must be John. Morgan tells me you used to be a magician on the telly? Well done." He turned to Elaine. "And you must be the lovely Elaine I've heard so much about. Do have a seat. And Merlin, wonderful to see you. Nice owl."

"Is Morgan coming?" I asked.

"She'll be here in a minute, just meeting the others."

"Others?"

The door opened and Morgan came in followed by Cas, Sebastian and Tree.

"Oh, good," Morgan said when she saw me. "You're here already. Just wait a moment for the others and we can get started."

Martin Springborn buzzed his assistant and asked her to organise more seating.

"Did we really need everybody?" I asked.

"Ratings, dear," said Morgan. "You and your crew are ratings dynamite at the moment. Don't you read the news?"

"Been rather busy. What do you mean my crew? Makes me sound like a street rapper or something."

"That's good. I like it." Morgan turned to Martin. "Can we use that? Merlin and his Street Crew? Got a sort of a ring to it. What do you think?"

"I like it. I'll put it to the Focus Group. Now, let me tell you what we have so far." Martin pushed his chair back slightly from the desk and aimed a remote control into the air. The lights dimmed and a screen sprang into life. It took up most of the end wall. "We already have Jayed Flayme." The face of Jayed Flayme filled the screen. An anorexic looking blonde with inflated lips and blue contact lenses. "MC Deepcut booked this morning." The screen changed to show the face of an African/American with shaven head and a tattoo of a snake curling around his neck and up his right cheek. "We're hoping to get Sheridan Baxter, the newsreader, and that Conservative politician fella', never remember his bloody name."

"Boris Johnson?" I offered.

"No, not him. The stupid one who keeps making racist comments." He pressed his intercom button. "Who's that idiot politician we're booking for the big one, Steph?"

"James Fanshaw," returned the speaker on his desk.

"That's the man. Great television to set him up with Deepcut and Merlin. Might even get a punch-up out of it."

The door opened a fraction and Stevie's head peeped round. "Is this the right room? Oh, hi, Cas." She waved at Cas.

"Come on in," said Morgan. "We've only just started."

The door pushed fully open and Eric and Colin followed her in.

"This is fun," said Elaine into my ear.

"I need a drink," I replied.

"Jolly good idea," said Martin. Clearly I hadn't spoken as quietly as I'd thought. Martin pressed his intercom. "Steph, bring those bottles of Moet in, there's a love. Should be cold enough by now."

"Okay, now we're planning to start shooting the first show in two weeks if those buggers at the Ministry of Defence get their fingers out. I tell you, if Russia ever wants to invade they've only got to wait until September because the whole Civil Service fucks off to the Caribbean or somewhere for the month and the British army can't order a new ballpoint pen until somebody comes back to sign the purchase requisition."

The door swung open once more and his assistant wheeled in a chrome trolley laden with Champagne bottles and glasses.

Martin continued with his slideshow of fading celebrities as his assistant poured the champagne. He went through the filming schedule and explained that this special Celebrity Time Diggers was running as a triple show special and a later special of Morgan's Spook Hunter would follow the haunted treasures after they are dug up and transported to the waiting museum vaults where they would be exorcised by Morgan.

"But we don't know if there's anything there?" said Colin. "The torque might be all there was."

"Trust me," said Martin. "There will be treasure. Have you ever seen an episode of Celebrity Time Diggers where no treasure was found?"

"No," confessed Colin. "But then I never watch it anyway. How can you be so sure?"

"We always have... what shall I say... contingency plans."

"You mean... but that's dishonest."

"It's just television. If you want reality, look out of your window, but don't watch reality television."

He continued to explain the shooting schedule and everybody's part in the upcoming fiasco. He had planned set pieces involving Stevie and Eric marking out star maps on the grass, Tree going into a trance and communing with an archangel or two, Cas and Sebastian dowsing for ley lines and Merlin swinging his pendant and generally looking mysterious.

"It's going to shoot the ratings through the roof," he said. "We'll blow Strictly Come Dancing out of the ratings charts. We'll probably even hit the newspaper headlines. Martin Springborn discovers King Arthur's tomb."

"Ahem!" said Morgan.

"Okay, okay, Martin Springborn and Morgan Faylon discover King Arthur's tomb."

For the first time, Merlin stopped scribbling in his book and looked up. "You're dealing with dark forces. The prophet has warned." He waved the battered Fifty Shades of Grey in the air. "The King must rise and all those who stand against him shall feel the nipple clamps."

"The nipple clamps?" I asked.

"Hmm." Merlin studied his book. "Maybe that bit's not quite right."

***

After we finally managed to escape the lunacy, we convened in a nearby Chinese restaurant. Cas, Sebastian and Tree just snatched sandwiches-to-go and dashed off to Paddington to catch the next train.

We sat down at a table. I needed a coffee. I quite enjoy a lunchtime drink but large quantities of Champagne on an empty stomach was not a good idea.

"No pets allowed," announced the waitress as she came for our orders. "What is that anyway? An owl?"

"It's a new treatment," said Elaine. "It's to help victims of PTSD return to normal life."

"With an owl?"

"They're very calming creatures. And intelligent. They're also allowed to go places where dogs aren't permitted."

"Really?"

"Yes," said Elaine. "I mean, when did you last see a sign which said No Owls?"

"Hum... well I suppose it's alright. PTSD? Was he in the army or something?"

"Special forces," I said. "But don't say anything."

The waitress pulled out her notebook. "I won't say a word. Nobody would believe me anyway. What would you like to order?"

I ordered Cantonese beef with noodles and the same for Merlin and the waitress gathered the rest of the orders.

We sat and chatted about the meeting until our food arrived. My beef and noodles tasted as good as it looked. Merlin grumbled about the lack of pizza as he studied his plate.

"It's a Chinese restaurant, Merlin," I said. "They don't do pizza."

"Why are we here then?"

"Because we don't all want to eat pizza for every meal."

"But flat food is the food of the gods," he said. "It has all your meal there, in a round, convenient disc and it fits perfectly in a box."

I turned to the waitress. "It's the PTSD. It comes in waves."

"Do you think the military will let us look around their base?" asked Stevie after the waitress had gone. "I'd love to see the Rendlesham UFO."

"I expect the Americans have it by now," said Eric. "That's how they developed Stealth Plane and the iPhone."

"Morgana wants to destroy the King." Merlin carefully removed the noodles one by one and poked them around the plate. "What creatures are these?"

"Noodles," I said. "And I'm not sure that it's her intent to destroy Arthur but that's almost certainly going to be the result."

Elaine peered at me over her coffee cup. "So, you agree with Merlin that the King is in danger?" She raised a quizzical eyebrow and smiled.

"That's not what I said. Well, not what I meant. What I meant to say was that *if* there is anything there of archaeological value and note I say *if*, then leaving it in the hands of a publicity mad self-appointed ghost hunter is probably not the best idea."

"Of course you did."

"King or not, I'm not happy about being a party to this circus."

"But if we don't go along with it, Morgan will call her chum, Captain whatsisname and we'll all be straight back in some cell or other facing charges of treason or something."

Merlin slammed his book on the table, Myrgrath startled and flapped from Merlin's shoulder and flew to a wooden beam straddling the roof space above us. "We must save the King. It's in here." He tapped at the book with his fork and added sweet and sour sauce to the already, rapidly deteriorating cover.

"We could hide anything we dig up," suggested Eric.

"That's ridiculous," I said. "How could we do that, they'll have film crew all over the place watching our every move."

"That's not such a crazy idea." Elaine's eyes brightened. "I've seen the programme—"

"You've watched that programme?" I feigned great shock. "I thought you had better taste."

"If I had better taste, do you really think I'd be sitting here with you lot?"

"Good point."

"Anyway," she continued. "It may look tidy on the screen but I think in reality it's all set up."

"Celebrity Time Diggers? A set up? I'll ring the papers at once."

"Shush, bear with me. They always have so many people running around; the cameras can't follow them all. I think everybody does their digging and if they find something, the cameras come over and they pretend to dig it up again."

"I suppose that makes sense," I said.

The waitress came over with a concerned look on her face. "I'm sorry, the manager's asked me to tell you you'll have to leave. Your bird is disturbing the other customers."

I glanced up. Myrgrath sat on the beam, his claw and beak tearing apart what, from here, looked like a spare rib. A crying child at the other end of the restaurant gave a clue as to its original location.

"Sorry," I said. "It's still in training."

We stood to leave and the owl swept down and landed neatly on Merlin's shoulder. It seemed to nuzzle at his ear.

"Myrgrath has spoken. He says we need John's magic to rescue Arthur," Merlin said.

I stared at the owl and the owl stared back. There was something very strange about that creature.

The bird lifted gently and hovered just in front of Merlin's face. They stared at each other for a brief moment then Myrgrath flew out of the door.

"Myrgrath has gone now," said Merlin.

"I can see that," I said.

"No, you non-understanding human. Myrgrath has gone. He has delivered his messages and now he goes to Albion. He will not be back."

"I wish he could have done that *before* we got thrown out," grumbled Cas. "I hadn't even started my prawn balls." He popped a spring roll into his mouth.

***

In the days that followed, we managed to relocate Breakfast to a temporary home at the Camden Petting Zoo, a facility set up to teach underprivileged kids about animal care. He seemed upset when we left him and whined at the gate of his pen. I nearly weakened but the mental image of Mrs Chamberlain with pitchfork strengthened my resolve.

Merlin continued to settle in to life in London and there were even times when we had almost normal conversations. As I grew to know him better, his obsession about King Arthur began to seem less random. He spent time showing me in detail his workings out in the paperback book. Each time I tried to find fault with his conclusions, I couldn't. His system of counting letter sequences within the text continued to throw up names and places that tied in to the areas we'd been and especially where we'd found the Saxon torque. The professional cynic in me drew odds with the man I'd once been. What had happened to the young, optimistic stage magician who, along with his soul mate, had once found his own magic and taken it to the world?

"Either Merlin is becoming saner or I'm gradually losing my marbles," I said to Elaine one morning as we strolled the Embankment.

"Does it have to be one or the other?" she said.

"What do you mean?"

"I've given my life to people who struggle with the world in which the rest of us live. They're never as far away as we would like to believe."

"I don't understand." I sidestepped a cyclist and was just wallowing in the glow of self congratulation at my agility when I cracked my shin on a metal bollard.

"Are you alright?" Elaine said. "I heard that clunk from here. Nothing broken?"

"No, all okay." I put on my best super-hero mask. "And besides, I've got another leg."

"You were saying?" she said.

"Um? Oh, yes, what do you mean they're not as far away as we'd believe?"

"Most people like to believe they are immune from the problems which affect those with mental difficulties. Yet deep down, subconsciously, we all recognise the reality that we are all probably only one crisis away. We look at these poor troubled individuals and see our own vulnerability. A marriage break-up, redundancy, death of a spouse?" Her eyes searched mine. "So we keep our distance and build walls. The more different we can make them, the safer we become."

"So you're saying I'm just as crazy as Merlin?"

She turned to face me, came close enough for me to feel her warmth and then poked me in the chest. "Don't be flippant, you know what I mean. Merlin has what he believes is his reality, you have what you believe is yours. The elephants that walk in line can only see the backside of the one in front. It's only the one who steps out of line who can see all. Maybe it's time for you to step out of the line."

Chapter Eighteen

Elaine and I were on our way to the supermarket when the phone call came.

"The dig starts on Tuesday," Martin Springborn said.

"Next Tuesday? That's a bit short notice isn't it?"

"It's all to do with the MOD. They had a gap in their diary. Apparently they're not keen on publicising their wargame schedules too far in advance in case the Taliban invade Salisbury while they're on the golf course."

"Okay, luckily my diary's fairly clear. Where do we go?"

"We're putting you all up in the Shrewton House hotel. All expenses paid so enjoy yourselves. You're booked in from Monday. See you there." The line went dead.

I turned to Elaine. "That was Martin. Apparently we're—"

Elaine's phone rang. "Yes? Oh hello, Martin... Tuesday?... Shrewton House hotel? Great. See you there."

The Shrewton House hotel stood in magnificent grounds on the edge of Salisbury Plain. Victorian architecture overlaid with a hundred years of modernisations and additions. By the time we arrived on Monday evening it seemed most of the others were already there. Cas wandered out of the bar when he heard our voices at reception. He carried a glass of what looked like champagne in one hand and a joint in the other.

"Hey," he greeted when he saw us. "Cool place. You're late; we started the party without you."

"Party? We didn't know about a party?" I said.

"Well sort of improv' really. But you know, when the drinks are free, there's always going to be a party."

"I think we'll just take it easy tonight. Been a long drive and we don't know what tomorrow's going to bring."

"Well, suit yourself, man. Got some cool smoke if you'd rather?"

"Are you sure you should be doing that?"

"Hey, chill. We've got the whole place, nobody else here but us dudes."

Elaine and I were given a double room, rather presumptively I thought, and Merlin had a room in the annexe.

We'd just unpacked when the room telephone rang and Martin announced we were due in the Oaks Conference Room for a briefing in twenty minutes.

"Can I leave you to it?" Elaine asked. "Only I've got some... um... shopping to do... a long way from here. They don't need me; I'll just clutter up the place. Ask stupid questions, that sort of thing. I'll only embarrass everybody."

"Embarrass this lot? That would be worth seeing." I squeezed her hand. "Besides, it will be an experience."

"Okay," she relented. "But don't expect sparkling."

We took our seats at a horseshoe arrangement of tables in the huge conference room. Bottles of Evian water had been placed at precise intervals and a pad of A4 paper and pencil provided at each seating position. I scanned the room. It seemed that apart from Martin Springborn and Morgan Faylon, everybody else was already there. There were people I recognised such as Sheridan Baxter, the newsreader, Jayed Flayme and Tory MP James Fanshaw plus a few people I didn't.

"Who's that?" I whispered to Elaine and nodded towards a

man in his twenties who wore a white puffy anorak three sizes too big and a tattered blue baseball cap.

"Isn't that Twentypence Atomik? The rapper or something? I think he was at Glastonbury Festival last year."

"But he's white."

"Observant one aren't you?"

The door opened and Martin and Morgan strutted in to take their places at the centre table.

"Good morning, Time Diggers." Martin dropped a leather briefcase on the table in front of him. "We'll whizz round the table for some quick introductions then crack straight on. We've a lot to cover, so please take notes. Morgan, would you set the ball rolling?"

Morgan steepled her fingers. "Good morning, everybody. I'm sure you all know me; I'm Morgan Faylon, producer and presenter of Spook Hunter. I'm the co-producer of this special Celebrity Time Diggers." She nodded towards Sheridan Baxter on her left.

"Good evening, I'm Sheridan Baxter and this is the six o'clock news... sorry, my little joke. I'm not sure why I'm here really. My agent arranged it all, I don't really do digging. I hosted Gardener's Question Time once so I suppose that's why I was invited."

"Good morning, people. I'm sure you all know me. I'm James Fanshaw, Member of Parliament for Hillsbridge West. I'm delighted to be here with this fine group of ordinary people. These sorts of events are a wonderful counterpoint to the heady world of Whitehall. Quite delightful. Grounding, one might say, if you'll excuse the pun."

"Prat," Sebastian announced.

Martin gave Sebastian a withering stare.

"What?" Sebastian looked offended. "Well he is, isn't he?"

Martin ignored the comment and nodded towards the next person on the table. A short man with rosy cheeks and just a little too much and too perfectly dressed yellow hair.

"Hello, everybody. I'm Desmond Smiley; call me Des, host of Kid's Challenge. Anybody give me an 'I Can Do it'?" He stared around the room to a collection of confused faces. "It's the catchphrase. I Can Do It? Come on, somebody must have seen the show? With Godfrey the gopher? Gopher it? Really? Nobody?" He looked quite crestfallen and I might have felt sorry for him if I could have got past the yellow hair.

"Moving on," Martin said, putting an end to Desmond's suffering.

"Yo, Bruvs. Wassup?" the rapper said. "Y'all know me cus I'm the money, doin' the thing, right with me homey. Y'all my homies. Sure thing, boomya!"

"Sorry," said James Fanshaw. "Is he speaking English?"

"It's rap, man," said Cas. "Voice of the streets. He's the dude."

Fanshaw looked confused. "But he's white."

Elaine nudged me and whispered, "See, he noticed as well."

I suppressed a giggle.

"This is Twentypence Atomik," said Martin. "He's a last minute replacement for MC Deepcut who we had to pull due to a... erm... little incident with the Heathrow Border Police and a gold plated Uzi."

"Man's a legend," said Twentypence. "And he don't depend on the way of the trend, he's the king with the bling and he don't take no crap from the man in the cap."

"What *is* he talking about?" said Fanshaw.

"I think that was probably his introduction." Martin looked quizzically at Morgan who nodded an affirmation. "Good, now if we can focus? We have a lot to cover." He looked at me and raised an eyebrow.

"My name is John Barker. I used to be a stage magician and I haven't the faintest idea why I'm here. I don't dig, the man who lives downstairs might object, and the closest I get to reality television is the Nine o' Clock News."

"I remember you," said Desmond. "You did that thing with the Statue of Liberty."

"That was David Copperfield," I corrected.

"Merlin," Martin said. "Why don't you tell everybody a little about yourself?"

Merlin looked up from his scribbles. "Why?"

"So everybody will know who you are."

"Everybody knows who I am. Advisor to Arthur. Time wasting nonsense and he's not invited." Merlin aimed his pencil towards Martin. "Nor that demon woman who sits at his side. I know her machinations, it's all in here." He tapped his book.

The introductions proceeded around the room and when finished Martin called for the lights to be dimmed and a huge screen revealed itself from behind a wooden facia. The presentation started with a panning shot over Salisbury Plain which then settled on the area we had been digging.

"This is the location of our Celebrity Time Diggers Special," said Martin. "For those of you who don't know, some items were recently discovered here which we believe belong to the grave of a Saxon king. We have every reason to believe that this is the location of the burial site of King Arthur."

"Are you insane?" said Baxter. "King Arthur is mythical. I can't lend my name to this nonsense; I'm a serious news broadcaster. I'll never be taken seriously again." He stood up. "I'm sorry, gentlemen... and ladies... but I will have to take my leave."

"I'm afraid that's not possible," said Morgan. "You signed a contract." She tapped a pile of paper in front of her. "Leaving now would finish your career anyway so you might just as well play the game."

Baxter sank slowly back into his seat.

"Okay," continued Martin. "The Ministry of Defence have granted us three clear days--"

"Just like Time Team," Colin interrupted. "Always wanted to go on that."

"It's nothing like Time Team," said Martin. "They have—"

"I always wanted to go on Celebrity Chef," said Desmond. "Thought that was where I was going to be honest. My agent told me—"

"Gentlemen, if we could—"

"Diggin' in the ground, takin' it down, the ground , the hole, the chain gang an take me, it shake me but ain't never gonna break me—"

"Somebody shut him up."

"Gentlemen," Martin slammed the flat of his hand on the table. "Look, here." He rummaged in his briefcase and came out with a plastic twelve inch ruler. "This is the Talking Stick. The only person allowed to speak is the person holding the Talking Stick."

"Oh, cool," said Cas. "Like the Apaches."

"No, it was the Cherokee, the Apaches used a Talking Feather," said Tree.

"I thought that was the Eskimos?"

"Where are they going to get a feather?"

"Please," Martin raised his voice to a badly concealed shout. "The Talking Stick? I have the Talking Stick."

"No you don't," said Merlin with an air of authority. He banged Harold loudly on the floor and the room fell silent.

185

"That is just a child's plaything. This..." He lifted Harold in the air. "This is a Talking Stick."

The room waited expectantly.

"Doesn't say much does it," Baxter said finally.

Merlin glared at him and pointed Harold in his direction. I half expected a thunderbolt to appear out of the end of the stick. Or at the very least, a puff of smoke. I certainly wasn't prepared for what actually happened. In the silence of the room I clearly heard the words, "Bring me soup," come from the stick.

I looked around the room, checking the expressions on the faces around the tables. It seemed everybody was as stunned as I was.

"Did I just hear..." Colin started but then gave up as words failed him.

"I heard it too," said Sebastian. "Clear as anything."

Merlin put Harold back on the floor and continued with his scribbling as if nothing had happened.

"Did that stick just speak?" said Martin.

"It seems so," I said.

"And did it just say something about soup?"

"Yes, I think it said, 'bring me soup'."

"Bring me soup?"

I played the sequence back in my mind. Could Merlin have been doing some sort of ventriloquism?

"You heard it too, right?" Elaine asked me. "I mean, I wasn't imagining it, was I?"

"No," I said. "You weren't imagining it. I heard it too but I'm sure it's a trick. Just got to figure out how he did it."

"It's a very random trick," she said. "And what's this about soup? The world has been waiting for centuries for proof positive of the supernatural and when it finally arrives, it's in the form of a walking stick demanding soup?"

"What sort of soup?" Cas asked. "I mean, I would never just ask for soup. Would anyone? You'd want to know what it was going to be."

"Is that really the issue here?" Morgan asked. "I mean, if there's one thing I've learned from my years of dealing with the supernatural, it's that it's... well... supernatural. It doesn't conform to our norms and values. I remember once when—"

"It's a bit of an issue if you're a vegetarian," interrupted Cas. "Or a vegan. What if somebody goes and presents you with a bowl of oxtail just because you didn't specify what sort of soup?"

"Can we *please* move along?" Martin hand squeezed his pencil until his knuckles whitened. "As wonderful as a speaking stick is, and I'm sure there's a perfectly rational explanation, we only have this room until midday and we have a lot to get through."

"There you go with this obsession for so-called rational explanations," Cas said. "Where did that ever get anybody with the Twin Towers? That's what I want to know."

Martin's pencil splintered into two separate parts and flew into the air. He gave a forced grin. "Anybody got a pencil?"

Elaine stood. "Will everybody please get a grip," she said. The room fell to silence under her uncharacteristic assertiveness. "I know most of us don't want to be here, that some are here under threats and coercion." She touched my hand. "And I know some of you are here to revive flagging television careers or just seeing an opportunity for profit or fame but if we don't get on with this then half of us are going to end up inside Wormwood Scrubs or something and the rest of you will be consigned to the darkest corners of some obscure satellite channel which only shows reruns of Friends and Celebrity Crocodile Wrestling."

"Will I still get to launch my own perfume?" Jayed's first contribution to the proceedings brought with it a bemused silence which hung ominously in the air like a dog fart at a vicarage tea.

"The filming schedule, we need to understand how this is going to work." Martin shuffled the papers in front of him. "Has anybody got a pencil I can borrow?"

Morgan handed him a pencil and he underlined then double circled the top item on the list in front of him. "*Rule one*, nobody digs up anything unless the camera is watching." He glanced around the room as if expecting a challenge. "*Rule two*, if you *do* accidently dig something up, bury it again until the camera is watching."

Colin looked up. "But surely—"

"*Rule three*, in the event of nothing being found we have a box of antique stuff our crew will bury on Day Three for the nominated celebs to find."

"What if—"

"*Rule four*, all finds are to be handed in immediately to the assay team. And we reserve the right to do random searches when exiting the site."

"That's fascist, you can't do that," Sebastian said. "This is not Trumpton Land."

"Which brings me to *rule five*, anybody who doesn't like rules one through four, can catch a lift back to Captain Bedivere's little establishment where I'm told he has some rooms waiting." Martin's eyes roamed the room. "Any takers?" He paused. "Jolly good. We'll crack right on then shall we?"

He returned to the screen and added his own commentary to the images. For the next hour he talked about camera angles, dramatic moments, engineered conflict and the importance of the right celebrity featuring at the right moment.

I lost concentration about twenty minutes in and wondered idly how I'd got myself into this mess. I should have just carried on driving that night. Merlin would have been alright and I'd still be doing the rounds of the séances. I glanced at Merlin. He was engrossed in his notes, drawing arrows and loops across pages of Fifty Shades which were increasingly detaching from the cover. Maybe he would have been alright but I doubted it. Whoever he really was and from wherever he had come, he was not equipped for this world.

"And finally," Martin said, words always guaranteed to snap one's attention back in boring meetings. "Due to the importance of this event, the syndicated channels want to strip it over the three days. That means we need good clear footage as the editing team will have very little time to prepare the film for same evening transmission. Ladies and gentlemen, the eyes of the world are upon us, let's go dig up history."

The meeting wrapped up with Martin reminding us of the need to be bright and early next morning as the coach wouldn't wait.

As we filed from the room I caught the attention of Cas, Sebastian, Tree, Colin, Stevie and Eric, quietly suggesting we meet in the hotel bar at seven.

"What are you up to?" asked Elaine.

"Fancy a quick tour of the antique shops in Salisbury?"

***

We arrived in the hotel bar at seven as arranged. The others were already there and at a guess, they were all several drinks in. I glanced around the room, but there was no sign of Martin or Morgan or any of their team. Good. I collected us some beers then joined the others round a large table.

"What gives, dude?" asked Cas. "This is all very Secret Squirrel."

I dumped my box on the table. "The whole purpose of us doing this is to help Merlin in his mission, right?"

"And to keep out of prison," suggested Colin.

"Quite. Now, he believes that Arthur's bones are buried under Salisbury Plain and they need to be taken to... um... Tower Wendy?"

"Trewar Venydh," corrected Tree. "It's a place in Cornwall."

"Huh?"

"It's the old name for Tintagel."

"You never thought to mention this before?" I tried to keep the frustration out of my voice.

"I couldn't." Tree took a large bite of her mushroom and kale baguette. We had to wait for a good minute while she chewed her way through the mouthful before continuing. "The angels only just told me."

"The angels told you?"

"Of course. They apologised for the time they took. I think they've been on a mission but of course they don't tell me their business. At least, not until I'm at the purple vibrational level. But secretly," she glanced around as if looking for eaves-droppers, "I think they're keeping an eye on Tony Blair. They told me once they were worried he was going to get out again."

Colin pulled out his smartphone. "I'll check on Wikipedia. Hang on... T.I.N.T.A.G.E.L... searching... Here we go; it's a mini vibrator you stick on your tongue when you... oops... no that's a Tongue Tingler, sodding auto correct. Here it is, Tintagel, Cornwall. Reputed to be the birthplace of King Arthur, old Cornish name, Trewar Venydh."

"See," Tree said, sweeping the escaped baguette crumbs back onto her plate. "The angels know."

"Hmm." I thought for a moment. "That changes things. I was hoping that if we found these bones, or whatever, that at least Merlin wanted them putting somewhere quiet. But Tintagel is one of the busiest tourist sites in England."

"Can't you just do some magic or something," suggested Sebastian. "You used to do all that magic stuff. Should be easy. Piff poof paff." He waved his fingers in the air.

"Piff poof paff? I was a stage magician, an illusionist. Not Harry bloody Potter."

"Later," said Elaine. "Let's tackle one thing at a time. First, we have to get the bones off the site without anybody seeing. Assuming that is, we actually find anything. Let's not worry about what happens after that, it might not happen."

"Right." I opened the box and reached inside. "We went and bought these earlier. They're just some trinkets, Roman coins, old jewellery, that sort of stuff." I placed a handful of coins and a couple of bracelets on the table.

Colin picked through the collection. "Tat," he announced. "Nobody will believe that comes from the grave of a Saxon king. Look." He held up a coin. "This is a Romulus Augustus. See what I mean?"

We waited in silence for a while then I said, "And?"

"And? By the time he was on the throne the Romans had left England by around thirty years."

"Sorry, I'm still not getting this."

Colin tutted as if talking to a five-year-old. "How did they get into a Saxon grave on Salisbury Plain? They're clearly imported by coin dealers. They are not natural to this country."

"It doesn't matter," said Elaine. "All we need is something to move the attention of the experts away from where we are. It will keep them amused for a while."

"You should have taken me with you," Colin muttered. "I'd have made sure we had something contemporary."

"Really, it will work."

"You're asking me to sacrifice my principles." Colin actually managed a pout. "I'll be the laughing stock of The Chipping Sodbury Numismatic Society."

"You collect tyres?" Cas looked confused.

"No," I said. "Numismatics is about coins. You're thinking of pneumatics."

"Oh, cool. Thought that would be a peculiar hobby but you never know people. Had an auntie who used to collect golliwogs. She suggested I take them into school one time for Show and Tell. That wasn't a good day. I had to stay after school to take 'Inclusiveness' lessons."

"Anyway, to get back to the plan." I held up the trinkets. "Unless anybody wants to come up with genuine Saxon stuff, we're using these. If we find any bones then we get these bits to the opposite end of the field and plant them. At the signal—"

"What's the signal?" asked Eric.

"Um..."

"How about semaphore?" suggested Eric.

"Does anybody know semaphore?"

Only Eric raised his hand.

"A wolf whistle?"

"An owl is better."

"In daylight?"

"We could wave a flag."

"Too obvious. What about waving a spade."

"How would we know when to be looking for a waving spade?"

The suggestions fell silent for a moment then Elaine offered, "We could always send text messages."

More silence as the dawning of the blindingly obvious filtered round the room.

"Right," I said. "When... If somebody finds bones, send a text message then the ones furthest away will dig up the fake treasure and get everybody's attention that end. That should give us enough time. Any questions?"

Several people started to speak at once. "Great," I said. "Then in that case, I'll see you all tomorrow."

Chapter Nineteen

The morning brought a light shower before sunrise but by the time we'd arrived at the site, the sun was already making a tentative appearance. As we approached we were directed to park in a small taped-off section just outside the fence and not far from The General's shack. He stood defiantly with spear in hand and watched the arrivals as if assessing the evolving threat level.

After we'd parked we followed the red-taped pathway that led through a newly created gap in the main fence. I'd caught bits of the odd episode of Celebrity Time Diggers and I'd never thought about the infrastructure behind the screen. When watching on the television all one tended to see was the featured celebrities, lots of muddy holes, the resident expert and of course Martin Springborn himself, whose manic laughing at the muddy celebs always made me want to punch his smug face. Having now met him in person that inclination had, if anything, strengthened. A large marquee dominated the skyline and several other smaller tents gathered closely to it like a small family. A catering truck, already fully in operation, dispensed bacon sandwiches and coffee to a team of technicians and a camera crew who looked like they had been there all night. Lighting rigs stood sentry, awaiting the inevitable dark clouds that would be sure to grace this English summer's day at some point and the whole area had been cordoned off with yellow hazard warning tape and signs warning of mines and other unexploded ordinance beyond the perimeter.

We were guided into the large marquee where a dozen trestle tables were arranged into two rows down the middle, presumably awaiting the arrival of freshly unearthed treasures to be cleaned, poked, sorted and catalogued.

"Excellent, glad you could all make it," Martin greeted. "Now, just a few house rules and we can get digging." He waved towards a table laden with coffee pots, bottled water and biscuits. "Help yourself to refreshments whenever you want. Portaloos are behind the equipment tent and don't venture out of the taped area. I'm told there are still a lot of mines out there. Now, if you notice anything even slightly interesting when you're digging, you plant one of these red flags." He held up a red flag to show us what a red flag looked like. "Then you signal for Walter, our resident archaeologist, who will assess what you've found. If Walter thinks it looks promising he'll arrange for the camera crew to take position before you continue. Do not dig anything up without alerting Walter first. Are we all on board?"

Muted grunts and nods signalled consent.

"You are to stay with your assigned partner." He pointed to a whiteboard on an easel which displayed the pairings. I couldn't read it from where I was standing. "And you are only to dig in the area you have been designated. No random holes. Well that's it. We've been allowed three days by the Ministry of Defence, after which time they start moving the bombs back so probably best if we're all cleared up by then. Any questions?"

"What if we feel the spirits guiding us to dig somewhere different?" Tree asked.

Martin seemed lost for a moment, but then said, "Talk to me first, maybe we can accommodate the... um... spirit world."

"I'm sure we can listen to them." Morgan slipped in through a gap in the tent flaps behind Martin. "But we need to be on our guard, the spirits of the next world may not want us to disturb their rest. They may try to deceive."

"Dumblewits," Merlin announced. "The King is here and he'll not tolerate playful nonsense from sprites or imps. Now, if you all stop your twiddle-twaddling so we can tend to Arthur's destiny and rest him where he belongs and not in this playground for minor despots and rear battalion noise makers." Merlin marched out of the tent, pausing only to tip over the white board as he went.

"Well, I'd say that seems to bring things to a natural conclusion," Morgan said. "Let's go stir up the ghosts and find some treasure."

To my annoyance, I'd been teamed up with James Fanshaw, the Tory MP whose right wing views would have made Hitler pause a moment. I looked to the far end of the field and saw Elaine struggling to help Jayed Flayme put on a pair of wellington boots. Maybe I'd got the better deal but it was a close-run thing. Merlin had been left to his own devices to wander the field and do his Cynbel dangling. He'd complained that he didn't need to do it as he already knew exactly where Arthur was but Martin wasn't listening and insisted he do more dangling as it was good television. Colin had also been left to wander the site and had been issued with a brand new metal detector to play with. He'd proudly informed me it was the best there was, a Minelab CTX 3030 which apparently could find a pin in the Sahara. The only other person free to wander was Tree. She'd been given strict instructions to alert the camera crew when she felt like going into a trance or talking with angels. Despite Sebastian's complaints that it just didn't work like that and angels don't just turn up to order, he'd been overruled and paired up with Twentypence Atomik.

We'd been given a couple of spades and a red flag then allocated specific areas in which to commence our digging. The turf had already been removed in the initial dig sites, presumably to save camera time rather than our hard work. Our area was some distance from where we had found the torque so that put us into one of the diversion locations.

I threw the spade in the ground and turned aside a pile of earth. Fanshaw lit a cigarette from a packet and stared around the field. "Country life, you can't beat it," he said. He flicked at his plastic lighter which stubbornly refused to light. He tossed it at the hole I'd started. "Becoming one with nature, this is what makes England great. Don't suppose you've got a light, old chap?"

"No, sorry. I don't smoke." I picked the lighter from the hole and dropped it in my pocket. "You could ask Sebastian. He's usually got some matches."

Fanshaw waved towards Sebastian and Twentypence. "I say. Do you have a light?"

"Sure, cool. Could use a rest." Sebastian handed his spade to Twentypence and ambled over, pulling a joint from his pocket and lighting it as he approached. He tossed the matches to Fanshaw. "That guy's a dick," he said as he nodded towards Twentypence. "He thinks he's a black gangsta from Chicago or something. Told him to look in the mirror."

"How did that go down?" I asked.

"Don't know. Can't understand a word he's saying."

"He's what they call a Malteser." Fanshaw lit his cigarette and tossed the dead match in the hole. He seemed to be trying to fill the hole faster than I could dig.

"A Malteser?" I queried.

"Black on the inside, white on the outside. Street slang. We encountered the term in a diversity workshop I had to attend. Waste of time, full of illegals, but jolly good PR and at least there was some tasteful totty there to brighten the day."

"That wouldn't be a Malteser," I said. "A Malteser is black on the outside and white inside."

"Could be a liquorice torpedo," suggested Sebastian after a moment's thought and a deep pull on his joint.

"Are they white?" asked Fanshaw. "Only I don't recall anybody being described as a liquorice torpedo in my workshop. I think I'd have remembered that."

Sebastian took another breath and held it for a moment. "They're all colours, man," he said through a cloud of smoke. "Pretty sure there'd be some white ones there. They have blue ones that I do know." He handed the joint to Fanshaw who took it without thinking.

"We need to look like we're doing something." I turned another spade full of soil out of the hole. "Shouldn't you be over there at your spot?"

We all looked towards Twentypence who was already waist deep in his hole.

"Nah," said Sebastian. "He's on a mission. I'd only get in the way."

"Looks like he's trying to tunnel out." Fanshaw drew absently on the joint. He paused and held both hands up to see the joint in one and a cigarette in the other. A moment's hesitation and then he tossed the cigarette into my hole and took another pull on the joint. "Probably best to stay out of his way. You know what they get like."

I heard movement behind me and turned to see Eric approaching with a roll of white sticky plastic tape unravelling on the ground behind him. Eric stopped in front of my hole. "Have you finished here?" he asked. "Only I'm laying this to follow the Silbury Ley. It cuts right through here."

"Well can't you go round?"

"Of course I can't go round." He sounded affronted. "The whole point of ley lines is that they're straight."

The camera crew appeared. "What's happening here?" asked the man with a furry microphone on the end of a stick.

"It's a hole," offered Fanshaw and attempted to smother a giggle.

"We've only just started," I said. "Nothing yet."

"They're right on the Silbury Ley," said Eric. He turned to look at the camera and froze.

"Don't look directly at the camera," said the man with the microphone.

Eric continued to stare at the camera as if hypnotised.

"Please?" The man waved his hand in front of Eric's face but there was no longer any sign of sentience in Eric's eyes. He motioned to the cameraman to cut away.

The camera swung to face Fanshaw just as he took another pull on the joint. Fanshaw flapped his hands to disperse the billowing cloud.

"This is a bit of a change for you from your constituency in Hillsbridge," said the man with the microphone. "I understand your family can be traced back to the Normans. Does this sort of endeavour make you feel more connected to your roots?"

"Ah, yes. We have roots in my family, we always have had. Which is why my party can offer stability and continuous... osity with a sense of history which is... that's to say..." he slipped his hand behind his back and flicked the joint backwards. It fell on Eric's roll of plastic tape. "That with forward progress, robust planning and... going forwards from this point... Sorry, what was the question?"

Sebastian slipped away from the group and headed back towards Twentypence whose head was now only just visible above ground level. Clods of earth flew out of his hole with the regularity of a metronome.

"Your history, Mister Fanshaw. You were telling us how your family history connects you."

"Spot on. Yes, Noblesse Oblige. Of course it falls to one to give a sense of stability to the... to the... is there something burning?"

We all turned to the smell. Eric's roll of plastic tape was hissing and spluttering and giving off a spiral of oily smoke which drifted skywards. It gave a little whumpf and flames jumped into the air. We all started back a step but remained captivated by the little fire. Clearly whatever tape Eric had got hold of to map out his ley lines, it was highly inflammable. The flames spread from the spool then ran along the ground following the line he'd laid earlier.

Eric finally snapped out of his trance and with remarkable speed, set off after the burning trail, every so often catching up with it enough to attempt to stamp it out. At one attempt the burning tape stuck to his shoe and he ran across the field dragging a burning tail behind him until somebody appeared with a bucket of water to end the torment.

"And cut," said the man with the microphone.

***

By lunchtime we'd dug a shallow trench which led away from the direction of Cas's position. He and Sheridan Baxter had been allocated the area which lay the closest to where the torque had been found so at some point one of us needed to dig there without supervision or cameras. That would be the difficult bit. The impossible bit would come later when we would need to remove anything we found from the site without anybody noticing.

We all gathered in the main marquee and ate sandwiches whilst looking at the array of treasures removed from the various digs. Bottle tops certainly led the field in terms of sheer quantity but the variety of objects found was quite surprising. A liberal sprinkling of rusty nails told of some wooden construction that had probably existed here at some point but had now sunk back into the earth. Several unidentified bones had been arranged on one table, probably not human but too damaged for me to identify. A collection of little bits of twisted metal that probably came from farm machinery were being washed by a crew of helpers and separated into little plastic boxes with labels, identifying from where they had originated. But beyond that and an assortment of relatively modern coins, there was little to suggest a Saxon burial site.

I sidled up to Cas. "How's it going?" I asked.

"I think I'm going to bury that newsreader in the hole when I've dug it. He just sits there telling me stories about how he once met Gaddafi and what a nice man he was really."

"Have you found anything yet?"

"What, you mean other than a pompous prig full of his own sense of self-importance whose ideas are more outdated than anything we're likely to find here?"

"Yes, other than that."

Cas glanced around the marquee. Partly satisfied by the absence of either KGB or CIA he came closer and reached into his pocket. "I found this. Don't know what it is." He pressed an object into my hand and gave another furtive scan of the tent.

I risked a look. It was a muddy, rusty and badly pitted piece of metal about five centimetres long. There appeared to be some detail on the surface; it would need a good clean.

"Could be a spear head I suppose." I picked at the dirt with my fingernail. "Or part of a combine harvester. Who knows?"

"Ah, there it is!" Merlin pushed between us. "I've been looking for that." He snatched the object from my hand.

"Hey, you can't do that," I said. "Besides, somebody might see."

"But it's mine." He spat on the object and wiped it free of mud. "I lost it... oh... a long, long time ago."

"What is it?" asked Cas in a stage whisper that would have easily carried to the upper circle.

"It's my dagger, fool." Merlin wiped the item on his sleeve and held it in front of Cas. "Surely even a half-brained dead mule could see that. Now, where's the rest of it, boy?"

Cas flustered. "The rest? That's all there was."

"It had a nice handle. Finest English oak, beautiful grain. Held the face of a wolf. What have you done with it? I hope you haven't lost it."

Martin appeared out of a small group and headed towards us. Damn. Too late, he'd seen the object. "What have we got here and why isn't it on the table for cataloguing?"

"It's mine," said Merlin.

"How can that be?"

Merlin held the rusty blade towards Martin and I thought for a moment I might have to leap in to save Martin's life. I also thought for another moment if I should bother. Fortunately, I didn't have to make that decision.

"You see this here?" Merlin pointed to a nick in the edge of what had probably been the blade.

"Yes," said Martin.

"Well, there you go. That proves it." He dropped it in his pocket. "If you find anything else of mine, I'm over there, I have work to do." He pushed his way through the people thronging the tent and disappeared.

Martin turned to look at us. "But, how does that...?"

"Don't ask me," I said. "If he really is Merlin it could well be his. Who knows? And if he isn't Merlin... well, do you want to argue with him?"

"Where did you find it?"

Cas started to speak and I kicked his ankle. He glared at me but didn't speak.

"It was in our trench." I tried to avoid Cas's look.

"It was?" queried Fanshaw.

"Yes," I said, thinking quickly. "Don't you remember? You were smoking that... cigarette at the time. The big cigarette."

"What? Oh, hell. Yes. That's right. We found it in our hole. Near the... Near the whatsit."

Martin looked at me. "Why did you not put down a flag and call Walter?"

"Didn't want to bother anybody," I said. "Thought it was just a bit of old metal."

"It may have escaped your notice but bits of old metal are exactly what we're here to find."

The sound of wailing from outside interrupted the interrogation. Everybody headed for the exit. Tree was walking in a tight circle, her arms held high and her eyes appeared closed. Sebastian held her elbow, ready to steady her in the event of a fall. She wailed again. It sounded like speech but quite incoherent.

"She's channelling," I heard somebody say from behind us.

She fell to her knees with Sebastian lending support. Her

203

hands threw up above her head and a string of unintelligible words spilled from her.

"She's talking in tongues," said the voice behind me. "I've seen this before. It's the language of the angels."

The camera crew scuttered into position and Martin flapped his hands encouraging them to move closer.

Morgan appeared from one of the other tents and ran to crouch at Tree's side.

"What are they saying? Who are you in contact with?" she asked Tree.

"She's talking with Arella," said Sebastian. "I recognise the language. She's the messenger."

More wails and gibberish followed from Tree and then she suddenly drew to her feet and set off across the field. Morgan took a moment to realise what was happening and then set off after her, closely followed by the camera crew and a large group of the curious.

"Cas, can you go and stand guard near Tree? Send me a text message if they start to come in my direction," I said. "Let's take advantage of the distraction."

I found Colin and took him over to where Cas had been digging.

"Is that machine really the business?" I asked Colin.

"It's a Minelab CTX 3030! It's equipped with Smartfind 2 technology and a – "

"Will it find buried stuff?"

"Yes."

"Good, you've got until that lot get bored of angel noises to find something here."

Colin carefully strapped the machine over his shoulder, put on the headphones and then proceeded to twiddle knobs whilst watching what appeared to be a video game on the little screen.

"Any chance of speeding this up?" I glanced nervously at the group gathered around Tree. There was still much activity but that could all change at any moment.

"I have to calibrate it. What are we looking for?"

"Arthur," I said. "Have you not been paying attention to any of this?"

"I know that. Of course I know that but I need a setting. Gold? Silver?"

"Bones, I expect. Have you got a setting for bones?"

"No. How about relics?"

"That'll do. Quickly, before they notice."

Colin fiddled with the controls some more then swept the plate across the area. At the second sweep he froze.

"There's something here," he said. "It's big and circular and I'm not getting any closer. The last big and circular thing went bang, if you remember?"

"Show me where it is."

Colin pointed vaguely at a patch of ground and stepped backwards. "I have something urgent to be doing... um... over there." He pointed to the far corner of the site, tucked the detector under his arm and headed off.

I noticed that the angel channelling display still held everybody's attention and decided to risk investigation of the disc. I dug the spade gently into the soft earth. This was a patch that had not yet had the turf removed beforehand so I removed it with care and put it to one side. Without the help of the Minelab ZX81, or whatever it was, I had no idea exactly where the object was. I just trusted that the M.O.D. had cleared all the mines from the area. Surely they would know where they all were? Wouldn't they?

I part scraped and part picked at the earth until I realised that approach was going to get me nowhere, at least not this year, and that a slightly more adventurous strategy was called for. I took the trowel I'd been issued and crouched over the fresh earth. A few gentle prods indeed reinforced Colin's assessment of a buried object and it didn't take long before I had a rough idea of where it was and how large. At a guess, it was about 20 centimetres wide and lay three or four centimetres under the surface. Perfect size and positioning for a landmine.

I glanced over my shoulder to ensure that nobody was looking then dug the trowel deep under the object. The M.O.D. would have kept detailed records; they'd never have let civilians on the site if there was even the slightest chance of any errant mines remaining. I wriggled the trowel a bit. No feel of it contacting anything which meant I'd penetrated beneath the object. That was reassuring as it meant the object wasn't very thick and landmines were certainly substantial items. I had no real grounds for that assumption other than a childhood diet of fairly dodgy American war movies.

I moved the trowel around and felt resistance as I lifted it. Okay, I was firmly underneath a small circular object buried in a minefield. What could possibly go wrong here? I started to lever the trowel upwards.

"What you doin'?"

I jumped. The trowel jumped. The object jumped out of the hole. I rolled over the grass and put my hands over my head and waited. No bang. I peeped through my hands.

Cas stood over me, he held two cardboard mugs. "I brought you some coffee," he said. "You do take sugar, right? I only put one in just in case you don't."

"What are you doing here? You're supposed to be keeping guard?"

"I got bored. What's that?" He pointed to the muddy disc which now lay on the edge of the hole.

"I don't know." I shuffled closer to the object. "I don't think it's a mine."

"Looks like a frisbee, bit small though so it probably isn't. Did they have frisbees in Merlin's day?"

I picked it up and pushed some of the mud away from the surface. "It's metal and it's old," I said.

"What are we going to do with it? Aren't we supposed to put a flag down?"

"Definitely not. This is the area the torque came from, then the knife and now this." I pushed more mud away to reveal a bronzy coloured disc in the middle. "If there is even the remotest chance of Merlin being right about Arthur, which is still insane, then this will be the spot. We need to keep everybody away from here while we find out what else is under here." I pointed at the hole.

"We could tell them there's nothing here," Cas suggested.

"We could." I looked over towards where Elaine and Jayed were digging. "Or we could employ a little misdirection. You stay here and look like you're digging, but don't."

Cas looked puzzled.

"Just stay here," I said. I slipped the disc into my shirt, the mud felt cold against my skin. I pulled my shirt closed and headed across the field.

By the time I reached Elaine, Jayed had disappeared. "You on your own?" I asked as I approached.

"Yes, she's gone off to find the first aider. Broken another fingernail. She's driving me nuts, just talks about shoes all the time."

"Do you like shoes?"

"I *wear* shoes. They're not the reason I get out of bed in the morning. Did you know there's a make of shoes called Miu Miu?"

"No."

"Neither did I until this morning. I thought that was a recreational drug, always had a steady flow of service users in the centre who'd taken too much of it and they certainly weren't interested in shoes."

"Probably wasn't the shoes they'd been sniffing."

"I doubt it. What brings you over here?"

I pulled the disc from my shirt. "What do you reckon this is?"

"Where did you find that?"

"In Cas's dig. Also seem to have discovered Merlin's long-lost penknife there as well so I'm guessing that's where we need to be digging."

Elaine studied the disc. "Bit like a saucepan lid. Did they have saucepans then?"

"I don't know." I noticed the angel chanting had finished and people were beginning to drift away. "I'm sure they had pots of some description, I know they had soup."

"Why haven't you given it to Walter?"

"Because we want to keep everybody away from there. That's where Merlin thinks Arthur is and if we tell them about this we'll never get the chance to find out."

"How do we do that?"

I handed Elaine the disc. "Here, you take this, give it half an hour and then discover it." I pulled a handful of Roman coins from my pocket and tossed them into Elaine's trench. "These'll help."

"Oh, hi, John."

I turned to see Jayed returning. She had a big bandage around her left hand and held it slightly raised.

"Been in the wars?" I asked.

"Not really into gardening. I've got a little man who comes

208

in on Tuesdays." She looked into the hole. "Oh, look, somebody's dropped some money." She stepped into the hole, her stilettoes sinking in the soft earth. "Find a penny, pick it up," she said as she gathered up some of the coins I'd just deposited. "That's lucky, I forgot my purse. I'll go get us all some tea." She strutted off across the field.

"Or we could not bother waiting half an hour," I said. "Quick, take this and bury it as best you can before somebody notices she's paying for her tea with two-thousand-year-old coins."

A shout from the tent signalled we had just run out of time. Elaine dropped the disc in the hole and we both kicked as much mud over it as we could in the few seconds we had.

"That'll have to do it." I gave her a quick kiss. "See you later."

I managed to get back to Cas just before the circus broke. It seemed like the whole tent emptied at once and a stampede of people headed towards Elaine. For a moment I feared she'd be trampled in the melee.

"Did you find out what it was?" asked Cas.

"What? No, start digging quickly."

We both set to with our spades and attacked the ground with a ferocity which gave no thought as to the existence of any undiscovered mines. The noise grew at Elaine's end of the field and I risked a glance. Walter, Morgan and Martin were holding court in the centre of the crowd while the camera crew pushed towards the hole. Somebody was busy putting posts and red tape around the general area while somebody else was laying big plastic sheets on the ground. They looked like they were going to be busy for a while. I returned to my digging.

"Whoa!" Cas stopped digging and crouched down. "Something here, man."

I looked at where he was now poking with his trowel. He eased a small lump of something out of the earth.

"Stop," I said. I took the object and studied it. It was about the size of a playing card although a fair bit thicker. I pushed the mud away from the surface and discovered it wasn't actually solid but a bit like a large, squared-off ring.

"What is it?" asked Cas.

"I don't know. Might be a buckle or something." I dropped it in my pocket. "Let's keep at it while we have chance."

The noise from the other end of the field suddenly grew and I looked over to see much movement and jostling for position. A lighting rig had now been aimed at the hole and a trestle table was being set up.

Back to our hole while our luck held. We continued to dig but now with trowels to minimise risk of damage to anything found. We were about half a metre deep when my trowel found something of a much larger size.

"Have a look at this, Cas." I scraped dirt from the object. "What do you think?"

"Lump of wood?" Cas offered.

"Not sure." I traced the trowel along the length of the buried shape. It was about thirty or forty centimetres in length and about the thickness of my spade handle.

"Can you get it out?"

I glanced over the field. Jayed was busy posing for the camera crew, flicking her hair back as she spoke to the microphone.

"Let's give it a try," I said.

We both crouched in the hole and dug round the thing as carefully as our paranoia would allow. Finally we had enough of it visible to see what it was.

"Holy fuck," said Cas. "That's a bone."

"Looks like it," I agreed. I tugged gently and it came free of the earth. "Could be an arm, maybe a forearm but then again it could be a pig's leg. I really don't know."

"What do we do?"

"We have to take it and hide it." I glanced across the field. People were starting to drift away and a small group were making their way to the marquee. "Here, put it in your coat."

"I can't do that," Cas protested. "It's a bit of a dead person. That's not right. Bad juju, man."

"Oh, for goodness sake." I stuffed it under my shirt. "You fill this in then. Put the turf back and make it look like nothing was here."

"What are you going to do?"

"Plan B," I said.

Keeping a watching eye on the group milling around the tent, I made my way to the western-most corner of the field then slipped through the taped barrier. This is the area that they hadn't cleared of mines so I had to walk very slowly and carefully. My one comfort was the network of tracks made by the army vehicles which I assumed had driven round here when they'd been preparing for this event. If I stayed in the tracks I should be fairly safe, I tried to reassure myself. Alternating my gaze from the tents to the tracks to the metal fence, I made slow progress but at least I still had a full set of appendages so far. As I neared the fence I gave my best impersonation of an owl hooting. This was as far as plan B had been prepared. We'd hoped we'd not need it.

I was answered by an equally unconvincing hoot from the other side of the fence and the General came into view just beyond the barbed wire.

"Got something I need you to take for us," I said quietly. "Can you catch?"

"No."

"Can you pick things up you've missed?"

"What is it?"

"A bone, I think."

"Human?"

What do I tell him? Best be honest. "Think it might be," I said.

"Cool," the General said. "Only got animal bones here."

I glanced back across the field and then swung the bone as gently as I could across the fence.

"Ow," said the General.

"Sorry. Can you hang on to that until we can get to you?"

"No problem. I'll put it with the rest."

If this really was the last remains of England's greatest ever warrior king this wasn't a particularly regal ceremony but needs drive. I picked my way back along the vehicle tracks and ducked under the plastic tape. I was back to relative safety.

Cas was still working in his hole so I made my way into the main marquee. The camera crew were focused on one of the tables in the centre of which lay the circular disc. Jayed fluffed her way around the people, trying to stay in camera shot, much to the annoyance of the cameraman who kept trying to cut away.

I found Martin. He was beaming like a child on Christmas morning.

"What is it?" I asked.

"Walter says it's the central boss from a Saxon shield. Probably around fifth century but they'll do more tests later."

"That's great. Where was it found?"

"At the south-eastern end. We didn't expect anything there. Last place we'd thought. That's why we put that dopey woman down there. Just goes to show."

"I assume you don't mean Elaine?"

"What? No, she's quite bright that one."

"I'll remember to tell her."

I headed off to find Elaine.

Chapter Twenty

That evening we convened in the bar to watch the evening's transmission. The hotel had tuned their 75 inch television screen to the Real Reality Channel where a dysfunctional family were currently building a chicken shed. We grabbed some drinks and found a couple of seats towards the back of the room, trying to ignore the disintegration of the human race being played out as entertainment on the giant screen.

"Long time since I've sat in the back row of the cinema," Elaine said. She placed her hand on my thigh and squeezed.

"Sorry I couldn't find anything more romantic; Zombie Flesh Eaters was sold out."

"Never mind, there's always the porn channel in the room later."

"You trying to shock me?" I asked.

"No, not at all. That comes afterwards."

Morgan stood in front of the television. "Welcome, welcome and thank you all for your support today. Although it's been a strange day for many of you, I think you'll see what a fantastic job the production team have done in such a short space of time. You'll be pleased to know this special has already been syndicated across twelve countries."

She started clapping and the celebrities joined in with much enthusiasm. I felt slightly horrified.

We sat through several minutes of advertising for a strange machine which claimed to give one a full body workout whilst sitting on the sofa eating pizza then the titles for Celebrity Time Diggers started rolling. The voiceover announced the special collaboration with Morgan Faylon's Spook Hunter and implored us to remember that everything we were about to witness was one hundred and ten percent genuine, although some scenes had been recreated for entertainment purposes.

The programme opened with Morgan talking to camera. "You are about to witness one of the most astonishing finds in the history of the human race," she said. "The discovery of the actual grave of King Arthur. Yes, you heard right. King Arthur of the Round Table was real and for years a team of top archaeologists and Supernatural Investigators have been painstakingly following the evidence that led us to this secret location somewhere in southern England."

The cameras cut away and scanned the field as it had looked prior to the invasion. A speeded up sequence then showed trucks arriving and tents being erected.

"Our investigators not only had to deal with the spirits of ancient warriors trying to protect their king, but from a more modern threat of a modern day minefield." A neatly spliced clip showed an explosion in a field, which if I hadn't known better, looked every bit like it had taken place at our dig site.

"We knew something strange was on the site when internationally renowned angel channeller, Tree Starflower, began communing with the angel Arella and speaking in the mystic language of the Holy Hordes."

We saw Tree waving her arms about and speaking gibberish. The film had been tinted slightly to give a more dramatic effect and noisy kettle drums, beat relentlessly in an attempt to engage our excitingness synapses. A voice off-camera yelled, "Look! What's that pushing up through the ground?" Cut to an image of my disc half buried but seemingly rising out of the ground under its own power. Neat trick but I knew exactly how it had been done. Just a variant on the Rising Card trick.

"Is this the place we were actually at?" asked Elaine.

"Some alternate, television-land version of it, I think."

"That's okay then, thought I'd gone to the wrong place."

Jayed Flayme appeared on the screen to applause from our little audience. She walked across the field, every so often stopping to investigate some item or other. The camera closed in as she crouched in a trench. "What is this?" she said to camera then reached down and picked up a coin. "It looks like a fifth century Roman coin from the reign of Romulus Augustus."

Cut to more gibberish from Tree, although it did look suspiciously like a repeat of the earlier clip.

Martin then appeared on screen and the cameras followed him as he strutted around the field introducing the carefully selected group of celebrities, all of whom had a special affinity for archaeology.

The camera closed in on James Fanshaw. "I understand your family can be traced back to the Normans," said the faceless interviewer. The camera clearly showed Fanshaw struggling to dispose of the joint as he burbled, giggled and blew a cloud of smoke at the camera. The room erupted into laughter.

"We could well be witnessing the end of a promising political career here," I said.

"With a bit of luck," Elaine said. "Man's a bigot and a dreadful misogynist."

We watched in stunned silence as Morgan spotted an ethereal shape near one end of the field and a wobbly-cam chased her across the field until the shape disappeared into a grassy patch. In came a faceless man with a spade, lots of exciting music and more shaky camera then Morgan reached into the newly dug hole and retrieved a long object from which she proceeded to remove the dirt. The camera closed in as she slowly exposed what lay beneath the coating of mud.

"This looks like a weapon of some description," she said.

Walter came into shot and announced it was a fifth century Saxon sword.

"I don't remember that?" I whispered to Elaine. "It certainly didn't come from either my dig or Cass'."

"Mine neither," said Elaine. "Could it be a plant?"

"Almost certainly."

Morgan explained to the camera how she'd felt a presence and then just caught a glimpse of something. "It wasn't fully corporeal," she said. "I think he was a warrior but it was difficult to see. He moved so fast and then vanished into the ground. I think he was trying to tell us something."

The film cut to a view of the sword displayed on one of the tables. It had now been cleaned and a close up showed ornate engraving along the blade. It looked like Elvish runes to me but surely they couldn't be that stupid?

The episode ended with the camera watching another hole being investigated with the voiceover telling us that work had to stop for the day but something strange was certainly buried in this place. We were all implored to tune in to tomorrow's episode to find out what was there.

The titles rolled to muted applause and people started to filter out of the room. James Fanshaw was speaking fervently on his phone as he hurried from the room.

"Fancy a Cornish pasty?" I said. "There's a nice quiet pub just back down the road. Be nice to escape this lot for a while."

"A night at the movies and a meal out. Was a girl ever so adored?"

"I'm just an old romantic at heart."

Chapter Twenty One

Day two started with one man down. James Fanshaw had been urgently recalled to his constituency office for a meeting with senior party members. Martin took me to one side to explain that I would now have to be on my own, and I reassured him that somehow I'd survive the trauma.

I picked at my dig just enough to keep me out of any direct interest while keeping an eye on Cas and Baxter. Cas had been given repeated instructions to make sure he dug up nothing of interest and that if anything *did* turn up, he had to bury it again immediately. I'd worried a bit about Baxter paying too much attention but he showed no interest in the hole at all and continually followed the film crew around offering them advice.

I'd given Elaine a bracelet and a couple of rings from my stash and told her to drop them in the hole during the lunch break. Cas had been issued with some bottle tops and empty beer cans to 'dig up' as a diversion.

The morning's highlight came when Merlin decided a whole section of the centre of the site needed to be cordoned off.

"It's the Great Decagon," he said. "One of the conjunctions is just..." He paced a few concentric circles whilst Cynbel swung wildly from its string. "Just here." He ground his heel into the earth to mark the spot.

"That's where the Silbury Ley intersects too," said Eric.

"What's the Great Decagon, Merlin?" asked Martin.

"It's sacred," said Merlin, as if that satisfied as a complete answer.

"Can anybody tell me what the Great Decagon is?" Martin asked.

One of the production crew pulled out his smartphone. "I'll ask the internet. Here we go; it's a ten sided shape with equal sides."

"I know what a decagon is, stupid. I wanted to know what the Great Decagon is."

"It's the huge geometric shape which centres on Whiteleaved Oak and at each intersection is an ancient site," Eric said. He caught Martin's look of puzzlement and quickly added, "Whiteleaved Oak, it's a small village exactly where the borders of the old counties of Hereford, Gloucester and Worcester join. It was laid out by visitors from space."

"Rubbish," said Merlin. "The ancients set the points, Glastonbury, Stonehenge, Goring Temple, all the others. I was there. Aliens, pfaff. Why do idiots have to invent such pigswill? If you can't understand the obvious when it's in front of you then leave the thinking to those born to think."

"It had to be aliens," Eric insisted. "They are the only ones who could have seen it. It's too big to be understood by ordinary people on the ground."

"Did I mention ordinary people?" Merlin snapped. "What have ordinary people got to do with it? What have they got to do with anything? Seems to me they're only interested in collecting shiny things and making war."

"That's not fair," protested Eric. "Humans have created some—"

"Do be quiet, I'm trying to follow my ancestors," Merlin

interrupted. "Here, have a shiny thing." He took a coin from his pocket and tossed it at Eric's feet.

Eric waited until Merlin had turned away then picked up the coin and put it in his pocket.

Merlin studied his notebook, scanned the horizon and then dug his heel in at another point. He took a few steps forwards and stopped again.

"Here," he said sweeping his arms around the small area he'd marked. "We must keep this place pure. It's a point of great power and not for mortals to disturb with their little spades and flags."

Martin signalled a couple of helpers to tape off the area and the camera crew pointed their camera at the grass.

"This is the point at which one of the conjunctions of the Great Decagon is sited," said the man with the microphone. "This has just been positively verified by our on-site shaman."

Merlin's head perked up and he wandered over to the camera crew. He raised Harold into the air then drove the end of the walking stick into the man's foot and then walked away.

The man jerked in pain and then fell to the ground, massaging his foot. "What was that about?"

"He's a Druid, not a shaman," I said. "He gets touchy about these things."

Merlin's Great Decagon conjunction remained taped off for the rest of the day, but nobody really understood why and nobody actually entered the cordon. Although, several people did wander over to stare at it from time to time as if expecting something to happen. Nothing did.

Straight after lunch, Jayed Flayme squealed and within seconds, a large gathering jostled for position around her dig site.

The camera crew pushed their way through the people and Martin and Morgan vied for prime camera position. Excited shouts came for the centre of the group so no doubt one of the trinkets had just been discovered.

Cas, Colin, Sebastian and myself set to work at Cas's dig. We laid out a tarpaulin and threw earth on it at a furious rate. I figured we had maybe thirty minutes of clear time before interest waned at Elaine and Jayed's site so we had a lot to do. We dug a bit, we detectorised a bit and then we dug some more. Several interesting artefacts turned up but we just put those to one side; they might be of use later.

The first bone turned up after about ten minutes. It was small and might have been something from a hand or a foot or even the remains of a pork chop, I wasn't good with anatomy. I dropped the bone in a black plastic bin bag. It felt rather disrespectful, especially if these *were* the last remains of a king but we had little choice. Time for respect later. Colin's machine sounded as if it was in a constant state of distress but we had no time to check. If there was a mine still here somewhere it would be likely a noisy discovery.

More trinkets emerged. A wide semi open tube that might have been some sort of bracelet, an assortment of unidentifiable bits of metal and something which was almost certainly a spearhead. We piled these up to one side as we continued to dig whilst all the time keeping a watching eye on the circus at the other end of the field.

Sebastian opened his rucksack and distributed cans of beer. He fluffed his rucksack into a suitable pillow, lit a joint and settled back with beer in one hand and the joint in the other.

"Comfortable?" I asked.

"I'm not really built for digging. I'm more of a researcher." He handed the joint to Cas.

Several more bones emerged and we dumped them unceremoniously in the bin bag. One bone in particular though gave me pause. It was clearly a finger bone, the size and shape gave a clue but the clincher was the large metal ring which encircled it. I stopped and stared at it. I didn't have time to clean the ring but it seemed chunky and held what I guessed was a large stone of some description. It felt very strange to hold. This was part of a human who had walked probably over a thousand years ago. What had this finger held, touched, caressed all those centuries ago? No time for sentiment. I slipped the ring in my pocket and dropped the bone in the bag.

The full impact of what we were doing came when Colin's detector started emitting a high-pitched wail that threatened to alert anybody within a five mile radius.

"Sorry," Colin said as he manically twisted and turned various controls on his machine.

We all paused and held our breath as if the reduction in overall sound levels created by our lack of breathing would somehow counteract the detector's screams. Fortunately, everybody's attention still seemed focused on the handful of cheap trinkets at the other end of the field.

"What caused that?" I asked Colin.

"Not sure. It's very big and it's only just under the surface. Be careful." Colin took a step backwards.

"We haven't got time to be careful." I poked my trowel around the buried lump. It was certainly metallic and about the size of a football. I dug around it and then prised the trowel underneath and attempted to lever it out. It started to move.

"Stop!" yelled Cas.

I jumped back from the hole. "What's up? Is it a mine?"

"No, look." Cas pointed to the other end of the field where the onlookers to the latest finds were already dispersing.

"Oh, shit." I looked at the hole. "We need to cover this all up again. Colin, grab the bag and hide it somewhere, Cas help me cover this lot over again."

Elaine looked like she was heading our way so I signalled for her to hurry. She looked confused but ran over.

"What's happening?" she said.

"We've found something big." I said.

"Not big like a boat or a train," Cas clarified. "He means big like in, wow, man, that's fucking awesome."

"Thank you, Cas I'm sure Elaine understood that. Elaine, can you run interference if anybody heads this way?"

"Okay."

I looked at Sebastian. He appeared to be asleep. I poked him with my foot. "How many more cans have you got in there?"

He propped himself up on his elbow and opened the rucksack. He peered inside and then checked his watch. "Enough to last 'till about fivish, maybe sixish at a push. Probably best say fourish just to be on the safe side. Although—"

"Chuck 'em over here," I interrupted. "In the hole."

Sebastian sat up and blinked at the sunlight. "In the hole?"

"We need lots of metal stuff in the hole, quickly."

"We're burying beer?"

"We have to divert any interest from this dig. Need to keep the focus over at Elaine's."

"How does burying beer help? I'd have thought that would be suspicious in itself," Sebastian said. "I mean, did they have Carlsberg Extra Strong in ancient times? Unless somebody came back from the future, like in that movie... um, what was that called?"

"Back to the Future?" offered Colin.

"Twelve Monkeys," Sebastian said.

"I don't remember Bruce Willis burying cans of Carlsberg Extra Strong," said Cas.

"Can we have this conversation later?" I glanced across the field to where Elaine was doing her best to stall Martin and Morgan who seemed intent on heading in our direction. "Give me the beer cans, quickly."

Sebastian tore the ring-pull from one of the cans and dropped it in the hole. "More realistic this way." He downed the contents in one and dropped that in the hole as well.

"Hmm," I said. "You're probably right. Give me one here."

We drank as quickly as we could and threw the cans in the hole. But as fast as we drank, Sebastian kept producing more from the rucksack.

"How many more have you got in there?" I noticed my words weren't quite as tidy as normal, a little fuzzy round the edges.

Sebastian peered into his rucksack then pulled out another four cans. "Getting there."

"That's like Mary Poppins's handbag," Cas said. "You got a ladder in there as well?"

"I don't know, I can't see for all this beer."

Sebastian and Cas erupted into giggles. I glanced over to Elaine. She was still standing in the way of Martin and Morgan but now Morgan seemed intent on sidestepping Elaine's attempts. We were out of time.

"Come on, guys. Let's cover this all over or this lot is going to get discovered and stuck in a vault somewhere." I picked up a spade and shovelled earth onto the pile of beer cans.

Colin helped and Cas chucked another empty beer can in the hole. I took a handful of small change from my pocket and scattered it across the earth and then threw another spadeful on top.

"What's happening here?" Morgan said.

I looked up from my work to see Morgan and Martin staring at our dig. Behind them stood Elaine, she was making gestures of sorry.

"We were just going to call you," I said. "Colin's detector is showing something here." I waved a little red flag at her.

Martin looked at Colin. "Well, what is it?"

"What?" Colin looked bewildered.

"Here, Colin," I pointed at the area we'd just covered up. "You said there was something there. Lots of metal stuff?"

"Oh, yes. It's big." He looked at me and saw me shaking my head. "Small. Not big."

"Well," said Morgan. "Which is it? Is it big or is it small? We didn't fund you two grand's worth of electronics if it can't tell the difference between big and small."

"Right," said Martin. "Let's dig it up shall we? And where's that bloody wizard? He's supposed to be here."

Morgan set off across the field to find Merlin.

Martin waved towards Walter and the camera crew, indicating they should come over.

"Okay, where is it?"

"Colin," I said. "Show Martin where you saw the metal."

Colin paused a moment then aimed his detector towards the position where we'd found the real treasure.

I shook my head and with my foot, nudged the detector towards the buried beer cans. "No, I think it was here." I gave Colin a quick smile. "Why don't you switch your machine on and try here?"

"I'm feeling a bit sick," he said.

"Oh, for heaven's sake," snapped Martin. "Just get on with it."

Walter and the camera crew arrived just as Colin switched

on the detector and gave it a sweep over the area I'd indicated. The machine buzzed feebly.

"Okay everybody stand back," Martin said. "Right, Walter, I want you scraping the dirt away as this idiot waves his bloody toy about. Make sure it makes a lot of noise, right?"

Colin nodded and the camera crew readied. The detector gave off a little whimper.

"Is that it? Two grand and the best I get is something that sounds like a dying mouse? How's that going to go down on a fifty-inch TV screen with knock-your-balls-off plasma sound?"

"But maybe it's thin metal? Buried deep? About half a metre deep?" offered Colin.

"Hang on." Sebastian took a little wad of mud and worked it into a ball. He pulled a fifty-pence piece from his pocket, wrapped the mud around it and then stuck the little package to the bottom of the detector. "Try that."

Colin switched on the machine again and it gave off a deafening squeal.

"That's more like it," said Martin. He looked at the cameraman. "You getting this? Right, detector man, wave it around a bit. That's it, good. Walter, you're on. Let's see what's here."

Walter knelt on the ground. "It looks like it's been dug fairly recently," he commented.

Martin looked at me.

"We started digging, we forgot. It was just a bit. Once we heard the detector noise we got over excited," I said. "But then Colin reminded us we were supposed to get everybody here first. So we stopped." I looked at Colin who just nodded.

"Well, no harm done. Walter? What you got?"

"Not sure." Walter poked a little pointed trowel into the ground. "There's definitely something here."

"Well dig it up, man. We're on a clock here."

"He's here!" Merlin arrived and pointed exactly to the patch where the bones were.

"What's over there?" Martin asked Colin.

"I really am feeling rather sick," said Colin. "I think I may have had a bit too much beer."

Martin glared at him.

"Last night," I said. "We had a bit of a session last night. Didn't we, Colin?"

Colin nodded.

"Just wave your detectoriser over there for a moment."

Colin looked at me with pleading, what-do-I-do-now eyes. I sent Colin a telepathic message to switch the detector off and pretend. Colin looked at me and wrinkled his eyebrows. I made a sort of switching-off movement with my fingers and hoped Martin wouldn't notice. Colin wrinkled his eyebrows again. I mouthed the words 'Switch it off'. Colin vomited all over the area where the real treasure was.

I grabbed the detector and put my arm round Colin. "Why don't you go and have a bit of a rest." He wobbled across the field.

"I'll do it," I said. I looked at the control panel on the detector. It reminded me of a flight simulator I'd once sat in at Farnham Airshow. There wasn't even a button marked off or on. I did, however, notice a lead running from the footplate thingy to the mission control centre thingy. I pulled it out then waved the machine over the area where Merlin pointed and which was now covered in vomit. Silence.

"Nothing there," said Martin. "Come on, Walter. Let's see what's here." His focus returned to the original spot.

The camera moved closer to witness this monumental event. Walter poked his pointed trowel deep and dug around his first contact. He reached down and pulled out one of the beer cans.

"Is that it?" Martin said.

Walter pulled another beer can from the hole followed by a couple of my coins and then another can.

"How old are these cans?" said Martin.

Walter picked one of them up and scraped off the mud. "Hmm, I'd say... about... Certainly no older than a year."

"And the coins?" Martin asked. "At least tell me they're Roman."

Walter cleaned one of the coins on a cloth. "Queen Elizabeth," he said.

"Well, Elizabethan, that's something at least."

"The Second."

Martin signalled the camera crew to cut. "Scratch that," he said. "Wasting my bloody time on some squaddie's rubbish tip."

Martin and his entourage set off back to the main marquee.

"That was close." Cas relit his joint as he watched them go.

"Too close," I said. "But hopefully they'll have lost all interest in this particular patch now."

"He's here," said Merlin.

"Yes, we know," I said. "But we need to leave him there for the moment. Keep him safe until we can move him."

"I'll wait here." Merlin sat on the ground by the freshly dug earth. "It's my place."

***

At lunchtime, I found Elaine hiding in one corner of the main marquee.

"You alright?" I asked.

"Yes, fine. Just keeping out of the way. Martin keeps coming over to see if we've found anything else and Jayed won't shut up about her plans to adopt an Angoran orphan."

"Is that the rabbit or a goat?"

"I think she means Angolan orphan."

"She'd probably be safer with a rabbit."

Elaine took my hand. "We need to talk about Merlin," she said. "He's gone very quiet."

"You mean, he's not his usual cantankerous, belligerent self? Yes, I'd noticed that as well. Don't worry, I'm sure he'll be back to irritating and rude by teatime."

"I'm just wondering whether now we've found Arthur's bones, he feels somewhat missionless."

"Oh, sorry. You mean you *really* want to talk about Merlin?"

"That's what I said."

"Well, firstly, we don't know those actually *are* Arthur's bones. Could be anybody's. Could be a Neolithic farmer."

"What, with all that armour and stuff you said was there?"

"Might not be armour. Might be bits of a combine harvester."

"Don't be daft." She looked me straight in the eyes. "When did you start believing him?"

The suddenness of that question stalled me. "What on Earth makes you think I believe him?"

"The fact that now you're trying to protect him rather than get rid of him."

"That just means... It's just that... Well, um..."

"Go on."

I grabbed a can of beer from the huge ice bucket. "Look, I've been chasing fakes and fraudsters for a very long time. I can see them from a mile off. Usually because they have their

230

grubby hands outstretched. But even if they're not after your money then it's fame or power or their own TV programme. These people are not complicated. Once one sees through their motives it's not difficult to see their methods." The cold beer hit the spot beautifully. "But Merlin, he's caused me problems from the moment I met him. He doesn't like people, he doesn't ask for anything and just wants to be left alone on his mission. A mission that's going to get him locked up in a secure wing somewhere the moment we stop trying to help him. He can't function in this world, let alone manipulate it. He's totally dependent on our rag-tag little group, even though he seems to think we're all idiots. Although..."

"So," said Elaine. "He's either genuine or he's completely barking."

"But if he's completely barking, as you put it... by the way, is that a recognised mental health professional term? If he's barking then where did he come from? How does he know all that stuff? Oh, sure, I could probably reproduce most, if not all, of the magic he does but that answer requires me to believe he's capable of that level of skill. No... It takes years of training and I know all of the people capable of doing that. And I tell you, he's not one of them."

"So that leaves only one conclusion then?"

"There you go, you see? Yet it can't be."

"Why?"

"Because... Because that would mean..." I rummaged in the ice bucket for another beer but could only find soft drinks left. I pulled out a fizzy bottle of something that looked like the colour I imagined nuclear waste would turn if it had been left out in the sun for too long. I didn't have a great deal of respect for my insides at the best of times but even I'm not going drink something that colour. I put it back.

231

"Because that would mean that perhaps Amy was right?" Elaine finished my thoughts for me. "And that maybe there is a bit more to this world than we can put under an electron scanning microscope or explode in the Hubble collider."

"It's the Hadron collider. The Hubble is—"

"Shush now," Elaine interrupted. "Maybe it's time you risked unlocking some of these doors you've been frightened of for so long."

"That's dangerous. There's lots of crazy behind those doors."

"Oh, your bus went straight past crazy three stops ago."

I felt sure I should have been offended by that. "What do you mean?"

"Your level of anger at the world for one. That's not right. And what makes you think the only things that exist are the things which you personally believe in? Who gave you the job of Reality Censor? If it doesn't pass John Barker's obsessional scrutiny then it doesn't exist."

"Don't hold back, will you?" I said.

"I wasn't going to. Your fear of emotional involvement borders on the pathological and yet—"

"Ah, there you are." Morgan to the rescue. "John, I need you to stir up Merlin a bit more, I've seen more animation in the House of Lords."

"We were just talking about him," I said. "Weren't we, Elaine? You just mentioned he was looking a bit flat."

Elaine narrowed her eyebrows at me in a message which said, "I haven't finished with you yet."

"Exactly," said Morgan. "We need him a bit more activity focused. After all, he's the reason we're all here."

"I'll have a word with him."

"That would be good. Eric and Stevie have found a ley line

232

which nobody knew about before; apparently it joins Tintagel to Stonehenge and runs right through this site."

"Tintagel?" I said.

"They're calling it the Pathway of the Dead," Morgan said. "It joins up with the Avenue at Stonehenge, where they used to take the bodies. You must have heard about it, one of the most haunted places on Earth. I did a special there two years back, you must have seen it, everybody did. Anyway, we're going to do a Psychic Lifting. Merlin doing his stuff in the background would add a bit of extra zing on the video."

"Zing? Merlin?"

"Good, have a word with him. There's a love." She patted my shoulder and then disappeared into a group of people at the other end of the marquee. "Darlings, there you are."

I looked at Elaine. "Fancy trying to persuade Merlin to zing?"

"I'm afraid you're on your own with that one." She kissed me quickly. "Look after him."

I grabbed a couple of hotdogs on the way out and found Merlin sitting cross-legged by Cas's dig.

"Lunch?" I handed him one.

"No pizza?" Merlin opened the bread roll. "What part of the animal is this?"

"Probably best leave that as one of life's mysteries."

Merlin sniffed at the hotdog then took a large bite. "It's food. Almost."

"Are you planning on just sitting there all the time now?"

"No. I'm going to take Arthur to Trewar Venydh."

"Not yet. And we can only do that if the Evil Twins over there don't realise he's here," I said. "If they find the bones, they'll have them locked in a private museum before the hole's filled in."

Merlin looked up at me, a darkness hinting in what little I could see of his eyes under those eyebrows. "We will stop them," he said, with a tone which carried more of a threat than anything I'd ever heard uttered in any Tarantino movie.

"Yes, but we need your help. I need you to put on a show."

"Do you see a minstrel here?"

"No, not that sort of show. I meant—"

"A witch burning then. We have a spare one." He gestured towards where Morgan held court.

"No, we're not burning any witches." I looked towards Morgan. "However tempting. I need you to do something mystical and magical. Something that will get everybody's attention."

Merlin thought for a moment. "I could turn her into a chicken," he suggested.

"What? No, you can't do… Can you *really* turn somebody into a chicken?"

Merlin gazed up at the sky. "I don't know. I've never tried. Do you want me to try?"

"No. I just want you to do some chanting and stuff. Make a noise, attract attention." I caught his glance. "And no chickens."

***

Cas, Colin and I readied ourselves by the burial site. I'd briefed Merlin to do his bit at the far end of the field. Tree had agreed to fake an angel encounter, although I hadn't the faintest idea what that would involve. Eric and Stevie were already marching up and down with dowsing rods, stopping every so often to plant coloured flags in the ground. Attention had already drifted to the far end of the site, leaving us in peace over the real grave.

234

I watched as Merlin strode across the field, chanting and waving Harold in the air. He really did look every bit the medieval wizard. The camera crew followed him and Morgan and Martin hovered, calling muted instructions to everybody. Merlin stopped, paused for a moment then jammed Harold into the ground. A small bang erupted from the contact point and everybody jumped back apace. Myself included. That was impressive and totally unexpected. Flashbang paper and an electronic ignition running up through the walking stick would certainly achieve that effect but I wasn't convinced that Merlin was that technically competent. Maybe Martin's Special Effects people had set it up to give some interest should nothing be uncovered. Yes, that must be it.

"Now," I said to Cas and he threw the spade into the ground.

We took turns digging and watching out while Colin waved his detector around, guiding us as to where to dig next. We turned up some interesting metal objects and a few bones but didn't stop to examine them. Whoever this person had been, king or not, he'd certainly been important. It felt very odd to be dragging these objects through time and into the twenty-first century.

A loud kerfuffle at the end of the field snagged my attention. Merlin was shouting loudly and waving Harold in the air. Tree was sitting in a meditation position on the grass; she appeared to be crying, while Eric seemed to be berating the camera crew. Well that certainly constituted a diversion, albeit not quite what I'd had in mind.

"Keep going, Cas," I said. "We've got a break."

We hadn't. The kerfuffle suddenly changed direction and started heading our way. Hell, what had caused that? Then I noticed the chicken. It ran, as best as a chicken can, directly towards us, hotly pursued by Martin and the camera crew. A chicken. He couldn't have done?

"Cas," I shouted. "Put it all back."

"What?"

"Put it all back in the hole. They're all coming over here."

"Seriously? After all my work?"

"Yes, seriously. Now would be good."

The chicken continued straight for us then leapt over the hole in one fluid, flapping leap and headed towards the perimeter fence.

I knelt on the ground, trying to conceal our treasures whilst pushing dirt back into the hole.

"Did you see a chicken?" Martin yelled as they approached.

I pointed towards the fence. "It went that way."

Cas paused and said, "Was that a chicken?"

"Hmm? Oh, yes," I said. "Do you think it looked like anyone we know?"

"It reminds me of a girlfriend I once had." Cas leaned on his spade as his head followed the group hurtling by. "Same colour hair."

"Come on, and make it quick. We've got to cover all this up again."

The chicken scurried through a gap in the perimeter fence and disappeared into the brush. The group came to a frustrated standstill by the fence, craning to see where it went.

"Dig it up, put it back," Cas muttered as he threw a spadeful of dirt over the treasures. "Can't you just magic it out? You're a magician."

"I'm not that sort of magician."

"We could always get Merlin to magic it out."

"Even if he could, I don't think encouraging Merlin to attempt something like that would be entirely wise."

Martin and the camera crew abandoned their chicken run and grouped around our dig. I tried to block the camera as they tried to film inside our hole.

"What's with the chicken?" I straightened and continued to kick dirt into the hole as inconspicuously as possible.

"Damn thing stole an antique ring and ran off with it," Martin said. "What's happening here?"

"Nothing much." I picked up a muddy beer can and gave it to him. "Just more of these. What antique ring?"

"We were just doing a bit of filming in case things went tits-up and we needed a filler. Morgan hypnotises a chicken and it finds an ancient ring. Looked good on paper. Who'd have thought a fucking chicken could move so fast?"

"I see, so you brought the chicken with you?" My stress levels receded slightly.

"Of course we brought it with us. Not much chance of finding a random chicken when you need one." He studied the muddy beer can for a moment then tossed it back in the hole. "I'd give this one up if I were you." He waved at the film crew to follow him and they traipsed back across the field.

"That was close," I said. "For a minute I thought… Cas… What's that in your belt?"

Cas looked down. "Oh, that? It's my sword. Cool isn't it?"

"Not really. It looks just like one we dug up five minutes ago which I thought you'd reburied."

"Really?" Cas feigned surprise. "No, not this one. This one I've had for…" He caught my look. "Well, okay, to be honest, I forgot it was there. I just wanted to try it out, you know how it is. I've never had a sword, not a real one."

"What if they'd seen it?"

"Well, they didn't, did they? I think it makes me look like Captain Jack." He pulled the sword from his belt in an

237

attempted flourish. It flew from his hand and pierced the ground at my feet.

"Captain Birdseye more like. Put it back in the hole and cover it over."

I needed to work out another way of getting the bones away. A bigger diversion, that's what we needed.

Chapter Twenty Two

When digging had finished for the day, we all headed back to the hotel. Martin informed us all that the evening's episode was broadcasting at eight o'clock and we should all gather in the lounge again.

I took Elaine to one side. "We need a bigger diversion," I said. "Tomorrow is the last day. If we don't get the bones away then, the army will cover the area in mines again and that will be that."

"What are you planning?"

"Not sure yet but I have a vague idea. I'm going to drive up to London this evening; I've got a lock-up there with all my magic stuff in it. I'm fairly sure I can cobble something together to divert attention long enough to get the bones away."

"But that'll take you all night."

"No, not in the evening. Clear road and a bit of luck, I reckon I can be there and back before ten. Midnight at the latest."

As it happened, the traffic was on my side for once and I made the round trip in just over four hours. By eleven, we had a hotel room full of magic gear. Elaine and I sat on the floor and sifted through it and by midnight, we had the beginnings of a plan.

The next morning we rose early and headed to the site before it was properly light. Although a substantial fence surrounded the area and was protected by a security guard, it wasn't really a problem for what we needed. Most of the preparation could be set up outside the fence and the guard was from an agency, working minimum wages and he probably had a day job as well. I risked a peek through the window of the Site Security Hut. Mixed Martial Arts videos cycled on YouTube on a laptop in front of the sleeping guard.

"All clear," I whispered. "He's asleep."

It took less than thirty minutes to prepare the equipment. The set up was in reality quite simple: a couple of smoke machines, a wireless speaker and a remote controlled projector. It was hiding the gear which took the time but by the time we'd finished it was pretty much invisible unless somebody actually tripped over it.

"I'm still not quite sure how this is supposed to work," Elaine said as we finished setting up.

"It's just an updated variant on the Pepper's Ghost illusion from the Victorian period. Simple really."

"Of course it is. Now, who on Earth was Pepper and what does his ghost do?"

"Hmm, Professor Pepper wasn't the ghost. He was the person who devised the illusion. It makes an image of a ghost, or anything, appear on stage. You've heard of the expression Smoke and Mirrors?"

Elaine nodded.

"Well, that was him. I can go on."

"Please don't."

We went back to the hotel for breakfast and then left once more for the dig site with everybody else. I'd decided that it was best to run the illusion as early as possible, while the sun was still low and playing shadows through the nearby trees. The long shadows would aid the effect somewhat. We'd all had a quick chat as to our individual roles and as I looked around the group once more I realised the insanity of what we were attempting. We were going to steal the bones of a fifteen-hundred-year-old Saxon king from under the noses of an archaeology team complete with television crew. And in broad daylight. What could go wrong here?

Immediately after Martin's morning briefing, Tree moved to her position just beyond Elaine and Jayed's dig site. At exactly eight-thirty, she started her wailing and just as I'd hoped, all eyes turned in her direction. Rule one in the magician's handbook: make the audience look somewhere else while you do your trickery. In this case, our trickery was quickly removing the contents of the grave, separating bones from treasure, making one disappear whilst the other appears. I'd done similar illusions hundreds of times but never under conditions like this.

Tree raised the volume a few decibels and threw her hands to the sky. I pressed one of the buttons on the remote control and waited. For a while nothing happened and I began to worry but then gradually, a mist started gathering just beyond the southern perimeter fence, about a hundred metres beyond where Tree was giving the performance of her life. My smoke machines drifted subtle clouds across the still dewy grass. Just enough to do the job but not enough to look like a fire.

"What's that mist?" Elaine said, just a little too loudly. A cold knife prodded at my soul as I involuntarily remembered just how well Amy had always delivered her lines. I pushed the thoughts away.

"That's very odd," somebody else said, and then all attention turned to the mist.

I pressed the second button on the remote and again nothing happened for a moment. I listened carefully then very faintly, I heard the sound. A clinking, beating sound which I'd set to gradually increase in volume.

I put my hands up as if shielding sunlight from my eyes. That was the cue for Cas and Colin to get to work. I didn't look. Rule two in the magician's handbook: never look at things you don't want your audience to see. And I really didn't want anybody looking towards the northern fence. I had to trust they could dig everything up in the time we'd allocated.

The noise grew in volume and as I looked at the others around me, I saw that several others were beginning to notice. A rhythmic, clinking and crunching drifting from the direction of the mist. Time for button three. The projector sprang into life and Pepper's ghost entered its latest incarnation. Shadowy figures slowly coalesced as they marched across the field just beyond the perimeter fence. Faintly at first, just moving shadows in the mist, then bit by bit, they came into view. The ghosts of hundreds of ancient warriors marching across the field, their armour clinking in time with their footsteps as they moved.

I risked a quick look around. All eyes were transfixed by the scene. Okay, it seemed like I still had my touch. I did have a slight panic though and wondered if anybody there had ever seen Warlords of Mercia. I'd been rushed and that was the only movie of which I could find a decent clip on YouTube. The mist helped of course, and the surroundings. It's not as if they'd been told we were about to watch a movie and who could name the title the quickest.

I needn't have worried. The awe which fell over the people gathered there was tangible. The camera crew seemed as captivated as everybody else and even Martin was motionless for the first time I could recall. "You getting this?" he called to the camera crew.

"Yup."

"Well make sure you do."

"We're getting it."

"Just checking."

Morgan was the first to shift the focus. She moved in front of the camera and in a low, conspiratorial whisper explained to Television World what was happening. "The ghosts of hundreds of brave warriors are marching from their graves. It seems we were right and this is the site of a ferocious ancient battle where the fallen still refuse to lie down. Their spirits march here, tirelessly searching for their comrades."

I felt a tap on my arm. I didn't look but I knew it would be Cas.

"Got it all," he said.

"Great. Get the treasure over to Elaine, she knows what to do. Did Colin get the bones?"

"Yeah, already lobbed 'em over the fence."

"The General?"

"He was there, all ready. Threw the bag over to him first go and he's carted it off somewhere. I love it when a plan comes together, mwahaha!"

I heard Cas move away and guessed, hoped, he was headed for Elaine with his bin bag full of one of the greatest archaeological finds of the century. I hit the master off-button and watched as the mist dissipated and the figures faded away. Not a bad job considering the time constraints.

Once the spell had broken people moved towards the fence, staring to see if the apparitions would make a return appearance. I risked a glance to Elaine's dig site and noticed Cas and Colin there, shovelling earth back into the hole as if they were trying to cover the entrance to hell before the devil noticed.

Two hours later, Jayed squealed with genuine surprise when she pulled a piece of metal from the earth. I remembered that piece from the first time we'd dug it up. To me, it looked a bit like a beer can split lengthways but I guessed it was probably a piece of armour meant for the arm or leg.

The find gathered an immediate crowd as everybody was still high from the earlier show. Walter did a long piece to camera, showing the semi-cleaned object but I was too far away to hear what he was saying about it. He did look unusually animated though so it was probably something important.

As the afternoon moved on, more treasures came up from Elaine and Jayed's dig and everybody pretty much ignored the other sites. Around five, we were given the instruction that we were now finishing and the Bobcats moved in to start re-levelling the field. We gathered around Morgan and Martin as they did their final session for the camera. A large trestle table had been positioned in front of them with the treasure laid out. It looked a bit like the last table in a car boot sale which had just been rained off but I knew the items there were probably going to set historians flapping for years. I was however, impressed with the helmet, which only three hours ago had contained a skull. I'd been worried that Cas, lacking both time and finesse, might have damaged one or the other. I owed him a drink. Or a joint.

"This has been a remarkable dig," Martin said to the camera. "We started with lots of false alarms but then suddenly we struck this." He waved his hands over the table. "It seems like an early Saxon grave for somebody of extremely high status but the strange thing about this site is that we have found not a single trace of the occupant. At first it seemed that this might simply be a stolen hoard we have discovered but Mystic Morgan and her team of psychic investigators have uncovered a deeper and more disturbing secret. Over to you, Morgan."

"Thank you, Martin. Yes indeed, the reality behind this site makes this one of the most extraordinary cases ever in the science of ghost hunting."

"*Science* of ghost hunting?" I muttered.

"Shush." Elaine jabbed an elbow in my ribs.

"We witnessed the ghosts of warriors walking and now we have an empty grave," Morgan continued.

"Empty, apart from this collection of armour which rivals the find at Sutton Hoo," Martin said.

"Exactly," said Morgan. "So what happened? According to the Archangel Gabriel, with whom our world renowned Angelologist, Tree Starflower, has been in communication, the warriors came back to collect the remains of their king and take him to Valhalla."

"Angelologist? Valhalla?" I said quietly. "I'm sorry, I *am* trying but—"

Another jab in the ribs from Elaine. "Well try harder."

"And while we can't say definitively that this is the grave of King Arthur," Morgan said. "In my professional opinion, there is no doubt."

"I think I would have to agree with that assessment, Morgan," Martin said. "As an archaeological historian, I only examine facts, provable facts. But here the evidence is overwhelming; this is a Saxon king's grave of major significance. The remarkably accurate historical texts presented by Merlin and the film evidence of the marching ghosts, I would have to agree that there is every possibility that we have just proved the existence of King Arthur here today."

"What the hell is an Archaeological Historian?" I said.

"Accurate historical texts? He does remember that's Fifty Shades of Grey? I mean—"

Elaine grabbed my arm. "Come on. I'm taking you away from here before you blow it all by telling them how you did it just to prove they're idiots. Which would kind of destroy all we've done."

"They're not idiots," I sulked. "They're conniving, cheating, money-grabbing shysters who wouldn't know an ethic if it beat them round the head with an honesty stick."

"You're ranting now, John."

***

As soon as we left the site for the final time, we made our way round the northern section of the fence to the General's encampment. He appeared with his homemade spear ready to do battle.

"It's okay," I said. "Just us."

"Ah, I was expecting the SPG."

"SPG?" I said.

"Special Patrol Group. Hard bastards but they're not taking me again."

"The police anti-riot squad or whatever they were. That SPG? But weren't they disbanded in the late eighties? Too much bad press, overly aggressive, that sort of thing?"

The General looked puzzled for a moment. "Disbanded?"

"Yes, they used to go to work with baseball bats, if I remember rightly."

"And you say they were disbanded in the eighties?"

"Yes."

"What's the time now?"

I looked at my watch. "Just after six."

246

"Ah, that explains why they've not been round for a while. Can't be too careful though. You sure they've not just gone into hiding?"

"Pretty sure. Have you got the bag of bones?"

"You mean the King?"

"Yes."

"No."

"No? Cas threw them over to you earlier. You were going to look after them."

"But he told me not to tell anybody."

"He didn't mean me," I said. "He meant anybody else, like... I don't know... the police or something."

"Oh, he should have said. I might have got confused."

"Can I take the bones now? Please?"

"Roger that." He disappeared into his shack and came out a moment later with a small green metal box. "I put them in here. More respectful than a bin bag."

"Thanks." I took the box and peeped inside to make sure they were there. I reached into the box and with oh-so delicate fingertips, removed the hand grenade nestling under the bones. I gave it to him. "You might want to hang on to this."

"Oh, thanks, I wondered where that had got to."

"I'll bring you a new box."

"Don't worry," the General said. "I've got lots of them. Every time they come over there playing their soldier games they leave these behind."

I took another quick peek in the box to make sure there were no bullets or whatever left. All seemed okay so we thanked the General and headed off back to the hotel.

***

That evening, we all settled in the conference room for the showing of the final part in the Celebrity Time Diggers Special. Drinks were on Martin and they flowed freely, although the smell of cannabis smoke suggested that Cas had chosen an alternate route to inebriation. The sequence of events had been rearranged for 'Dramatic Effect' and the marching ghosts had been edited towards the end. Lots of panoramic sweeps of the site, celebrity posturing and close-ups of muddy holes occupied the first part. The kleptomaniac chicken had been dropped but we still had the section with Martin talking to Cas and I just after we'd reburied the armour. It was at that point that Morgan leapt up and flew out of the room as if she'd suddenly remembered leaving the milk on.

The finding of the armour had been placed before the ghost marching as Martin felt the film had a better flow that way. That suited me, one of the tricks magicians use to confuse people who've just witnessed a trick is to persuade them events happened in a slightly different order. This makes it very difficult for people trying to later work out how a trick was done.

Much was made of the finding of the armour peppered with plenty of accidental shots of Jayed's £50,000 cleavage and Morgan's leather clad backside. Elaine hardly featured apart from a few shots of her holding a spade occasionally while Jayed pouted to camera. My appearance was a twenty second clip of me wiping mud off a beer can. I was grateful I didn't need this programme to leverage my career. The final big build-up centred on the ghost marching which, although I say it myself, looked remarkably convincing on the screen.

The film finished amid a round of applause and Martin stood to thank everybody for their participation in, what he claimed, had been the most historical event in history. He hesitated for a moment as clearly Morgan had been scheduled to make a statement at this point then lamely finished with 'It has all been lovely', and he wished us safe onward journeys.

Our little group gathered in the bar afterwards to discuss the next phase. Taking the bones to Trewar Venydh, or, as we now knew it to be, Tintagel.

"I guess we set off first thing tomorrow," I suggested. "We can have this all done and dusted by evening and get on with our lives."

"What life is that then?" Elaine asked. "More medium busting?"

"No, I'm done with that. Thought I'd move to Spain. Buy a small farm and grow some olives. Or maybe Wales. Not so much difficulty with the language there."

"Wouldn't be so sure on that."

"What day is it?" Merlin looked up from his book.

"Thursday," Colin said.

"When is Thursday?" asked Merlin.

"Huh? Today. That's what I said," Colin answered.

"Is that the Hunter's Moon?"

"What?"

"Oh I see," said Stevie. "He's talking about a Hunter's Moon. Very spiritual days. It's the full moon nearest the autumn equinox."

"What's this about, Merlin?" I asked. "Is it important?"

"The caves will only open during a Hunter's Moon," Merlin said. "Look." He held up what remained of his paperback and I saw his usual markings across the page highlighting equidistant letters. I looked closer. The little circles joined up HUNTERSMOON.

"But it's a popular tourist spot," I said. "I'm sure the caves will be open all year."

Merlin stared at me. "I'm not talking about the trivial touristy comings and goings of gawking idiots. I'm talking about the caves themselves opening to commune with me. They will only do this on the Hunter's Moon."

"This could be a problem," I said. "Does anybody know when the next Hunter's Moon is?"

"I've got an app," said Colin. "Use it mostly to tell me good fishing nights but it's got that sort of stuff on it too." He pulled out his smartphone and tapped the screen. "Ah, no signal. I'll go upstairs, had a signal there earlier."

Just as he left the bar the door swung again and Morgan billowed in like an approaching thunderstorm. This didn't look good.

She came directly over to my table and slammed an A4 photograph down in front of me. It shook my beer causing it to spill. I watched as a dribble hit the edge of the piece of paper.

"Want to tell me what this is?" she demanded.

I stared at the picture. It was very grainy and blurred; I guessed it was a screenshot of something. I studied it for a moment.

"Isn't that Cas?" I said.

"Yes. See anything else?"

"It's at the dig. Yesterday was it?" I couldn't see where this was going but I knew it wasn't heading anywhere pleasant.

"Look closer."

I studied the photograph some more. Cas and Colin stood by the hole we'd been working on. Cas leaned on the spade smiling into the camera while Colin seemed to be staring at Cas's midriff. Nothing else. Or… what was Colin staring at so intently and just what was that in Cas's belt? Oh hell.

Morgan noticed the change in my eyes. "Ah, I see you've found the problem. Do you want to tell me what it is?"

"Um… it looks like a sword. Could be a stick though, maybe it's a trowel. Who knows?"

"Oh I think we can take a fair guess." She slapped another sheet of paper down on the table.

I slid it towards me and it dampened as it dragged through the spilt beer. It was a picture of the table containing the treasure. In the centre of the display was the same sword.

"See the puzzle?" she said.

"No," I lied.

"Let me help you." She slid the pictures together in front of me. "You see, this sword attached to Cas is the same sword as the one on the table. So when I saw the film earlier, I thought to myself, I know where I saw that before."

I started to speak but she pressed her hand on top of mine, a clear signal that it wasn't my turn to speak.

She continued, "Now, my question is, how could we dig up a sword in the afternoon which we'd already filmed dangling from one of your scruffy hippy mates four hours earlier?"

"It's a puzzle," I agreed.

"Indeed. If I was a cynic," she tapped the picture of Cas and Colin with a red fingernail, "I might be tempted to believe that Frodo and Sam here had dug this lot up from one place and buried it somewhere else."

She sensed my need to speak and squeezed my hand with a force that somebody her size shouldn't have been able to apply.

"Now, why would anyone do that?" she asked. I sensed this was a purely rhetorical question and let her continue. "Because they were hiding something that was buried with the armour."

"Oh, that's a bit—"

She lowered her head until her face was level with mine. "Where's Arthur's fucking body?" she snarled. I was sure her eyes turned red as she spoke.

251

"What body?"

Her voice dropped to a hiss. "How do you think you lot got out of the police cells? Me, that's how. Me and my brother, Commissioner Ifan Murdrydd of the Metropolitan Police. If you don't tell me where that bastard king's body is now, one phone call and you will be back there again, this time with an extra charge sheet including breach of the Official Secrets Act and grave robbing."

"That's a bit harsh. We were only—"

"Tell me."

"Upstairs in my room. It's not a body though. Just a few bones. Might even be an animal, I don't know."

"Come," she commanded.

I led her up to our room and showed her the green box. She lifted the lid and then turned to me and smiled.

"See, that wasn't so hard." She picked up the box with surprising ease and disappeared along the corridor.

I returned to the bar and explained to Merlin and the others what had happened. The door swung open once more and we all braced for another onslaught but it was only Colin.

"Tomorrow," he said.

"What?" I asked. "What about tomorrow?"

"The Hunter's Moon, it's tomorrow. That's a bit of luck isn't it?"

Chapter Twenty Three

We sat in the bar nursing our drinks.

"Well, that's messed things up a bit," said Cas.

"I will slice pieces from her soulless heart and feed them to the dogs while she watches," Merlin said.

"I think I'll call it a day," said Colin. "It's been fun. Well, actually, no, it's not been much fun. In fact it's been a bloody nightmare so I'm going to bed now and in the morning I'm going home."

"Can't you do anything?" Elaine asked. "I mean with your magic or something? We've come so far it seems a shame to give up now."

"Give up?" I said. "Morgan seems to be in league with the New World Order or the Illuminati or at the very least, the Masons. I think tactical withdrawal is more accurate. I have no desire to spend the rest of my days in Guantanamo Bay."

"That's America. Here it would be... oh I don't know... Belmarsh?"

"But you can do escaping magic," Cas said. "No prison could hold you."

"I'll ask the angels to spread some light," said Tree. "We need some soothing energy."

"Cas might have a point," Elaine said. "Is there nothing you can do? Can you hypnotise them or do a trick with the box?"

"Magicians are good at tricks with boxes," Cas said. "Saw

one in Southend once. He put a girl in this box... or it might have been a boy... no, it was a snake. Put the lid down and when he opened it... poof! There was a rabbit... or it might have been a pigeon. Anyway, it was pretty impressive, never forgotten that."

The conversation continued to deteriorate but Cas had sparked something. The glimmerings of an idea. I'd just thrown a load of my stage equipment in the back of the car while I was at my lock-up. I hadn't paid too much attention; I'd just thrown in everything which I thought might be vaguely useful in setting up the Pepper's Ghost illusion. There must be something I could use. I needed to switch a box; that was fairly standard illusionist fare. Okay, what did I need? Identical looking box and contents and a means to pull off the switch.

"I might have a plan," I said. "I need to go back to the General and get another one of those boxes. Then we fill it with something that looks like the bones we dug up. I think I might then be able to switch the boxes."

"Sounds cool," said Cas.

"I could just send her to the caverns of Morgdrygal," offered Merlin. "I can seal them for nine centuries."

"That sounds better," said Cas.

"Does that get the bones back?" I asked.

"No," said Merlin.

"Maybe we'll call that option 'B' then," I said. "I'm going to nip back to see the General and pick up another of those boxes. Can somebody raid the kitchen and find some bones we can use?"

"Bones," said Cas. "Cool. Leave that to us. They had spare ribs on the menu earlier."

I grabbed Elaine's hand. "We're not sunk yet, you up for a drive?"

"Got nothing else to do."

"Great, oh, and Cas, do try to stop Merlin smiting anybody. At least until I get back."

We headed upstairs, quickly briefed a very reluctant Colin and headed to our room. I sifted through the pile of magic kit I'd stacked in the corner of our room earlier. The only item I found which might be vaguely useful was a false bottom suitcase. That would have to do; I could probably improvise something with that.

The drive to the General's shack took less than twenty minutes but it took me thirty more to explain to him I needed another of the empty boxes. He insisted I took three, save me coming back, he explained. I checked them for errant hand grenades and thanked him again for his help.

When we arrived back at the hotel bar, our group were the only ones left. The barmen looked slightly irritated as Elaine and I entered as I guessed he was looking to close up.

Cas and Colin sat in a corner, they looked pleased with themselves. Too pleased. They were also sporting fresh mud stains on clothes and faces.

"Anybody dead?" I asked.

Cas shook his head and emptied his glass. "Nobody new anyway." He waved his glass towards the barman who tried hard to conceal a scowl and failed.

"Did you find any suitable bones?"

Cas appeared to stretch out a bit and I felt something touch my foot. I looked down. He nudged a black bin bag against my leg with his foot.

I bent down to take a peek in the bag. Definitely bones. Only these weren't spare ribs, or indeed anything even vaguely pig-like. They were also covered in mud. Odd! I looked closer.

I'd had a worry that using bones from the kitchen would only pass a casual glance and the lack of anything resembling a skull might prove problematical if Morgan paid any more than just passing attention. The good news was that I didn't need to worry anymore about the absence of a skull. The lifeless hollows from a mud-caked skull stared up at me from the bottom of the bin bag.

I closed the bag carefully. "Um… They're not from the kitchen, are they?"

Cas grinned widely and shook his head.

Elaine bent down to take a look before I could warn her. "Oh, I see," she said.

The barman headed our way with our drinks and I stuffed my foot on top of the bag, holding it shut.

I thanked him and then turned to Cas. "We're all going to hell. That's if we don't go to prison first. Or both. You have to put them back."

"Why?"

"Because you can't go round digging up bodies, that's why. I don't even want to think where you got it."

"But we've done it before," Cas protested. "You didn't complain then."

"When?"

"Arthur. You dug up Arthur first and put him in a bin bag."

"That's different."

"Why?"

"Because… well… he's been dead a lot longer, that's why."

"So how long has a body got to be dead before we can dig it up again?"

"I can't believe I'm having this conversation," I said. "Elaine, help me. Explain it to him will you?"

"Well, he has got a point," she said.

"Not helping. This is probably somebody's father. Or mother. Do you even know what sex it is?"

"Is that important?" Cas asked.

"I don't know. I'm sure it should be."

Elaine touched my arm. "It's just a pile of bones. There's nobody there."

"No one's going to miss him," said Cas.

"It was a very *old* grave," said Colin. "We didn't want to risk digging up anything recent."

"We're not ghouls," said Cas. "That would be gross. And probably smelly."

"I think his name was Nathanial," said Colin.

"Really?" said Cas. "That's a cool name."

"Nathanial Weatherbridge. That's what it said on the headstone. Nathanial Weatherbridge, sadly missed by his wife Agnes and their five children. I can't remember their names though. I think one might have been Emily."

I sank my beer in one and called for a large gin. The increasingly grumpy looking barman nodded.

"When are you going to switch the boxes?" Elaine asked.

"The only time is at checkout tomorrow. I can't do anything before as Morgan will have the box safely in her room and after checkout, it will be in her car with her."

"That gives a very tight window. Can't you pick her room lock? I thought you did lock picking?"

"I can but the hotel keys are cards, not traditional keys. I can't pick those."

"We can create a diversion," offered Cas. "I could do my clown dance. I made some good money with that last year at Glastonbury Festival. Do you want to see it?"

"Maybe we'll say yes to a diversion but I think we'll pass on the clown dance. We need something a bit more subtle."

"I will bring a thunderbolt down and cleave the demon woman in four parts to scatter her to the corners of hell," Merlin said.

"I think we might put that idea in the same box as clown dancing," I said. "We need subtle. Maybe a noise outside at just the right moment to make her look. Only needs about five seconds for me to make the switch. Five seconds, we don't need Gerry Cottle's Circus or the Four Horsemen of the Apocalypse. A clattering dustbin should do it."

"Dustbins are wheelie-bins now," said Elaine. "They're made of plastic, they don't clatter anymore."

I stared at Elaine with my best pissed-off stare and she grinned back at me.

"Maybe a car pulling up outside Reception just at the right moment," I said. "That's subtle. People always look to see who the new arrivals are. Sebastian, can you drive your van up at exactly the right moment?"

"Sure," said Sebastian. "No worries. When's the right moment?"

Right there, that was the problem. We had no way of controlling at what time Morgan would check out.

"I know," said Cas. I braced myself. "We could use walkie-talkies. Easy."

"Only one small problem with that plan, Cas," I said. "We don't have any walkie-talkies."

Elaine took her mobile phone from her bag and placed it on the table without saying a word.

"Or… we could use our phones," I said.

The plan was drawn. I stand near Reception and when Morgan starts checking out, I press 'Send' on a phone call to Sebastian who then pulls up outside. That would just snag her attention long enough to use the false bottom suitcase. It was a natty little gadget. A clever system of flaps on the bottom allowed it to be placed over an item which would then become locked inside the case until a small lever was activated. Whatever one placed it over would simply disappear. It had originally been designed for luggage thieves in places like airports or railway stations but magicians had long ago purloined the idea for entertainment purposes.

By seven in the morning I started loitering in the Reception area. By nine, I'd consumed five coffees and was beginning to feel quite wired. Morgan turned up at just after nine. She placed the small box on the ground next to her black, calf leather suitcase. I moved up behind her as if I'd just arrived to check out as well. She turned briefly to give me a forced smile then returned to discussing the extras on her account. I pressed send on the pre-programmed call and put the phone to my ear. My hand clutched the handle of the case, ready to drop the counterfeit box. I heard the engaged tone in my ear. I pressed end and immediately redialled. Still engaged. Morgan was removing her credit card. Redial. Still engaged. I looked at the box and wondered if I could pull the switch while she signed the bill. No, way too risky. I glanced around the room. Cas had arrived with Eric and Stevie. I left the trick suitcase standing in line behind Morgan and slid over to Cas.

"Sebastian's talking on the phone," I said. "I can't get through."

"I expect it's his mum. She calls him every morning."

"If we miss this chance, we're screwed. There's no way we'll swap the box after here."

"I'll go find him," Cas said.

"Subtle, remember."

I slid back into line behind Morgan who was tapping her red

claws on the counter as she waited for the card machine to process her payment.

Cas stood in the hotel doorway, waved his arms towards the drive and yelled, "Oi!"

There goes subtle. Morgan glanced briefly towards the door to see what was happening then returned her attention to the machine which had just started printing her receipt.

Cas yelled again and flapped his arms as if trying to take off. I heard the sudden revving of an engine outside and Cas jumped back in alarm. A cloud of dust and gravel from the driveway kicked up in front of the door as Sebastian's van hurtled past followed by a loud crashing of metal on metal.

Oh, good and subtle, Sebastian.

Morgan turned to look towards the door, and her mouth dropped open. "My fucking car," she yelled.

I made the switch.

"That fucking lunatic's smashed his bloody hippy wagon into my Range Rover."

She turned to look at me. I shrugged. She looked down at the box then back at me. I shrugged again. She bent down and picked up the box.

"Don't even think about it." She opened the top of the box and gave a quick peek. Seeming content, she tucked the box under her arm and ran outside.

Thank goodness we hadn't filled it with spare ribs and lamb chops. I said a silent thank you to Nathanial Weatherbridge

Chapter Twenty Four

We'd agreed to meet up at a Travel Eatery just outside Exeter so we could plan the next, and hopefully final, leg of this journey. We were the first there and as the others straggled in over the next thirty minutes I realised I was probably going to miss this strange bunch. Merlin had already finished his pizza by the time the others joined us. I resisted his pleas for another one; he was showing signs of having accumulated quite a bit of extra weight since we'd first met.

Sebastian was the last to arrive, which was hardly surprising given the current state of his van. In an argument between a thirty year old VW camper van and the latest Range Rover, the contest was a little unfair. He'd had to stop every few miles to let the engine cool down as the fan had buckled. I supposed it was one advantage of the air cooled engine, as had this had a more modern water cooled engine, damage to the front like this had suffered would certainly had stopped it running completely.

"So, what's the plan?" Cas asked.

"We just turn up and take the bones to the cave," I said. "Seems straightforward. Home for tea!"

Merlin pushed his paperback novel to me. "Here," he said. He stabbed the acknowledgements page of the book with a pizza stained finger, adding a red blob to the growing collection of stains throughout the book. "This is the time."

I looked at his circles and arrows across the page. Three sets of equidistant letters had been circled: HUNTERS, MOON and RISE.

"We have to be there at the rise of the Hunter's Moon?"

"It's written here," Merlin confirmed, adding another stain. "The most important prophecy of all, it's written on the first page of The Book. Hunter's Moon Rise."

"Does anybody know what time the moon rises?" I asked. "Colin? Does your app tell you that?"

Colin stabbed buttons on his smartphone. "Twenty oh five," he said finally.

"Looks like we'll have to hang around there all day," I said.

"Time for sightseeing," said Elaine. "I went there once many years ago. It's a lovely little town, very quaint, beautiful walks. We could have a cream tea."

With the end of this madness now in sight I felt a little more relaxed. In fact, I was feeling positively laid back. "Okay, that's a plan then. We head on down there now, have a relaxing day doing the touristy bit then when the moon rises, off to the caves, drop the bones and then home."

"Be a bit late then," said Sebastian. "I think we'll get a B&B and shoot back in the morning."

"That sounds like a good idea," said Elaine. "Make a mini holiday of it. Should be easy to get a room this late in the season."

***

We knew something was wrong as soon as we turned off the A39 and into the lanes. The traffic was heavier than it should have been for this time of year. Late summer usually brought welcome relief from long tailbacks and jams but as we approached Tintagel, the traffic continued to thicken. Around three miles from our destination we came to a halt. The lanes in this area were narrow and sparse with little chance of a detour; we would just have to wait it out. Fortunately, we had plenty of time until the rising of the Hunter's Moon. Even if we walked from here we'd still have time for a cream tea and a Cornish pasty.

Elaine climbed out of the car to secure a better view of the jam. "I can't see what's happening. It just goes on."

"Probably a broken down car," I suggested. "In these lanes a breakdown can cause havoc and it takes an age for a rescue truck to get through."

Sebastian tapped on my window. "Hey, man, any idea what's happening? My van's not coping with this stop start." He nodded towards his camper van behind my car.

"Think it might be a breakdown," I said. "We could be here a while you might want to make yourselves comfortable."

Sebastian returned to his camper van, took several deck chairs out and arranged them on the verge. The others joined him and before long they had a camping stove going with tea and joints easing the day. For the next hour we inched forwards a car's length at a time and each time, Sebastian and his crew edged their mobile picnic a few yards along the verge to keep up with the van. Even Eric and Stevie in their car behind Sebastian's van joined in, creating a sort a surreal roadside version of the mad hatter's tea party.

Finally we rounded a corner to see Tintagel peeking out from the folds in the hills about a mile in front of us. No sign of a breakdown, just nose to tail traffic.

"Something must be going on here," I said.

"I think I can see an advertising poster up ahead," said Elaine. "Can't quite make it out though."

We shuffled forwards until we were almost adjacent to the poster. I read the poster as we approached, not quite believing what I'd just read. I jammed the brakes to take another look. I felt, and heard, a crunch behind. Sebastian had just driven into the back of us. I got out of the car to see what the damage was. My black plastic bumper had a small kink and a scratch, I could live with that. I turned to inspect Sebastian's van and saw a bent panel dangling from a piece of wire emanating from the nearside wing of Sebastian's vehicle. Sebastian pushed it back in place and wriggled it to check its fit.

"You stopped," he said, accusingly.

"Sorry, is it alright?"

"Oh this?" He poked the panel. "It keeps doing that. Why'd you stop?"

"Look at this." I took him to the poster. "What do you make of that?"

"You're kidding?" he said as his eyes scanned the poster.

"What is it?" Elaine said from inside the car.

"It says, 'Welcome to Tintagel, home of the first International Merlin Festival'."

A toot from a car behind reminded me we were blocking the road. We jumped back in the vehicles and continued our tortoise creep.

"A Merlin Festival," said Elaine after a moment.

"*International* Merlin Festival," I corrected.

"They know I'm here?" Merlin said from the back seat.

"I don't think so," I said. "Just a coincidence. A strange, surreal and slightly alarming coincidence."

"I suppose it's the place for a Merlin Festival," said Elaine. "It always was a bit like that here. There's Merlin and Arthur stuff all over the place. Arthur's Tavern, Merlin's hall, Arthur's tea shop, Merlin's fish and chips. It's all to do with the legend."

"You mean the one that claims King Arthur was born here?" I said. "You do know that's just nonsense, don't you?"

"Who's to say?"

A man in a yellow hi-vis jacket and pointy wizard hat ushered us into a field where a hand written piece of paper on a post announced this as the Official Car Park for the International Merlin Festival. He relieved me of five pounds and sent us to the end of a long row of cars.

I grabbed the rucksack in which we'd placed the bones and we made our way out of the car park and down the lane into the village. All around us people flowed in the same general direction: families with young children, couples, small groups of friends and individuals. Many people were dressed as Merlin or other characters from the Arthurian Tales. There were also quite a few elves, hobbits, wookies and even the occasional Klingon. As we entered the village itself I noticed the roads had been closed off, turning the whole village into a pedestrian zone. That would explain the traffic problems.

Signs pointed the way to various attractions, including Merlin's Pig Roast, Merlin's Medieval Circus and Merlin's Oldé Beer Tent. That seemed like a good place to start. The beer tent was a huge marquee erected in a field which backed on to the main car park. Inside, were row upon row of long wooden tables and benches already thronged with people. We bought some jugs of Camelot Ale and found somewhere to sit.

"Well," said Elaine. "If we wanted somewhere to lay low for a few hours I think we've found the perfect spot. Who's going to take any notice of one more Merlin?"

"This is insanity," said Merlin. "What disease takes the minds of these people?"

"They're your fans," I said.

An overweight couple settled at our table.

"Howdy," said the man. His accent placed him somewhere in the American mid-west and his attire placed him somewhere between Numptyville and La-la Land. He was dressed as a schoolboy and wore a black silk cape with a red lining. He looked a bit like a cross between Angus Young from AC/DC and Meatloaf. Harry Potter had a lot to answer for.

"Hi," I said. "You from the States?"

"Sure thing; couldn't miss this." He held a hand towards me. "Name's Hank, this is my good lady, Nancy."

I took his hand; it felt pudgy and slightly damp. "John, nice to meet you." I introduced the rest of our group and surreptitiously wiped my hand on my jeans.

"You guys have so much history," Nancy said. "Merlin's so awesome. We don't have so much history back home, not like you guys. It's everywhere; even your trains are like something out of the history books. Our history is mostly just Presidents or Indians."

"And spacemen," said Cas.

"Spacemen?" Hank asked.

"Yeah, like Neil Armstrong and Buzz Lightyear. Who was the other one? Houston we have a problem, that one?"

"You mean Lovell?"

"No, not him. You know… Major Tom, that's it."

"Wasn't he a Brit?" asked Hank.

"Are you doing a tour?" I asked, in an attempt to rescue the conversation from the cul-de-sac it had just entered.

"Just here for this," said Hank. "Flying back Stateside tomorrow."

"You came all the way just for this?" Elaine sounded shocked.

"Yes, sir. It's not every day you get the chance to see real history."

"Come on, honey," said Nancy. "I think they're doing the sword in the stone." She squeezed his upper arm. "My big guy, you might win." She grinned and they set off.

Their places were immediately taken by two Merlins. They looked about twenty but it was hard to tell under the fake beards and large floppy hats. They ignored us and continued with a heated discussion they'd obviously started some time earlier. I tried to tune them out but became fascinated by their theories on the different types of dragons which had lived in Camelot. I felt Merlin stiffen and put my hand on his arm in an attempt to head off the inevitable.

I was too late.

"What fantasy is this?" he said loudly enough for the adjoining tables to all fall silent.

The two lads looked shocked at his outburst but Merlin had only just started. "Dragons? What nonsense do you speak? There are no dragons in Camelot. Stuff of childhood tales told by nurses to quieten their charges. Dragons indeed. Is there no sense in this world? When did people start believing in such tales?"

"In The Return of Arthur there was a Wyvern which Lancelot destroyed with a flaming arrow," one of the lads said. "Right into the throat. It's the only way to destroy a Wyvern."

"And in Merlin's Revenge, Camelot is attacked by a Wruenele Dragon," said the other.

"It completely destroyed the East Tower," added the first.

"Merlin's Revenge? East Tower?" Merlin stood up. "Camelot has no East Tower." He pointed at the lads but turned to me. "Who are these people and why are they being allowed to speak this rubbish?"

"Calm, Merlin," I said.

"You don't look much like Merlin," said the first lad. "I'm a much better Merlin. You haven't even got a proper beard."

"Or a decent hat. You need a hat to be Merlin."

I tugged at Merlin's arm and looked to Elaine for support. "We need to leave," I said. "Now."

Elaine stood just as Merlin brought his stick crashing to the table between him and the lads.

"Beard you say? Hat, is it?"

By now people had started to gather. Elaine tried to calm Merlin with a hand on his shoulder but he shrugged her away. He aimed Harold at the beard on the first lad. Sparks flickered in the beard and then it started to smoulder. The lad jumped back and threw the beard to the floor. Merlin immediately swung Harold to the second lad and his hat began to smoke. I grabbed it, tossed it to the floor then stamped on it.

"Beards and hats," yelled Merlin. He turned to the gathering group of onlookers. "Do I need a beard and a hat? Fools and knaves, is that all you think makes a Master Magician? Do I need a hat and beard to carry the Once and Future King to his last resting place in the caves of Trewar Venydh?" He waved his stick around the group and several people ducked. "Imposters! There is only one true Merlin and only one true King."

"Come on, Merlin," Elaine said. "We have to go. For Arthur, we have to go."

He stared at her his eyes wide. He suddenly looked like a child. "What is this place?" he asked, almost pleading. "Why are all these people here?"

Elaine guided him to the exit and I said to the group, "Sorry, he's had one too many. This ale, it goes straight to your head."

"But the hat? The beard?" said one of the Merlins. "How...?"

"Sorry, I told him he shouldn't smoke in here. Sorry." I followed the others out of the marquee.

I caught up with them as they rounded a corner to a side street.

"Hang on," I said. "Where are we going?"

"Just trying to get away from the chaos and all those people." Elaine kept a gentle but guiding grip on Merlin's arm. "He's likely to do something... something outrageous or... okay, I don't know what he's going to do but I'm sure it won't be good."

We headed down the lane until it opened up into a common. There were still people around but a lot less than further back in the village. At least there were no Merlins here.

The common sloped away towards the cliff top and we followed it down a way until we came to a group of large granite boulders which sat on the edge of the cliff, as if staring out to sea awaiting an overdue visitor. We sat on the rocks.

The wind blew through me, lifting the dirty clouds of the last few days. "How long until moonrise?"

Colin checked his watch. "Five hours, and a bit. Gets dark in about four hours."

"We can't sit here for four hours," said Elaine.

"Let's go get some ice cream." Cas lit a joint and drew the smoke deep. "There's a stall up the road selling Uncle Merlin's Magic Cornets. I saw it on the way down. The cornets are like magic wizard hats, clever, huh?"

"You go get yourself some ice cream," I told Cas. "We're going to book a room for the night, there's a pub just off the main street over there. They had a Bed and Breakfast sign in the window. What say we all meet up here at five? Gives us plenty of time to get down to the cave before it gets dark."

Merlin's Rest was a traditional English pub, full of oak beams and open fireplaces. It was also full of tourists.

"Sorry, love," said the girl behind the bar. "We're

completely full. It's this convention see? You could try Merlin's Tavern at the top of the High Street or Merlin's B&B just out of town but I wouldn't hold much hope. We were fully booked six months ago."

"Is everything here called Merlin's something or other?"

"No, not really. We're not supposed to say 'cause it spoils the fun but we're normally the Pilgrim's Rest." She lifted a wooden sign behind the bar to reveal a menu for the Pilgrim's Rest. She eyed us up and down. "You not dressing up? There's a prize for the best Merlin you know."

"Don't need to," I said and indicated Merlin. "He's the real thing."

She looked at Merlin. "No offence, but I've seen better. He hasn't even got a hat."

Merlin's Tavern, or as it was normally known, the Queen's Head, was predictably full. We decided to have a drink while we contemplated our next move.

We seized a just-vacated table by the door. The constant opening and shutting of the door was driving me mad after about three minutes but at least we were still for a moment.

"I don't fancy driving all the way back to London tonight," I said. "We can probably find a Road Lodge once we clear this place. Bound to be one on the A39. What do you say, Merlin, Road Lodge?"

"Do they have pizza and television?"

"Television, for sure, pizza… don't know. Probably nearby."

"Road Lodge is good," said Merlin.

"That's a swing vote," I said.

"Road Lodge, huh?" Elaine said. "You really know how to whisk a girl off her feet, don't you?"

"We could try for a Moto Lodge if you prefer? Bit more expensive but they usually have a kettle in the room."

"A kettle? Well, that clinches it. Moto Lodge it is then."

The door swung open once more and I glanced up.

"Ah, here you are," Morgan said with triumph. "Mind if I join you? It's been a hell of a journey. You wouldn't believe the traffic and the nightmare I had tracking you down. Do you know how many Merlins there are here?" She waved her hand towards the bar. "A glass of Merlot please." She pointed to our table. "In the end I bumped into that raggle-headed friend of yours, the one that's always stoned. He had a face full of ice-cream."

"Well, this is an unexpected pleasure, you here for the Merlin Festival?"

"Sort of," she said. "But I would like the real bones back please. If it's not too much of an inconvenience of course?"

"What do you mean?" I stalled and used my foot to shove the rucksack under Elaine's chair.

The bored looking girl from behind the bar brought a glass of red wine to our table, banged it down and announced, "It's not waitress service you know."

"Thank you, darling," Morgan said. "I'll be sure to leave you a very large tip."

"You took the bones, if I remember rightly," I said. "Under a series of quite nasty threats."

"Yes, I did, didn't I? Those threats still stand by the way if you don't return them." She took a sip of her wine. "Don't they understand about room temperature?"

"I don't understand," I said. "You have the bones."

"Yes, I thought that too. Until I checked the box and discovered that King Arthur had a gold wedding ring still on his finger."

"Oh, maybe he secretly married Guinevere?" I offered.

"I know, that's kind of plausible isn't it, but when I took a closer look, it was engraved, 'To my beloved Nathanial'. I feel that blows that theory out of the water."

"How did you know we'd be here?" I asked.

"Not difficult." She nodded towards Merlin. "That idiot kept babbling on about the caves of Trewar Venydh and in this modern, connected age which we inhabit, we really are only ever one click away from all human knowledge. Now, if you'll just let me have my property back you can carry on with your insignificant little lives and I can prepare for my exhibition."

"Does it matter?" Elaine asked. "I mean, what are the chances that those bones are really Arthur's?"

I felt Merlin bristle and laid a hand on his arm to calm him. We didn't need any more burning hats.

"It was just a Saxon grave," continued Elaine. "Important, yes, but they could be anybody's bones. Could have been a farmer. The only person who really holds any value in those particular bones is Merlin. Apart from his own beliefs, they're just another pile of bones and no different from the other set. Nobody will ever know."

"I will know," said Merlin. "The Prophet told me, she tells all who will listen." He waved the remains of the paperback at her. Several pages fell from the book and fluttered to the floor. "You would do well to listen too, I know you, as does the Prophet. She has words for you; they are in The Book, clear for all. Your days are numbered."

"You're not taking the bones, Morgan," said Elaine. "Merlin has a mission and we're here to help him see it through."

Morgan clapped her hands. "Bravo, spirit. I do like spirit. I always admire people who stand up for what they believe; you have a good sense of moral justice. And that's why you'll understand that we had a deal, I keep the bones, you stay out of prison."

"A deal is it?" Elaine leaned in towards Morgan, her eyes darkened. "Let's talk about another deal. We keep the original bones and you go away and leave us in peace."

"Now why would I do that?" Morgan asked. Her body language was still strong but her eyes had lost some of their previous confidence. Elaine had hit something but for the life of me I couldn't see what it was.

"Because your reputation is out there in television land for all to rewind and play again. Morgan the ghost hunter stating unequivocally that you'd witnessed ghosts marching and the vanishing warrior who'd risen from the grave. How do you intend explaining that the empty grave was really just turned over by a bunch of amateurs and that there was no ghost?"

Morgan hesitated, clearly Elaine had shaken her. "You forget; I control large parts of the media. I can spin this."

"And can you spin the screening of an old movie and passing it off as a horde of marching ghosts?"

"What do you mean?" Morgan gripped the edge of the table.

"The marching ghosts you filmed and put out publicly as evidence of your ghost hunting skills was a clip from… what was the movie, John?"

"Warlords of Mercia," I said.

"Yes, Warlords of Mercia," Elaine continued her attack. "If that comes out, at the very least you'll be facing a copyright action as I'm guessing you didn't have permission to broadcast that. At best, your career is over."

Morgan slumped back in her seat. "I think I underestimated you," she said. "You have a feisty one there, John. I'd hang on to her."

But Elaine wasn't finished. "And you might want to mention to your friend Martin, that if he plans on causing trouble then we will point out, very publically, that the treasure he unearthed had already been dug up in a different position then reburied. I think in professional archaeological terms that would constitute major site contamination. I'm not sure his career would survive that."

Morgan looked defeated. "What do you want?" she asked.

"Nothing. Nothing at all. Just go away now and leave us all alone."

Morgan sat for a moment. Then, without a word, she stood and left.

"Did she pay for her wine?" I said as I watched the door swing shut.

"Want me to go bring her back?" Elaine grinned.

"No, the look on her face was well worth picking up the bill for. That was all very masterful, where did that come from?"

"I work shifts in a place where the televisions are going all day. I think Law and Order has probably seeped into my subconscious."

"Come on." I picked up the rucksack. "Nearly time, let's have a wander."

Chapter Twenty Five

We bought some ice creams from Uncle Merlin's Ice Cream Shoppé then threaded our way through the people and back to the cliff top where we'd agreed to meet the others. We sat looking out over the darkening sea.

"What do you think is going to happen, Merlin?" I asked. "When you take Arthur into the cave, I mean."

"There will be a place to leave him. The Prophet wrote it. I leave him at the place that reveals itself."

"And you? Are you coming back with us?" Elaine asked.

"When my task is done, it is done," he said.

"Well, you're welcome to come back up to London," I said. "I've kind of got used to having you around."

Merlin didn't answer he just turned his eyes back to the sea.

"What about you?" I asked Elaine. "Back to Taunton, looking after society's lost and bewildered?"

"I think that career path is well and truly closed to me now. I didn't turn up to my disciplinary hearing; they take a dim view of that. I will be forever banished from the kingdom of Social Services and all its domains."

"You don't seem overly concerned."

"Time for a change. I suppose you'll be going back to being Angry Man, protecting the world from its own stupidity?"

"I think I'm done with that. Time I moved on too." The thought of letting go of my crusade had always somehow felt like betraying Amy's memory. Almost as if, once I stopped, I would finally be closing a door on her. Forever. But now, something had changed. Something was different.

"Do you believe him yet?" Elaine asked in a hushed voice.

"I think… I think… I'm not sure. I think I don't disbelieve him."

"Cop out."

"What about you? You deal with people all the time who claim they're somebody they're not. How do you choose who to believe?"

"It's not my place to believe them or disbelieve them. It's the same with Merlin. If he believes he's Merlin then that's good enough for me. My place is not to judge."

"That must be difficult?" I said.

"Not really. It only becomes difficult when one makes judgements. Tell me, why have you decided to… um… *not* disbelieve him, as you put it? Is it because you've been confronted with things you can't explain?"

"That disturbs me, sure. But on the other hand, neither can I explain how time works, where the other sock goes or why people kept on voting for Tony Blair. Merlin's different." I turned to look at him. He was still staring out to sea, oblivious to everything apart from trying to reach, with his tongue, the last drop of ice cream in the cornet.

I raised my voice above the gentle wind. "You can eat the cornet, Merlin," I said.

He turned to look at me, he clearly hadn't heard. "The cornet." I held mine up and took a bite; ice cream ran down my chin. "You can eat the cornet."

He finally caught what I was saying and bit down on the cornet.

I turned back to Elaine, dropping my voice below wind

276

level. "He has a different feel. Like he doesn't belong here anymore and he's just visiting."

"Maybe the world doesn't comply with your rules, John. Sometimes things don't fit, sometimes they just are."

"Fancy coming up to London for a while?" I asked. "Just to... I mean... you know, for a change. As you're sort of at a loss. No big deal."

"I think I'd like that." She took my hand. "Know any good pizza houses?"

"Oh, yes."

"We bought ice creams," I heard from behind me and turned to see Cas and Colin coming towards us. They balanced several cornets in each hand and proceeded to distribute them. "Uncle Merlin's. That's cool, huh? Only cheese and onion flavour, sorry, they've sold out of everything else."

"I wonder why that was the last flavour left in the shop," I said.

"I know, spooky, huh? Where's the others?"

I checked my watch. "Twenty minutes yet, they'll be here."

Sebastian, Tree, Eric and Stevie turned up on the stroke of six.

"I've got a wand." Sebastian waved what looked like an icicle; I guessed it was some sort of crystal. "Doesn't work though," he said and waved it in the air.

Merlin turned to look at Sebastian. "Fool," he said. "A wand needs setting first."

"How do I do that?"

"It has to feel attuned with its owner and settled in the environment."

"Huh?"

"Give it to me." Merlin held his hand out.

Sebastian handed the wand to Merlin who studied it for a

moment and then threw it over the cliff edge. "That should do it," said Merlin.

"Why would you do that?" asked Sebastian. "That was my wand."

"Because you are an idiot." He stood up. "Night's coming, it's nearly time. I have a circle to complete."

We followed the path from the cliff top to the beach. The small cove was already packed, to the point of finding it difficult descending the last few steps. People were scattered everywhere but some clusters were more densely packed than others. Several groups had built fires and at the far end of the cove a huge bonfire was already holding dusk at bay. I looked nervously to see if there was any evidence of either stakes or wicker men. I couldn't see either but it didn't necessarily mean there weren't any. Another group splashed in the crashing surf and judging by the squeals I guessed both large quantities of alcohol and the shedding of clothing were involved. A party atmosphere pervaded, tempered with a feeling of what I could only describe as eager anticipation.

I looked over to the cave. People milled around the entrance, jostling to get inside but the cavern would hold no more. From what I could see of the interior, it looked like Day One of the John Lewis Boxing Day sales.

"This is hopeless," I said. "What the hell is going on?"

"Beats me," said Elaine. "Can we ask somebody?"

I stopped a passing Merlin. He had a long grey beard which looked so real I was actually tempted to give it a tug to find out. The ubiquitous pointy hat, this one with painted stars, was just too large and fell forwards over his eyes. He carried a large wooden walking stick with an eagle carved into the handle.

"What's happening?" I asked. "Why is everybody in the cave?"

"Merlin's coming. Didn't you know?"

"Well, I kind of figured, being as how this is a Merlin Convention and all, but there's lots of him here already."

"No, *THE* Merlin. The one who's coming to reinstate Arthur as king and stop global warming. Don't you read Twitter?"

I pointed at Merlin. "You mean *this* Merlin?"

The Merlin stared at Merlin for a moment then said, "No, that's not him. He hasn't got a hat. Or much of a beard." The Merlin snatched a can of beer from another Merlin and they disappeared into the crowd.

"What are we going to do?" Elaine asked. "It's starting to get dark and the moon comes up in just over an hour. We'll never get in the cave."

"I don't know." I looked around. "Why are they waiting for Merlin? How do they know he's coming?"

"Lucky guess?" Cas suggested.

I looked at him. "Lucky guess?"

"Synchronicity, you know how it is; you're watching TV just thinking about your uncle you haven't seen for thirty years and then he rings the doorbell. Happens all the time."

"Synchronicity?"

"Yeah, it's not like it's a big thing. Doesn't mean anybody has said anything they shouldn't have or if they did then, you know... whatever. Anyway, why are you accusing me?"

"Who did you tell?" I asked.

"I don't know; I'd had a couple of flagons of Merlin's Special Brew. He had a pointy hat and a long beard. Not the Merlin's Special Brew that would be ridiculous, the Merlin."

I looked around the beach. Pointy hats and beards were much in evidence. "Why? Why on Earth would you tell anybody about Merlin?"

"Well, he was giving it all the bollocks about being on the same astral plane as Merlin and all that."

"So you told him about the real Merlin?" I caught Elaine's smile and added, "Allegedly real."

"I didn't think he'd go round telling everybody. He promised. Can't trust anybody these days."

"And what's this about ending global warming?"

"Now, to be fair, I didn't actually say that. He was banging on about Arthur's destiny and how he was going to save the world. I just sort of agreed and then we got to talking about which problems he'd solve first."

"So now they're all waiting for this real Merlin to come and we can't get in the cave because our Merlin hasn't got a pointy hat."

"Can't you do some magic?" Elaine asked Merlin. "That would prove who you are and then we could get in the cave."

"You want me to do party tricks?" Merlin shouted. "Party tricks are the domain of the charlatan and the knave. My magic is for the seasons and the crops, for kings and justice, not for entertaining children. Here," he pointed at me, "here's your conjuror, your sideshow man." He hoisted the rucksack over his shoulder. "Take me to the caves of Trewar Venydh, The Prophet calls."

"But that's what we were trying…"

Merlin started pushing his way through the crowds.

"John, you have to do something," Elaine said. "Moonrise is in about an hour and it's probably only going to throw light in the cave for a short time. If he's not in there… we'll… erm… Look, I don't know what will happen if he gets in there in time but I am certain that we're going to end up looking after him if he doesn't."

That seemed like a reasonable threat. "Okay," I said. "You

stay here, keep him here. I'm going back to the car. I've still got all that extra magic kit in there when I collected the Pepper's ghost stuff, there might be something I can use."

Elaine looked at her watch. "You'll have to hurry."

"I know. Cas, help keep Merlin out of trouble." I saw the glimmer of confusion on Cas's face and added, "Elaine, keep Cas out of trouble."

I forced my way through the tide of people pouring down the steps and made my way as quickly as I could back to the car. I was severely out of breath by the time I arrived. I checked my watch. That had taken me fifteen minutes but it was downhill on the way back so should be quicker. I rummaged through the boxes of props I'd randomly tossed in the car, grabbing everything I thought might be vaguely useful and stuffed it in a holdall.

As I pushed my way back through the narrow street, I mentally went through the items I'd brought and tried to think of what sort of illusions I could create with them. Invisible wire, a large cotton throw, flash powder, a couple of packs of cards. What the hell was I thinking? I was going to convince all these people that we had the one true Merlin by doing a few card tricks? I noticed a few people waving glow sticks and stopped one to ask where he'd bought it. He directed me to a small shop called Merlin's Toy Box where I bought a handful of them along with a large beach ball, a box of fireworks and a roll of sticky tape. I also noticed a rack of postcards showing views of the area. One in particular caught my attention. I was beginning to form the basis of an idea.

By the time I reached the cove there seemed to be more people than ever. It was like rush hour at King's Cross. I pushed my way through to find the others.

"Well?" asked Elaine.

"I have a sort of idea," I said. "How much time do we have?"

"Moonrise in…" Colin aimed his smartphone to the horizon. "Seventeen minutes."

I looked towards the horizon then over to the cave entrance. "That means the moonlight will be visible in the cave about ten minutes after that, I'd guess. And then… for maybe thirty minutes?"

"Who knows?" said Colin. "I don't think my Skywatch app has that setting."

"What are you planning, John?" asked Elaine.

I showed her the postcard. "Look, somebody has carved the face of Merlin in the rock face here somewhere."

"That's very interesting but how does that help?"

"It's a recent carving and quite small, so I'm guessing that the majority of people here don't know about it. I think I can use it. But first, we have to find it." I studied the postcard and tried to align the image with the rapidly darkening vista in front of me. "I think it's over there." I pointed to a gap between the rock face and a huge boulder.

We threaded our way to the place I'd guessed from the postcard and I studied the rocks in front of me. I saw nothing that resembled a face. "We all need to spread out a bit. It's definitely here somewhere."

It took a precious ten minutes to find it. Tucked between the cliffs and a massive rock and about head height, the carving stared out at me under the faint light of my phone. I looked around. Nobody seemed to be paying it any attention so my assumption that few people realised it was here was probably right. The gathered Merlins were probably not the normal visitor profile for an English Heritage site.

"How did this get here?" Elaine ran her fingertips across the carving.

"I don't know." I pulled a cloth from my pocket and handed it to her. "Here, just dry out the grooves in that sculpture."

Cas looked from Merlin to the carving and back. "That looks nothing like Merlin."

I sprinkled flash powder into the grooves. "It looks enough like him to do the job. Merlin, I need you to crouch down behind that rock over there."

I gave everybody quick stage directions and hoped for the best. There would be no rehearsals and no second chances. Get this wrong and Merlin wouldn't gain entrance to the cave, the bones would just be a bag of bones and I'd have wasted the last weeks of my life. Get it right and... What was going to happen if we got it right? I hadn't the faintest idea. Probably nothing. Just like every other fake and charlatan only this time, I was the fake, using trickery to convince an audience that something supernatural was real. I didn't want to think about that, I had a gig to do.

The moon was already on the rise by the time we had everything set.

Okay, here goes.

I'd already settled the gunpowder from one firework in a hollow in a small rock. A second firework lay in the centre of the pile. Good way to lose eyebrows. I lit the fuse on the second firework and stepped back just as the banger exploded loudly and the surrounding powder caught in a huge flash.

Silence fell across the cove as if somebody had just pressed the mute button. Everybody turned towards the source of the flash.

So far so good.

I nodded towards Cas and he shouted, "It's Merlin, he's here!"

People moved in our direction, I began my act. The floating

ball wasn't quite up to Palladium standard but given the circumstances, it looked pretty good. I'd sticky-taped several glow sticks around the beach ball and the light bleed actually made it look like the light was emanating from within the ball, just as I'd hoped. Two more glow sticks hung like a neon collar around my neck, spookily illuminating my face. The ball began to float between my outstretched arms. I heard murmurs in the crowd and it felt good to be performing again. The glowing ball danced and floated in the air just in front of me as I moved my hands around it. I'd never have got away with this on a well-lit stage but here, in the haunting light of the moon, it certainly looked impressive.

The ball headed towards the rock face where Merlin's impassive face laid waiting. I levelled the ball just below the carving and the flash powder I'd spread across the face flared. Merlin's face burst into brilliant white light and the shock to the crowd was clear from the collective indrawn breath. If this hadn't been quite so important I'd have really enjoyed this and even through the seriousness, I felt a grin trying to spread across my face.

Cas pushed forwards exactly on cue and ran his hand across the carved face. "It's Merlin's face," he yelled. "It's shaped into the rock."

I held my breath and waited for the cries of 'Fraud' or 'Fake' but they never came. Clearly my hunch had been correct. Few, if any, of the people gathered here were aware the carving existed. And as the noise grew, even if some knew, their voice would be drowned under the excited clamour.

The ball danced once more and as it rose, Elaine threw the large red silk sheet over it shouting, "It's changing. Get back!"

The people in the front actually obeyed and pushed back against those behind them. Good, compliance achieved. The silk covered ball bounced in the air as if trying to escape, and the glow sticks lighting the whole thing from inside gave a wild, almost demonic appearance. The ball ducked behind the huge rock then bounced up again where it hovered about two metres off the top of the rock with the silk tumbling in folds over the moonlit granite. I couldn't see but I just hoped that Merlin had done his bit. I let everything settle for a moment to build the tension. For a makeshift illusion it wasn't bad and it certainly had the desired effect. I waited, judging the silence to catch the psychological moment. The real skill of the illusionist. Not the elaborate rigging or the hand deceiving the eye. No, the real skill was in the timing. My years of studying the masters had taught me that. Harry Blackstone, David Copperfield and of course the master himself, Harry Houdini, they had all mastered the subtle art of timing.

Just as the whispers started, I grabbed the corner of the silk and pulled it away revealing the surprisingly imposing figure of Merlin. He stood bathed in the light of a bunch of glow sticks on the rock, his hand outstretched in the exact position the ball had occupied just a split second before, holding the skull of Arthur.

Merlin's deep voice thundered impressively, perfectly exploiting the acoustics of the rocks in which he stood. "Take me to the caves of Trewar Venydh," he boomed.

I waited. Everything depended on the next few seconds. Whispers. I could hear whispers rising but not what they said. If they were whispering about pointy hats or beards we were in deep trouble.

"It's Merlin," somebody shouted. "He's come."

Once the first voice had broken, the others followed. Group compliance.

"Let him through."

"It's really him, look!"

"He's the one on the TV."

"He has Arthur's skull."

Somebody pushed their way through to the front. He rubbed his hand over the carving in the rock then stared up at Merlin. I held my breath. "Merlin has returned," the man yelled. "He's come to return the true king.

And that was it. Crowd dynamics did the rest. An opening formed in the throng of people and Merlin was ushered forwards into the caves. We followed as best we could but this was now Merlin's time and events were completely out of my control.

I felt Elaine squeeze my hand. "You did it," she said.

"We did it," I said. "You persuaded me to help him. I'd have dumped him from the moment he pulled out that bloody book."

She leaned in to me and put her head on my shoulder. "I don't believe that for a moment. You needed to see where this road led just as much as he did."

Merlin shuffled forwards as people parted in front of him like a scene from a biblical epic. He made his way into the cave which was strangely illuminated by the glow of two hundred mobile phones. The internet was going to be busy tomorrow. He stopped at the back of the cave, knelt down and unpacked the rest of the bones. He showed a lot less reverence than I thought he would. The skull he placed on top of the pile and then he removed Cynbel, the ring, from his finger. He placed that on one of the finger bones then stood back. He faced the rear rock wall, outstretched his arms and spoke loudly in some language I couldn't begin to fathom. Celtic, I guessed, but it might just as easily have been Danish or Navajo.

Moonlight streamed in from the entrance of the cave and touched the bones. As Merlin continued to speak, the bones began to glow, orange at first then white and finally a brilliant blue.

And then they were gone. Just like that. No crafty movements, distractions or mirrors. They just went away.

Elaine whispered in my ear, "Did you set that up?"

"No, nothing to do with me." I looked at the solid rock where they had lain only seconds before. Solid, impassive grey granite which had probably been there before man had even clambered out of the cosmic soup.

"How did he do it then?"

I turned to look at her. Her eyes sparkled with mischief. "A good magician never tells," I said.

"You don't know, do you?"

"Nope, I haven't got a clue."

The crowded cave bubbled with excitement but surprisingly, the noise was low and respectful. A strange sharing among this strange group that something quite profound had just taken place.

Merlin turned to face the crowd. "John? John Barker? Is John Barker here?"

"What's happening?" Elaine asked.

"I don't know," I replied. I pushed my way through the people as they tried to clear a way for me.

I stood in front of Merlin and he leaned towards me, his eyes clearer than I had ever seen. "She told me to tell you something," he said quietly.

"Who told you? What?"

"She said to tell you, the magic is real, never lose it, never let the world take you."

My mind froze, synapses firing randomly as they tried to process the words. The words which I'd last heard spoken so long ago. So many years ago in another world. A world where all things had once seemed possible. The world I'd shared with Amy. The world I'd lost on a cruel parting defined by those very words. Her last words to me as she promised to breach the barriers of the next world to prove to me once and for all that the magic was real. I felt my legs go. Hands grasped at me, easing my fall to the wet shingles of the cave floor.

"John? John? What's happening?" Elaine's voice. I felt her arms around me. "Are you alright?"

I struggled into a sitting position. "Yes, I think."

"What did he say?"

"Some words I never expected to hear." I came up to my feet with Elaine steadying me.

"You sure you're alright?"

"I'll be fine. Everything's going to be fine. Just fine." I regained my feet and slipped my hands into my pockets so nobody would see them trembling. I felt something solid and pulled it into the light. A ring. Then I remembered. This was the ring I'd removed from Arthur's skeleton yesterday. I slipped it onto my finger where it once felt both comfortable and familiar, as if I had always worn it.

Merlin turned to face the rear wall once more. He walked forwards towards the wall. The silence thundered through the cave as the moonlight faded from the entrance leaving only the collective lights of hundreds of cell phones lighting Merlin's final walk. The three steps it took to reach the wall and the one step to take him through. Through the solid rock and into... where? Albion? Avalon? Or maybe just the collective insanity of hundreds of people all expecting something magical to happen.

I felt Elaine grasping my hand. "Time to go," she said. "It's over."

"No," I said. "It's not over. It's just beginning. Fancy a pizza?"